IGNITE

Hosting Gods

Book Two

By Lena Mae Hill

Ignite
Copyright © 2018 Lena Mae Hill

ISBN: 978-1-945780-46-2

Dedication

To all the readers who encouraged me to go on.

Table of Contents

Blurb

Gwen's barely gotten a taste of normal when her resident god shows up with an assignment. The bridge between the human world and the world of the gods is weakening, and the nine hosts of Heimdall must find each other if they hope to fix it. One small problem—Gwen and the Keens must travel to another world to find Heimdall's remaining hosts.

Gwen has always relied on books for her education, but no amount of reading can prepare her for what waits outside the human world. The people are different. The rules are different. She's different.

As Gwen struggles with her growing attraction to her stepsiblings, loyalties are tested and sacrifices made. But when the giant-infested Joaquin threatens to come between them, what will she sacrifice to unify the group?

Chapter One

Gwen

I groped across the bed, feeling for Xander in the dark. Only cold, empty sheets met my fingertips. I should have known he would run away from this. He'd accused me of cowardice, but he was the king of taking off on his motorcycle the moment things got complicated. I tried not to take it personally, even when it stung. It was a little more difficult this time, when he'd pulled his disappearing act after our first kiss.

My first kiss. My heart stutter-stepped at the thought.

I sat bolt upright. Shit. We'd *kissed.* I seriously doubted that was the kind of closeness our parents had intended when they got married.

Double shit. Our parents.

I dropped my feet to the floor, my heart pounding as I approached the door. After easing it open, I paused, holding my breath. The house was quiet now in the dark. Only a faint glimmer of moonlight filtered in through the third-floor window of Xander's bedroom. I stepped out into the hallway and tiptoed past my other stepsiblings' rooms. My relationships with them had been a bit tense since we'd found out a god had taken up residence inside us like some kind of parasite.

I glanced at their rooms, but my thoughts were focused on my mom. I wasn't worried about getting in trouble. Mom probably didn't even realize most parents disciplined their kids. She didn't make rules. I obeyed her wishes simply because I didn't want her to flip out. And she might if she couldn't find me. Heart racing, I hurried down the hall on tiptoes.

Zeke's door was cracked, a faint glow coming from within like he'd left a small light on. Peyton's door was closed, as were Eliot's and Finn's. My door stood open, and I could hear my mother's soft snores from within. I breathed a sigh of relief. She hadn't waited up for me.

My mom had married Neil for strictly parasitic god-related reasons, and they didn't share a bedroom. In fact, she shared a room with me, which meant that she'd gone to bed without me, probably wondering where I was. One of my stepbrothers had probably made an excuse for me, which was good. She would not be happy if she knew the truth. She'd warned me about getting close to them in this way.

I slipped through the door, wincing as it gave a slight squeak when I pulled it shut. Holding my breath, I turned and snuck toward the bed. The spacious room had never seemed so big, so cavernous. At last, I reached the edge and began to ease myself onto the mattress.

"Gwen?" Mom asked, her voice slurry with sleep.

"Yeah?"

"Where have you been?"

"I was out on the deck," I said. "Talking to the others."

Mom made a noncommittal sound and sighed deeply, already asleep again. I lay on the bed, staring at the ceiling in the darkness. I never lied to my mom. We were a team, the Two Musketeers. Guilt washed over me, and I considered shaking her awake and telling her the truth, apologizing for lying.

But she'd kept things from me, too. Like that I was born in Boston, and that this rich guy would have welcomed us into his home years ago, so we didn't have to live on the road for the past ten years. Ten years during which I thought it was normal to be uprooted every few months, to have no other friends besides my mother, and to be educated by dime store paperbacks. Thanks to Mom, instead of a life of luxury, I'd grown up with an unhealthy obsession with Scarlett O'Hara and the ability to make things awkward in record time.

Now that I had more, I didn't know what to do with it. I wanted a normal life so badly my whole body ached, but at the same time, I didn't trust this taste of ordinary. It couldn't last. Nothing lasted.

Finally, I fell asleep. In the morning, I watched Mom carefully as I dressed, waiting for her to confront me about my lie. But she just stumbled downstairs in her robe, bleary-eyed before coffee. In the kitchen, everyone was rushing around as usual. I'd been so busy worrying about Mom that I'd forgotten to worry about Xander.

He stood at the counter, a cup of coffee in one hand, wearing his usual leather jacket and a pair of dark jeans. His hair fell in thick, dark waves, and his ocean blue eyes locked onto mine the moment I stepped into the room. My heart skipped in my chest, and my feet tripped over themselves.

"Steady there," a deep voice said, and Zeke caught my elbow. My eyes stayed locked on Xander's. His expression was arranged in a carefully bland look. I squirmed under his gaze, sure he could see the confusion and hurt and hope mixing on my face.

Of course, I couldn't read him at all. I didn't know what I'd expected. He was still Xander. One kiss wasn't going to change that.

I dragged my eyes from his, turning my attention to the melee of activity in the kitchen. The amount of energy in the morning still made my head spin. Peyton chattered about some football game while she buttered toast. Neil handed out coffee. Zeke asked if I was okay, drawing me to the table to sit next to my mom. Finn rooted through the fridge.

Only Xander seemed to be still, an island in the chaos. Watching me as if he were waiting to pounce. Suddenly, my insecurity flared. What if I'd read him all wrong, and that kiss and heartfelt talk hadn't meant anything to him? I'd seen him kiss another girl. I knew how little that had meant to him. Why was kissing me necessarily different? It hadn't been his first kiss, after all. Who was to say he wouldn't go back to tormenting me today?

The thought made me want to flee, to get in Mom's car and run just like Xander said I always did. But I wouldn't give him the satisfaction of being right. Instead, I clutched the table as if it could hold me in place, anchor me to the spot so my feet couldn't take me far away from this boy who looked at me with that flat gaze that stiffened my spine with tension and fear of his judgement. My heart lurched as he pushed away from the counter and crossed the kitchen, heading for the door. I hadn't even gotten a hello.

At the last second, as he was about to pass my chair, he paused. "Want a ride?" he asked quietly.

"Hi," I breathed, my heart clutching inside my chest. I stared up at him like a complete, brainless idiot.

The corner of his mouth quirked into a smirk. "I'll bring the bike around," he said. "Don't make me wait."

A giddy smile tugged at my lips, though I tried to hold it back when I saw my mom watching. Xander was never going to be a sweet, romantic like Finn or even a flirt like Zeke, but he'd offered me a ride to school without his father forcing him to. I was pretty sure that was his way of letting me know we were cool. The tension flowed out of me, relief turning me into putty.

I took a minute to collect myself. Despite his warning, Xander could wait. Finally, I rose and said goodbye to my mother, who still watched me with that eerie, perceptive clarity. Slinging my bag over my shoulder I headed for the door, trying to look normal, whatever that was. Just as I stepped out of the kitchen, I ran straight into Eliot. His broad, strong chest collided with my cheek, his hands resting gently on my upper arms.

"You okay there, Gwen?" he asked, his brow creasing as he held me away and searched my face from behind his glasses.

"So okay," I said, my words sliding out on a sigh. Everything was okay when he was there. Even when Xander had been cruel, Eliot could always take away the sting. Now that they were both on my side, I was almost high with it. Was this what happiness felt like?

Eliot raised an eyebrow. "I see you patched things up with Xander."

"Yeah," I said, swallowing hard at the rush of emotion swelling inside me when I saw the concern in his warm brown eyes. I *had* been attacked by a giant-infested surfer just the day before, after all.

"Good," Eliot said, nodding. "You sure you don't want to ride with us?"

In that moment, all I wanted to do was stay, curl into his chest, and let him walk me around like he did at school. Everything in me warred with itself, wanting to be two places at once. It was too much for my brain, which just wanted to stop being pulled in a different direction every other minute by my hormonal body and fickle heart.

"I want to," I said, glancing at the door when I heard the purr of Xander's engine outside. "Tomorrow?"

"Keep your phone on," Eliot said, though it seemed I hardly needed it anymore. He had some kind of instinct for when I was in danger, although I had to admit, being able to actually tell him what was wrong would help.

"I will."

"Good," he said, his eyes cutting to the kitchen door before he leaned in to brush a quick kiss across my forehead.

Goosebumps exploded across my skin, making my toes curl in my shoes, and a gasp escaped my lips. Eliot studied me from behind his glasses like he was trying to solve some kind of equation. Then he shook his head and blinked a few times before heading into the kitchen. My eyes followed his tall, trim form for a second.

Still reeling from the newness of all this—I'd barely met a guy before in my life, and now I was swooning over four of them at once—I made my way outside. Xander sat astride his bike, the toes of his motorcycle boots skimming the ground. My cheeks warmed as my eyes moved over his knees, up his thighs hugging the bike, and to his hips that inevitably drew my eyes like a magnet.

"Get on, little girl," he said, beckoning me with a lazy wave.

"Don't call me that," I said, my feet unsticking as I jogged down the steps and crossed the gravel drive. I slung my leg over the bike and scooted in behind him, securing my thighs around his irresistible hips. "Ready."

He snorted. "I don't think so, little girl." He handed me a helmet, which I put on without a word, though he never wore one. I was pretty sure he had a death wish, but that didn't mean I wanted to join him—if a god's hosts could even die. I'd have to ask Heimdall the next time he paid us a visit.

If I'd thought that riding the bike with Xander had been exciting before, it was almost painful now. With every purr of the engine when he revved it, with every turn that made me lean in and hold him tighter, my body ached to be closer to his. I closed my eyes and leaned my cheek against his back, squeezing him as I pressed my body to his. By the time we pulled up at school, my breath was coming fast, and my hands had worked their way under his T-shirt. He

8

slid off the bike and held out a hand to me, the cocky smirk on his face telling me he knew exactly how worked up he'd gotten me.

A flicker of resentment went through me. I wouldn't be one of those girls like Jen who chased after him, panting for a bit of attention. Shaking myself out of my daze, I shoved a hand in my back pocket and tried to look cool like him. I threw my head back and shrugged for no reason. "See ya at lunch."

"Nah," he said. "Look, about what happened yesterday…"

My heart started hammering for a completely different reason. He couldn't just say those things to me and then take them back. It couldn't mean as little to him as Jen. It just couldn't.

I had to swallow twice before words would come, but I was in it now, and I couldn't backtrack. I was going to be Cool Gwen for once in my life. "What about it?" I said, shrugging again, like it had meant nothing to me, too.

"It happened, okay?" he said, his voice low. Around us, I could hear students getting out of their cars. Some of them were probably staring—Xander tended to draw attention. I couldn't see anything but his blue eyes, dark and intense today. He took my hand. "I'm not saying it didn't, or that it wasn't real. I meant it, Gwen."

My legs nearly gave way with relief. "Cool," I breathed, sounding anything but.

"But don't make a big thing of it," he said. "It is what it is."

I squeezed his hand gently, forgetting my act. "It is a big thing."

"I said don't make a big thing of it," he said, his voice as hard as it had always been with me before last night. He pulled his hand away, that curtain dropping over his face again.

I sucked in a breath, regretting that I'd pushed it. I couldn't go back to the way things had been—having him hate me, or act like it, had been unbearable.

"I'm sorry," I said. "I just meant... it was a big deal to me. Just so you know."

He smirked. "Oh, I know."

I gritted my teeth, wanting to have some kind of comeback, but of course, I didn't have one when I needed it.

"I wasn't talking about the kiss," I said. It was all I had.

"Sure you weren't."

He was right—and wrong. The kiss was a big deal to me, but so was his decision to open up to me, to tell me about his past. But he probably knew all that. To him, I was transparent. I hadn't had a whole lifetime of hiding my feelings the way he had. I had no defenses and he knew it.

"See you around, Gwen," he said, turning and sauntering off to join his friends, who were sitting on the tailgate of their truck, watching us and sharing a cigarette.

Well, at least he'd called me by my name this time. That was an improvement. It wasn't what I'd hoped for, but coming from Xander, I'd take it.

Chapter Two

Gwen

"Hey, Gwen," Zeke said, stopping at my locker before class. In his letterman jacket and jeans, with his broad shoulders and neat blond hair, he looked like someone out of a commercial. "You skipped out on us this morning."

"What?"

"You totally disappeared."

"Oh," I said. "I rode with Xander."

"I know that now," he said, giving me his puppy dog eyes. "Ride home with us?"

"Sure," I said, remembering Xander's dismissal in the parking lot. He'd said it meant something, but he apparently didn't want anything to change. My chest squeezed with pain at the memory. I wanted more, but I had to let Xander be Xander. I'd known who he was, how he was, and I'd let him get close to me, anyway.

"Cool," Zeke said, rewarding me with that movie star smile that made my knees weak. I was seriously in trouble. Instead of getting used to our connection, it was getting harder and harder to be around my stepsiblings without rubbing up against them like a cat in heat. The worst part of it was that I didn't think it was all Heimdall's fault. God or no god, I'd be attracted to every single one of them. How could I help it? They were each perfect in their own way.

Just then, I spotted the mean girls. Seriously, though, what could they do to me? After last night when I'd been tied to a chair and nearly had my throat slit, the threat of their taunts seemed silly. I turned to my locker, deciding to focus on controlling my raging hormones instead of what other girls thought of my jeans.

"God, she moves fast," Jen said. "Yesterday it was Xander she was running off with. Looks like it's Zeke's turn tonight."

"You think they each get a night with her?" Barb asked. "Or do they draw straws every night?"

"Dude," Zeke said, throwing an arm around me and pulling me close. "Don't talk about my sister like that."

"Not helping," I muttered, detaching myself from his arm. I'd thought they couldn't hurt me, but they'd moved on from my clothes. Now, they'd found something personal to tease me about. Something that hit a little too close to home.

"What kind of girl lets her stepbrothers pass her around?" their friend asked as they walked away. She said it loud enough that the entire hall could hear. I felt my throat tighten and my eyes prickle as people turned to stare. I faced my locker and shuffled through my books until my face was under control.

"Can I ask you something?" I said to Zeke.

"Anything, Baby Keen."

I lifted an eyebrow. "Really?"

"You don't like it?" He crossed his arms, making his muscles bulge. He wasn't flexing or anything, just standing there being Zeke. Add in the extra god-bond, and I was in danger of making Jen's words come true.

I shook my head to dislodge the hormone buildup blocking my brain from functioning. "I don't know, this might be weird. How do I know if it's okay to ask someone something, or if it's too personal?"

His brow furrowed, and he studied the ceiling for a second. "That's your question?"

"No," I said with a little laugh. The tension dissipated, my brain fog clearing as I slammed my locker and pulled my eyes away from Zeke's biceps. "Why don't you have a girlfriend?"

"Oh," he said, falling into step beside me. He scooped my books from my arms as we headed for my next class. "I guess... I mean, there's only like twenty kids in each grade at this school, so that makes the dating pool pretty small."

"Still," I said. "Say there's ten girls in each grade, and four grades in this school, that's forty girls."

"And there's four of us," he said. "Five, if you count Finn, though he doesn't really like girls. I mean, he's not gay. He's just not interested."

"So you'd never date anyone your brothers had dated," I said slowly. "Or Peyton."

"Dude, that would just be weird. It's like, incesty or something, right?"

"Sure," I said, suddenly wishing I had my books to hug to my chest. Here I was lusting after all the Keens, thinking the feeling was mutual. But in reality, we couldn't even date if he liked me. We were legally related. It was bad enough that I'd kissed Xander. What would people think if I walked around school holding hands with my stepbrother? What would our parents do?

"I'll see you at lunch, Baby Keen," Zeke said, stopping outside my classroom and handing back my books.

My heart squeezed. If he didn't like me that way, why did he give me a nickname? Why did he smile at me that way?

Maybe he only likes you because of the god.

"Yeah, see ya," I said, turning and making my way to my desk. My heart was hammering at this new possibility. It was hard enough to separate my own attraction to them from the pull of the god. Now I had to wonder if they felt anything for me beyond wanting to be close because we shared a deity.

A minute later, my eyes were drawn to the door. It was empty, but that charged feeling had started, making the fine hairs on the back of my neck prickle. Peyton came flouncing in the door in her cheer uniform, her pink ponytail swinging behind her. Her legs were perfectly shaped, small but muscular, her golden skin seeming to glow even in the dull fluorescent light.

It's just the god, I reminded myself, closing my eyes and taking a deep breath. It was bad enough that I was attracted to four guys. Add a girl, and it was getting plain ridiculous. I'd never even thought of being attracted to a girl before, and now here I was, ogling my stepsister. Maybe Jen and her friends were right.

"Hey," Peyton said, sliding into a chair behind me.

"Hey." I knew it wasn't her fault, but I kind of wished she'd go away. I wanted to get up and walk out, to go outside and find my mother waiting to drive away and disappear again. But she was done running, which meant I was done running. It might have been nice to have a say in that, but like always, my mother made the calls. For the first time in my life, I was starting to resent that. And then, of course, the guilt set in for resenting her. She couldn't help it that she was sick.

"You okay?" Peyton asked. "You're going to have so much fun tonight. I can't believe you've never been to a football game! This is like, the biggest high school tradition there is."

"I've never been to high school."

"I know, that's why you're going to love it. I'll be right there on the sidelines, so make sure to wave to me. And you'll get to see Zeke play. I'm so happy I get to share this with you. I'm going to make it my personal mission to take you to all the high school stuff you missed out on."

I knew football was a big deal in Wellfleet, but right now it seemed so trivial. A shiver went down my spine when a surfer strolled in and slouched into a seat. Joaquin, the surfer who usually flirted with me, had tried to kill me the day before. More accurately, the giant who had taken up residence inside him had tried to kill me. Now Joaquin was locked up in the Keen's basement while their housekeeper, who happened to be a dwarf, tried out rune spells to see if she could put the giant to sleep.

I wondered if our god could be suppressed. Though I liked all my stepsiblings, I wasn't sure I wanted to share something so momentous with them. I didn't want to be a god in the first place. I wanted to be a normal teenager. Although now that I was getting a taste of it, I wasn't sure it was really such a worthy goal. Normal teenagers seemed pretty awful. Even so, I wanted to make that choice, to make mistakes, and to experience the things I'd missed. Not experience life as a puppet to some god I'd never heard of until a few days ago.

I made it through the first half of the day, only to balk at the cafeteria. My eyes involuntarily landed on Joaquin's table, and coldness crept over me.

"You okay?" Finn's quiet voice asked behind me.

"Yeah," I said, relaxing in his presence.

"I'll grab you some food," he said, heading for the line.

I sat down at my usual table near the door. A minute later, Chelsea headed up the aisle towards me. She spotted me and slowed, resting her tray against the end of my table. "Hey."

I waited, tensed to jump up in case she wanted to throw her tray in my face like Barb had. A detention slip occupied one of the spaces on her plastic tray, and her nails were coated in chipped orange polish.

"I just wanted to say that I've been friends with Xander for a long time," she said. "And it really is time he put the past behind him."

"Okay…"

"But if you hurt him, girl, I will cut you." She picked up her tray and strolled out, leaving me staring after her. I tried to focus on the fact that she was being a good friend to Xander, but all I could think about was that she'd slept with him. Before I knew him, before he became the Xander I knew, she'd known him. He'd shared something with her that was so foreign to me that I blushed at the very thought of it. The intimacy was unfathomable. He'd been *inside* her.

Peyton bounced over and dropped into the seat beside me, startling me back to the present. Her bare knee touched my jeans. Her skin looked so soft. She was wearing some kind of lotion that made her skin take on a subtle sheen, and my fingers twitched with longing. I curled my hands into fists in my lap.

I will not touch my stepsister. I will not touch my stepsister…

"Aren't you excited?" Peyton asked.

I jerked my eyes up to hers, my cheeks flaring with heat. I felt like some kind of leering perv, staring at her legs while she talked to me.

"I'm sorry," I said. "I'm just a little distracted."

"I know," Peyton said, dropping her voice to a whisper as Zeke slid in on my other side. "Me, too. But we have to pretend everything's normal and that the absent student isn't tied up in our basement."

"Why?" Zeke asked. "This is so much bigger than Joaquin."

"Because we don't want Dad to get arrested," Peyton hissed.

"It's wild," Zeke said, shaking his head as the twins slid in opposite us with trays of food. "I can't concentrate on anything. I went to the wrong class second period."

I almost collapsed in relief. I wasn't alone. They were all struggling with this, too. It was so easy for me to forget that, to feel like I had all my life—dealing with my problems on my own and keeping my fears inside so they wouldn't set Mom off.

"Look, it's Friday. We only have to make it through today," Eliot said. "It's not like teachers expect *you* to have the answers, Zeke."

"Bro, I'm so distracted, I'm going to get sacked as bad as *you* would on the field tonight," Zeke said.

"Okay, you don't have to insult each other," I said. "We're all feeling the tension right now."

They both looked at me.

Peyton laughed and bumped her shoulder against mine. "They always talk to each other like that," she said. "It's how they show love."

"Oh," I said, feeling stupid and clumsy with my words. I picked up a roll and started tearing off pieces so I'd have something to do.

"We're all having trouble relaxing," Finn said, his fingers brushing the back of my hand to stop my nervous bread butchering. His kind eyes only made me feel more awkward, though. This was why I needed Xander. His cutting remarks and snarky sneers were the thing that kept me strong.

"He's right," Peyton said. "We all need to chill. We're going to kick Truro ass tonight, and that's all we need to worry about right now. That, and making sure you have the time of your life, Gwen."

She dropped her hand onto my knee and gave it a little squeeze. Warm tingles spread up my thigh.

"Exactly," Zeke said. "The guys will be with you the whole time. You're going to have a blast."

"I don't know," Eliot said, frowning at the three of us. "We probably shouldn't all be at the field at the same time."

"Damn," Zeke said. "You're right."

"Well, me and Zeke have to be there," Peyton said. "And Gwen."

"Xander won't want to come," Finn said.

"I wouldn't be so sure," Eliot said, studying me as he spoke. "There's a lot of things Xander wouldn't have done a few weeks ago, but I think he's changing his tune."

"Then I'll stay home," Finn said quietly.

"Cool," Zeke said, biting into a burger. "The rest of us will enjoy this game while we can. If we're really going into another world, who knows when we'll get to go to another football game?"

"Wow, so sensitive," Peyton said. "You always know just what to say."

"Oh, shit, sorry," Zeke said. "I wasn't trying to put on the pressure."

We all laughed, but it seemed forced. He was right. We'd found the giant, as Heimdall had instructed, but that wasn't the end. Who knew when he would come back asking us to perform some other task? The hole into the other world was still in Boston, and at some point, we were supposed to go through it. Another freaking world.

For now, our parents had told us to go to school, act normal, and try to recover from the attack the day before.

I smiled at Finn and touched the back of his hand. "Thank you," I murmured. I didn't know if he even liked football, but he was volunteering to be the one left out. This might be our last time to do something normal together, and he wouldn't get to be there. Although he didn't make a big deal of it, I knew it was a sacrifice.

Chapter Three

Gwen

A t the bottom of the stairs, I balked. Joaquin was standing there talking to Finn.

A cold chill shot straight up my spine. I didn't even like knowing he was in the same house, and I definitely wasn't ready to face him. I'd been prepared to go off to a fun football game, not confront my attacker. But I had no choice now.

"What are you—what is he doing here?" I asked, my eyes darting between him and Finn. The god had said one of us would betray the others. Was Finn still friends with this asshole after what he'd done to me? Was that the betrayal? Knowing a betrayal was coming made it hard to trust my stepsiblings. Part of me just wanted to get it over with.

Rosa stepped out of the kitchen, an apron tied around her short, round figure. "Don't worry, Gwen," she said, joining me where I stood clutching the railing. "I have put the giant to sleep inside him."

"It's still there?" I asked, pulling my hands into the sleeves of my jacket. I wanted to shrink inside it, to disappear so his eager eyes couldn't find me.

"Hey, Gwennie," he said with a dopey grin, like nothing had ever happened. I'd found him funny before, if slightly obnoxious and over-the-top. Now I couldn't see anything but a creep who had lured me to his house and threatened to make my worst nightmares come true.

"I haven't yet found a way to rid him of the giant completely," Rosa said. "I don't know if I can perform that kind of magic with the rune stones I have. But as long as the giant is bound in a sleeping spell, he is just Joaquin."

"How long does the spell last?" I asked, my stomach turning.

"I don't know," Rosa admitted with a frown. "It would be best to get him back to the world of the giants as soon as we can."

As much as I wanted to ask more questions, I had to focus on Joaquin right now. I didn't know how long we'd be stuck with him, but I knew this moment would determine the rest of our time together. I'd had some experience with creeps when we were homeless, and I knew not to show fear.

"Hey, Joaquin," I said, forcing my legs not to tremble as I moved across the sleek wooden floor of the foyer. "I see you're back to your old self."

"It wasn't very nice of your family to keep me locked up all day," he said. "Today could have been the most important day of my life."

I stopped in front of him, my heart hammering so hard I was afraid he could hear it. He just looked like regular old Joaquin, with his adorable smile and floppy surfer haircut. He seemed like the same boy who had flirted outrageously with me and made me laugh when I was overwhelmed on the first day of school by being such a cartoonish human being.

The same boy who turned out to be a knife-happy psycho.

He sported a black eye now, but Xander hadn't landed any other punches on his face. I didn't want to think about what the rest of him looked like. Xander had beaten him pretty badly. He winced as if in pain when Finn took hold of his arm, obviously not trusting Joaquin to behave himself.

"Too bad you had to go and attack me," I said. "Speaking of, shouldn't you still be tied up like a dog?"

"It's not my fault," he said. "The giant made me do that."

I didn't like fighting, but there had been times we'd had to get out of tough situations. I'd been in a scrape or two. Now seemed like a good time to make sure Joaquin knew that he wouldn't take me by surprise again. My mom had always told me to go for the groin. So I punched Joaquin in the crotch.

"Sorry," I said as he dropped to his knees with a howl of protest. "The god made me do it."

"Come on, Gwennie-Gwen," Joaquin said, looking at me and raising one hand in a supplicating gesture. "I thought we were friends."

"I did, too," I said. "Until you tied me up and tried to rape me and slit my throat."

"Dude. You're really going to hold that against me? I was possessed."

"I am, too," I said. "And you don't see me trying to murder anyone. Look, I get it. It sucks to have someone else driving you around and asking you do to things. But in the end, you could say no. They can't actually make us do anything."

Joaquin dropped his hand. His eyes flickered with this strange, haunted look before he climbed to his feet, his hands guarding his groin. "Then you really *don't* get it."

"I guess I don't," I said. I turned to Finn. "I'm going to the game. Are you sure you'll be okay here?"

"Sure," he said with a shrug. "We've been friends for years."

The words hung in the air between us. He'd been friends with Joaquin. Maybe he was still friends with him. I didn't know Finn all that well, but if anyone would be willing to forgive, it was Finn. He might be able to separate

Joaquin from the actions he'd taken when under the influence of a giant, but I couldn't. I wasn't that trusting. For the majority of my lifetime, I'd trusted only my mother. When I'd finally let down my guard and trusted someone else, I'd ended up tied up in Joaquin's chair with a knife at my throat. I wasn't going to be so quick to trust anyone again—especially him.

With a final confirmation from Rosa that she would be around to make sure Joaquin's giant was fully asleep, I headed out with Mom, Neil, and Eliot. When we stepped out of the car at the game, I could smell the salt of the sea on the chill evening air. A truck bounced into the lot, a load of our classmates from Wellfleet High tumbling out as soon as it stopped. Eliot gave my hand a quick squeeze, a secret smile tugging at his lips before he released his hold.

A delicious flicker of excitement began to build inside me. Not just from being near Eliot, but from the anticipation of the game ahead. I was doing what I'd always wanted—being a normal teenager. Going to a football game on a Friday night, walking with a cute boy, looking forward to seeing my new friends. Because that's what they were. My stepsiblings had embraced me, welcomed me. Even Xander had come around.

I could feel the charge in the air as we made our way across the lot to the football field. Footsteps thudded up the small metal bleachers ahead as families climbed up and down, finding seats and going to the concession stand. I let the excitement wash over me, luring me through the entrance where Neil paid our admission. A couple preteen girls ran past shrieking while two laughing boys thundered after them.

There were probably a hundred people on each set of bleachers, spread out along the metal benches, huddled in their jackets or wrapped in blankets. Eliot's hand grazed my back as we stepped onto the bleachers, and he ducked his head to speak into my ear. "We can leave if this isn't your thing."

"Football's not your thing?" I asked.

"I appreciate the talent and skill of athletes," he said. "But our school is so small, anyone who wants to play gets a spot on the team. Let's just say, most of them are not bursting with talent or skill. They just want something to do, and they know this will get them laid."

"Then I'm surprised you don't play," I said.

"I don't need football," Eliot said with a smug smile.

I wanted to find his arrogance off-putting at the least, but with his dark curls and that confident step, it was hard not to be taken in. He steered me to the bottom row, where some freshman girls started giggling as they scooted over to make room. I sighed. High school was getting less fun by the day.

But when I looked over, the girls weren't making fun of me. They were making eyes at Eliot, talking and gesturing too loudly as if trying to get his attention. He grinned at them, and a flicker of irrational jealousy went through me. I had no claim to him, and I had no right to be jealous considering I'd made out with his brother. But my heart didn't care about logic.

I elbowed him in the ribs. "Quit," I said. "You'll break their hearts."

Eliot glanced at me, his brows raised in surprise. "What's that supposed to mean?"

"Zeke told me about you," I said. "That you don't date girls, you just string them along."

"That's the exact opposite of what I do," he said. "I date a lot. I just date more than one person at once. Monogamy is unnatural for humans. When I'm interested in a girl, I tell her up front, the first time we hang out, that I'm going to be hanging out with other girls, too. If that's a problem for her, she can decide to back out before we get involved."

"That's all very logical," I said. "But what happens when feelings get involved?"

He blinked at me from behind his dark-framed glasses. "What do you mean?"

I twisted my fingers between my knees, avoiding his scrutiny. "I mean... what if someone thinks she can handle it, but then she gets jealous? Or what if she knows she wouldn't be okay with that?"

"Then we don't date," Eliot said slowly, his eyes steady on my face. "What's this about, Gwen?"

"Nothing," I said, crossing my arms and huddling into my lumpy jacket. Surely this couldn't be the betrayal Heimdall had warned of, but it still hurt. This was the second time today one of the Keen brothers had basically shot me down. But what else could they do? They were being rational, and I wasn't. I was listening to my heart, which wanted them all. They were listening to the world around us that said it could never happen.

My mom and Neil arrived with popcorn and drinks, as if to emphasize the impossibility of what I wanted. I could never have Eliot. What did it matter how many girls he dated, or if he dated them all at once, or if he checked out the freshman girls who were practically screaming for his attention?

The fact remained that he could have them, but he could never have me. Why shouldn't he have them? And why wouldn't he want to? They knew how to flirt. Even now they were swishing their hair, throwing popcorn at each other, and shrieking so he'd look their way, watching from the corners of their eyes and smiling when he did. They knew what it was all about. And they'd probably be fine if he dated the whole lot of them.

I had no idea how to do all that stuff. I'd never had a boyfriend. If I had one, I didn't think I'd really want to share him with even one of them. Which was silly. I liked other people besides Eliot. I had no right to resent him for wanting more, too. But just seeing those girls arranging themselves in pretty poses made me want to leap across the bleachers and yank their shiny hair out.

Instead, I reached up and began unfastening my own hair. A minute later, the whole mess of it cascaded down over my shoulders and back.

"Whoa," Eliot said. "That's a lot of hair."

Before I could drive myself crazy analyzing that statement, a hush fell over the crowd. I looked up, expecting the team to be emerging onto the field. No sign of them.

Then I felt it—the buzz in the bleachers under my feet and in my seat. The same feeling I'd had when I came here with my siblings before. It was almost like the frenzied atmosphere of the crowd, but this was lower, more intense. When I saw the girls whispering and pointing, I turned in the direction of their attention.

Xander stood on the ramp leading up to the bleachers, his eyes scanning the crowd. For a second, I could see the vulnerability in his gaze. Everyone in the stands was staring. This was a place where he had been king, and now he was the guy who smoked under the bleachers. He'd told me football hadn't mattered to him, he'd just done it to pass the time, but in that brief second, I knew he'd been hiding his true feelings.

The pain of it ripped through my chest, as if it were something I had lost.

"Xander," I whispered, pressing my palm against my belly.

His eyes snapped to me as if I'd spoken his name over the loudspeaker. A blank expression dropped over his face, and the pain was gone. He was just Xander, scowling savagely at some girls who waved at him as he made his way up the ramp, stepped around Mom and Neil, and planted himself beside me, squeezing me against Eliot.

"You made it," Eliot said, reaching around my shoulders to give Xander a soft clap on the shoulder. "Looks like I'm not the only one who noticed."

"I don't do football," Xander growled. "They probably think I'm going to blow the place up."

"But you're not," Neil said with a frown.

I bristled, putting a hand on Xander's knee and giving it a quick squeeze. I was pretty sure the buzzing in the bleachers intensified before I pulled away.

"Are we the only ones feeling this?" I whispered, turning to Eliot.

"I don't think so," he said with a slight frown. Most people had gone back to making noise and stomping, but a few people motioned at the metal bleachers and looked freaked. I didn't blame them. I was a little afraid we'd electrocute someone.

"Zeke said the lights went out before, and that stuff sometimes happens at the games. Should we all be here—even with Finn gone?"

"Gwen!"

I looked down to see Peyton bouncing on her toes at the railing. She had a pair of pompoms that she was shaking together in front of her chest and a rub-on tattoo of a silver oyster on her cheek. I waved.

"Are you having fun yet?" she called up. "We're about to get started. Relax and enjoy it, 'kay?" She couldn't say more, but I caught her eye.

Enjoy it because we never know when our god is going to show up and tell us our time in this world is over.

So I tried. I ate popcorn, drank a soda, and huddled between my stepbrothers. When the team came out, everyone stood and cheered, and I stood with them. For a second, I felt self-conscious standing there screaming for something that wasn't even real. It was just a game. But then Zeke turned and found me, and his face broke into that dazzling smile. The girls beside us started squealing, maybe thinking he was smiling at them, but I knew.

He threw his arms up in a gesture of victory. I lifted my fingers in a tiny wave, a smile breaking over my face before I could help it. Then he pulled on his helmet.

"Is he going to get hurt out there?" I asked as he raced across the field, looking up at the ball instead of back at the three-hundred-pound slab of opponent barreling down on him. I grabbed Eliot's hand, my fingers digging in to anchor myself.

"He'll live," Xander said. "It's football, not a duel."

"There's a high probability he'll get bruised up," Eliot said, squeezing my hand. "But he'll soak after the game, and he'll be fine by the next game."

I winced as the opponent crashed down on Zeke. He looked so big at home, all muscles and broad shoulders. But here, compared to these guys, he didn't look so huge. I could barely see his feet sticking out from under the tank that had run him over.

"Why is everyone cheering?" I hissed at Eliot. "He could be hurt."

Xander snorted.

"He got a first down, and he kept the ball," Eliot said. "That was a successful play."

"You mean he's going to have to do that again?"

Eliot laughed, putting his arm around me. "All night long. That's his job. He's the running back. He gets the ball and carries it as far as he can."

"Can't he have a less dangerous job?" I asked, tearing at a thread on my jeans. I was going to unravel my entire pants by the end of the game.

"Like that one?" Xander said as the guy trying to throw the ball got slammed to the ground.

"That's what Xander used to play," Eliot said. "QB."

I turned to Xander, who was watching the game with a slight smirk, as if it were all beneath him. But his gaze moved around the field like he was planning out the next ten plays. I saw something else behind that smirk. Longing. Loss.

I touched his knee.

Without taking his eyes off the field, his fingers closed around mine, and I felt what it was like to be someone else's anchor. It was scary but also made my chest swell with importance. He didn't let go until the team ran off the field, and a brass band took their place. Neil turned to say something to Xander. His eyes dropped to our linked hands, and a frown furrowed his brow. I pulled away, shoving my hands under my thighs.

Crap. I absolutely had to get better at hiding things— not just my feelings, but this new thing with Xander. I didn't know if it would ever go further than it had the night before or if that would happen again. But whatever was between us, I didn't think it was parent-approved.

Peyton and the cheerleaders jumped up and started doing cheers, which everyone in the stands seemed to know. Her pink ponytail swung as she danced, her slight curves alluring as she moved in a sultry rhythm, the light glimmering on her sleek skin. Her eyes met mine, and time seemed to slow, her hips gyrating slowly, her pink mouth moving. I could no longer hear her, could only watch her skirt rise and fall on her thighs as she bent and twirled.

A hand squeezed my elbow, and I jolted to attention, my heart hammering. What the Helheim? My head was spinning. Eliot frowned at me. He'd obviously asked me a question, but I hadn't heard it. His eyes darted to Peyton and then back to me. Did he know? Could he tell what had distracted me?

"Gwen?" Mom asked, leaning forward to peer at me. Her eyes were wide, just short of panic. She didn't like crowds, even ones of a hundred people. That was ninety-nine too many.

I reached over and squeezed her hand. "Let me know if you want to leave."

"Do you want to leave?" she asked.

I shook my head. I wanted to do this, and she knew it. She also knew I'd be out of there the second she said the word.

Instead, she sat back, watching me carefully. I turned back to watch the cheerleaders. Okay, so now I liked a girl. Or did I? Was it just the god pulling us together, or did I really like her? And how would I know? Did I like girls, or just Peyton? Trying to figure it out was making my blood pressure rise. It was all too much.

Maybe I really was as bad as the mean girls thought. If my stepbrothers had offered, I would have crawled into a different one of their beds every night. And not just them. Peyton, too. But it wasn't about attraction. It was about wanting to be close to them, wanting to belong with them. Wanting to be part of the Keen clan—normal, admired, always protected. They had each other's backs, stood together no matter what. I wanted that, too. I just had to figure out how to get it, how to belong.

I swallowed, forcing my eyes away from Peyton. Alejandra was at the end of the row. Shit. Not only was I lusting after a girl, I was lusting after one with a girlfriend.

For the rest of the game, I managed to act like a normal human being. I felt my mother watching, but I joined in with everyone else, stomping the bleachers, standing when they stood, and watching the banks of lights blink on and illuminate the field. I felt a rush of excitement sweep over the entire stands, nearly buoying me off my feet when Zeke finally broke away from all the defenders and ran down the field, crossing one white stripe after another, ticking off the ten-yard increments until he rounded in the end zone and threw up his hands again, turning to find me as he had before. My heart swelled, and I wrapped my arms around myself as I smiled back at him. I knew that inside his helmet, his mega-watt smile was just for me.

Finally when the game ended, I followed the others out of the stands in a daze. The lights, the small-town crowd, the noise of cheering, and clang of footsteps on the metal bleachers—it was all building inside me along with the charge of being with the others. There was something in the air, the atmosphere of the night, that made me feel sad despite the team's victory over the other tiny school. Yawning parents carried droopy little ones out, but everyone my age seemed to be pumped up by the win. I wanted to be swallowed by it, to disappear into the crowd and absorb all that energy.

When I stopped at the bottom of the stands, Mom pulled me aside. "Did you see something?"

Yes, but not a raven or a giant or anything that would freak her out—just my stepbrother and stepsister looking painfully beautiful out there.

"No, Mom," I said, forcing a smile.

I wasn't the one who had visions, who went nearly comatose and came out screaming. I still remembered the first time she'd done that, the first time I'd really had to take care of her, though I was too young to understand that's what I was doing.

We'd just gone on the road for the first time, and we'd been in a grocery store when Mom zoned out so completely, I'd been afraid she'd died. I'd seen her stare off into space lots of times, but this was different. She was no longer making a game of seeing how much food we could get for forty dollars, checking labels, and having me painstakingly copy down the prices in my childish handwriting.

Numb with terror at having her ripped away, I'd whispered for her to wake up. Even then I knew as if by instinct that I had to protect my mother. I couldn't go running up to the cash register and ask the nice cashier to help me or even yell for Mom to wake up. I had to be very quiet while I tried to rouse her because if someone came and saw us, they'd know that she was broken. That would be bad, though I couldn't have said why or how I knew this. I just did.

And then she'd roused herself, shrieking about giants. Everyone had stared, and I'd grabbed her hand so tight she couldn't get away. She'd run from the store, dragging me behind her, before the manager even got to us. We hadn't eaten that night.

"You can go home," I said, putting my hands on her shoulders and keeping my voice firm. "I want to stay until Peyton and Zeke are done."

That wasn't exactly true. I wanted to stay, but mostly because sitting between Eliot and Xander all night had wound me tighter than I could bear. Mom's watchful eye had only made things worse. I just needed to be away from them—all of them—for a minute. A minute to breathe, to let all the tension slip out of me. A minute to be just me. As much as I wanted to be part of something bigger, I also wanted to still be myself. Sometimes I didn't know who I was anymore. It was like the god took over entirely.

"They have a car," Mom said, licking her lips nervously. People crowded around, chatting with their friends, taking selfies, cheering about the Wellfleet win. Little kids chased each other up and down the emptying bleachers, and someone was yelling about a party.

"I can ride with them," I said. "You shouldn't wait."

"I can't just leave you here by yourself."

"Mom," I said, squeezing her shoulders. "I'm fine. I'll be fine. I won't talk to anyone but the Keens, okay? I just want to stay a little longer. Soak this in. Trust me?"

After a long hesitation, she nodded. "Don't go off with anyone else," she said. "Even if you know them."

"I won't," I said with a shiver, thinking how stupid I'd been to walk home with Joaquin. Even someone who seemed like a harmless clown could turn out to be a psycho.

"Do you think it's okay if she stays?" Mom asked Neil. "Would you leave your kids here?"

"I do it every week," he said. "Gwen has a good head on her shoulders. She'll take care of herself."

I nodded to Mom, letting her go. I watched her walk away. She looked back over her shoulder, anxiety and doubt written all over her. I smiled and waved to show I was fine, and then we were separated by a group of yelling, celebrating kids from school as they left the stands.

Eliot broke away from the crowd and joined me, leaning down so I could hear him. "Zeke can drive Peyton home. We'll see them there."

I scooted away a step, but I didn't want to say something that would hurt his feelings. This was all dizzyingly new to me. I took care of Mom when she needed me, but feelings were not part of the equation. But Eliot would be okay. He didn't look like the type to get his feelings hurt. His looks combined with his wealth probably made it easy to walk through life with the kind of confidence that made him emotionally invincible.

"I… I'm going to stay," I said. "To congratulate them. I'll see you guys at home, okay?"

"Are you sure?" Xander asked, frowning at me.

"Yeah," I said. "You don't have to watch me every second. I learned my lesson, and I won't do anything stupid. It might be better for us to be apart, anyway. Let some of this charge go away."

"You're probably right," Eliot said, nodding. "The bleachers were buzzing with the three of us up there. Add in Peyton and Zeke…"

"I'm on my bike," Xander said. "It'll just be the two of us."

"Or if you need some quiet after all this, I can take you," Eliot said. "How about I won't talk to you all the way home?"

"No," I said, pressing a hand to his chest. "Let me stay. I want to celebrate their victory with them."

Eliot covered my hand with his, pressing my palm to his heart. I could feel it beating steady and strong under his sweater. He closed his eyes, drawing a deep breath. When he opened them, I caught a flash of something I'd never seen in Eliot before. I had no idea what that look meant. I was a socially stunted, facial-expression illiterate idiot.

An idiot who was completely overwhelmed by all these *feelings*. Mom and I didn't talk about feelings, unless we were feeling cold or hungry or something along those lines. Now my heart threatened to explode every time one of my stepsiblings walked by.

The moment Eliot and Xander left, I stepped away from the few groups of people still hanging out and found my way under the bleachers. It wasn't exactly quiet, but it was solitary. I leaned back against one of the support poles and closed my eyes. What was happening to me? People fell in love all the time, and yet, they kept their autonomy, kept their heads. They remained themselves. The truth was, I wasn't sure I even knew who I was. I'd never gotten to be anything other than Mom's protector and daughter. It had been enough. Now it wasn't.

The moment I opened my eyes, Zeke's form cut through the crowd, appearing as if from nowhere. He strode under the bleachers, grabbed me in his arms, and swept me around in a full circle, laughing and whooping. "We won!" he yelled. "Did you see that touchdown? I totally slayed."

"You totally did," I agreed, my glumness melting away.

He set me down on my feet. "It was all for you," he said, taking my face between his hands. "I was thinking about you sitting up there watching me every minute of the game."

And then his lips were on mine without warning, firm and confident. He kissed me hard and fast, like he had been waiting to do this for a long time. Like he knew I wanted it as much as he did. His hands held my face, and his body pressed mine against the metal beam holding up the bleachers. My hands found his hips, pulling him closer, wanting to feel every inch of his body: the tight muscles above his hipbones, the thick muscles of his back, the knotted muscles of his broad shoulders. I'd never even known I liked muscles, but they felt so good under my hands, so strong and commanding.

He sighed, responding to my grip on his hips by grinding slowly against me. My lips fell open in a gasp, and his tongue swept over mine, claiming my mouth. The intensity of the kiss increased as I let my hands explore his body. His tongue began to thrust against mine, his hand slipping inside my jacket to gently massage my breast. A flame ignited in my core, my body straining against his as my knees went limp.

I linked my hands around his neck and held on, letting his hips support my weight as he pinned me to the cold metal, the heat of him searing into me. His tongue stoked the fire inside me higher and higher until I thought I'd burst into flame. Somewhere, I heard distant screams, but my brain had turned off. Only my body mattered, the need pulling tight inside me.

"Hey," a voice yelled, and I felt the jolt as someone hit Zeke.

He broke our kiss, and I blinked at Peyton, trying to comprehend what she was saying. She was standing there with Alejandra while back on the field, people were yelling and gesturing. Spots of flame danced on the grass, and smoke billowed up from the overhead lights.

"What happened?" I muttered, shaking off the daze.

She glanced at Alejandra and then at us, biting her lip.

"Someone threw something on the field," Alejandra said. "All these little fires started in the grass. It was nuts! They all just burst up at once. Nobody knows who started them."

"The fire department is on their way here, but the fires are so small that people are just stomping them out," Peyton said. "This time."

I drew a slow breath as Zeke released me, making sure I found my feet. The cold air hit my body like a slap. My head cleared, and I caught the unspoken words behind Peyton's statement.

What about next time?

On the bright side, Alejandra didn't seem to notice or care that I'd been kissing my stepbrother. Even though he was a Keen, everyone else had been too busy looking at the fires to look for Zeke, which meant they'd been too busy to see us kissing.

On the not-so-bright side, I was pretty sure I knew exactly who had started the fires. This time, it had only taken two of us.

Chapter Four

Zeke

This called for a serious hot tub meeting. I wasn't even sure how it was possible to cause little fires everywhere, but Gwen and Peyton were sure it had been us. Maybe Heimdall wasn't cool with his pieces kissing. It wasn't like it was incest, since it was all pieces of the same thing. Which meant it was more like whacking off.

To be honest, I wasn't sure if I was cool with us kissing. I mean, it had been cool, don't get me wrong. Or hella hot, to be more exact. But I was pretty sure Dad would be pissed, not to mention her mom. Olivia had brought Gwen here so we could take care of her and protect her, not hook up with her.

I was all about protecting her, and I wanted way more than a hookup. It was super obvious that Gwen had never hooked up with anyone, though, and I didn't want to go breaking her heart if our parents put a stop to it.

Tonight was definitely not the time to make a decision. It was time to call our god. When Finn finally slinked out the door and climbed into the hot tub, I expected it to explode or something, but not much happened. Not that I wanted to explode, but I expected a god to do something spectacular like the pyrotechnics display.

"Are you okay?" Gwen asked Finn when he slid into the water. As a matter of fact, the dude had been acting a little weird lately. Weirder than usual.

He nodded.

Eliot turned to me. "What happened?"

"Apparently, we set the football field on fire," I said. "But I don't see how, since only three of us were there. Unless some of you snuck in to spy or something."

Eliot was looking at me in that way he had, like he could read my mind.

"Why would we spy on a football game?" Xander asked. "We were just there and we left. Since when are you paranoid?"

"Maybe you should tell him what you were doing when the fires started," Peyton said, smirking. "It could have been the spark between you that ignited the grass."

Gwen's face got all red, and she looked hella embarrassed. And sexy. Super sexy. I wasn't going to say anything because Dad had taught me that a gentleman doesn't kiss and tell.

"We...were..." Gwen said, looking down at the water like she wanted to slide under it and disappear. I tried to take her hand, but she crossed her arms over her chest. Her awesome chest that I totally wanted to touch again, next time with a little more privacy and a lot more time to enjoy it.

"Kissing," Peyton said. "They were kissing under the bleachers. Zeke was kissing Gwen." Apparently, Peyton didn't care about gentlemanliness.

"Okay, they got it," I said. "Can you stop saying *kissing* over and over?"

Everyone was silent for a minute. Then Eliot spoke up. "And yet, we're all together now, and nothing's happening."

"Just tell us what it means," I said. "You've got that look on your face like you're dying to share it."

Eliot shook his head. "I do have a theory," he said. "When something has happened, it's been a high-stress situation. Since we're all part of the same thing, to the god it's like internal turmoil when we have conflict."

"So it's building tension because there's tension between us," Xander said.

"Right," Eliot said. "Like that day we blew out the cafeteria windows. There was a pull between us before Xander came in. But when he came in angry, the windows blew and the tension snapped. Once we all went out and sat there together, we didn't start any fires. It was like the energy that had built from our friction had been spent."

"So we're not being punished for being together," I said. "We're being punished for being apart."

"Sort of," Eliot said. "It's just a theory."

"What about tonight?" I said. "There wasn't any tension. We were both into it. Right?" I turned to Gwen.

She turned that cute shade of pink again. "I might have had some internal conflict," she muttered.

"But there wasn't conflict between us," I said.

"I saw you," Peyton said. "So there were three of us there."

I frowned at her. "But the fires were already going."

"No," she said, crossing her arms just like Gwen. "I saw you, and then I heard a bunch of people screaming, and I went to grab Alejandra."

Had we been kissing that long? It felt like we'd barely gotten started. I could have kept kissing Gwen all night. Maybe it had been longer than I thought. I'd liked plenty of girls before, but this was different. I liked Gwen a lot harder, a lot deeper. It kind of freaked me out. I barely knew the girl, but I knew I wanted to know her better. And not just in the sex way. I wanted to know what music got stuck in her head, and what scared her enough to keep her awake at night. What food she craved when she couldn't sleep on those nights, and what could finally make her fall asleep. I wanted to be the one who could chase away those fears and put her fascinating mind to rest.

"Still," Gwen said after a slight pause. "There were three of us there. I think it's getting stronger. It used to take all six of us."

"Heimdall said we had a task after we got rid of the giant," I said. "Maybe he's telling us to hurry up."

"There's one way to find out," Gwen said, slipping her hand into mine. I cradled her fingers, feeling how small and delicate they were. It was like the last time, like we were plugging into a power source when we joined hands. When Peyton took my other hand, another part was connected. At last, the circuit was complete.

The water in the tub began to swirl, and that shiny golden dude appeared above us. "You have identified the giant in your midst," Heimdall said. "Well done, little humans."

I didn't know if I liked being called a little human, but I figured I shouldn't argue with a god, so I let it go. There were bigger things to worry about than my pride. I wasn't actually sure I could talk, anyway. I was pinned to the edge of the tub by all that shininess.

"What do you want us to do with him?" Eliot asked.

"Kill him, of course."

Peyton's eyes widened, and she exchanged a look with Finn, who had gone a little pale. This god was probably used to bloodthirsty Vikings jumping at the chance to murder someone, but Joaquin had been our friend. Sure, the guy was kind of a tool, but he surfed with us. We'd known him our whole lives. It wasn't his fault he'd been infested by a giant instead of a god.

"Any alternatives?" Finn asked. More than ever, I felt this connection with the others, as if we were all thinking the same thoughts at the same time.

"You must rid yourselves of him," Heimdall said. "Return him to his world if you cannot defeat him."

I wanted to say we could have, and we just didn't want to, but I figured it was better not to say anything than to give him a reason to think he'd picked the wrong hosts. The others might have had doubts, but I was stoked to find out I was a god.

"Assemble my pieces, and then you will be ready to complete your task."

"May we know what task you have for us?" Gwen asked.

"You must fix Bifrost."

"The rainbow bridge?" Eliot asked.

"It's not a rainbow," Heimdall shouted, and water shot up from the tub to circle around him. He moved his hand in an arch, and the water moved with it, making a rainbow shape between his hands. "It is made of the seething green sea, furious fires of red, and the blue sky itself."

"And we're supposed to fix that?" Xander asked. "I'm handy with a wrench, but I don't know about a tri-colored elemental rainbow."

"Not a rainbow," Heimdall thundered. The air around us trembled, and the water crashed back into the tub, blasting into our faces. The dude obviously had something against rainbows.

"The bridge," Eliot said. "How do we fix it?"

"You must use it," Heimdall said. "No one but a god may cross. When you have all my parts together as a whole, you will bring me across the bridge. In the past two thousand years while it waits for the gods to cross at Ragnarok, it has fallen into disrepair. Now, it will be strengthened each time you cross until it is strong enough to hold all the gods."

"When do we need to leave?" Gwen asked.

"Do not delay." The sun-like apparition began to spin. "You have your tasks set before you. Perform them well, my hosts."

"Wait," Finn said, but the glow was already so bright we couldn't look directly at it, and after a second, it blasted out like a star exploding.

"Well," Peyton said. "Looks like we'd better get ready to go to Boston and find this hole into the other worlds."

Chapter Five

Gwen

A week later, we were ready. I stood in my room, looking out the window. Mom sat on the bed behind me, rocking and muttering. When the gods and some other beasts had torn through into our world on the night I was born, she'd been gifted with the ability to see the future, including the apocalyptic end of the world at Ragnarok. I'd just always thought she was crazy.

Suddenly, she jumped up and came over to me. "Don't go."

I turned and studied her, my guard going up automatically. Though she'd never hurt me, in a way I'd always been afraid of her. I'd spent my life tiptoeing around, indulging her paranoia, trying not to upset her, and never having a life of my own. For ten years, I'd been hardly more than a hostage to her mental state.

I hadn't known better for so long. I was a child when we went on the road. She told me it was a road trip, and at five years old, I didn't argue. As I grew older, I didn't have friends or classmates with normal lives, so how could I have compared my life to anyone else's? I didn't know anyone else. As the years went by, I'd gotten used to it, maybe even grown numb to it. But that didn't mean I was okay. It didn't mean what she'd done was okay.

I'd always assumed she loved me as I loved her— fiercely and helplessly, having no one else. But lately, I had begun to resent the way she'd made all my decisions, manipulated me into doing as she wanted, and never let me experience a life of my own. If I could have convinced her to go to a hospital years ago, I would have. But she wouldn't go to a hospital. I had given up everything for her because of her stubborn refusal to get help. She hadn't given up anything for me.

She hadn't done what was best for me, even as I tried to do what was best for her, to accommodate her illness. All along, Neil had been looking for us. She'd run from him the night I was born. When my dad was killed, she hadn't looked up Neil. If he could find us by hacking into some computer, she could have found him. Instead, she'd kept running until *she* decided she was done, ten long years later. I would have been better off here, even if she'd had to dump me on his porch and run off on her own.

"Don't go," she said again, her eyes going far away as she clutched at my sleeve.

She was the child here. That's what I hadn't understood all those years. I should have made her get help. I hadn't realized that I had that option, that through the years, I'd become the stronger one. Now I knew—now that it no longer mattered.

"I have to go through, Mom," I said. "Heimdall's inside me. I can't just tell him to go away."

"You'll be hurt," she said, reaching out to touch my face. I used to long for those quick touches, the only human contact I got. Now they seemed so insufficient. I needed so much more than an occasional brush of the hand doled out like charity.

"It doesn't matter if I get hurt," I said. "The whole world will end if I don't go."

"It's dangerous," she said. "There's heartbreak there."

"There's heartbreak everywhere." I sighed and took her hands, softening towards her as I always did. It wasn't her fault that she was cursed with this sight any more than it was mine that I was a piece of Heimdall. Neil had said the visions had taken a toll on her mental state, and I couldn't fault her for that, either. Despite what she had or hadn't done, she was still my mom, and I shouldn't be so hard on her.

Her hands clenched around mine, crushing my fingers together painfully as she dragged me closer. "We could run," she whispered. "We can get in the car and go."

I pulled my hands from her. "No. I'm not running. That didn't solve anything. In fact, it probably screwed me up beyond repair."

My mother wasn't in any state to hear my words and react to them rationally. She was freaking out. Before she'd dragged me to Cape Cod and gotten married, we would have run when she got like this. "We'd be safe on the road," she said, as if she'd forgotten the past month had ever happened.

"Safe from what, Mom? From heartbreak? I'd rather take the chance and get to know what love feels like than be trapped in a car with a bunch of crappy, dated novels that don't tell a quarter of the real story."

"Are you in love?" she asked, her eyes suddenly clear and sharp.

Shit. I'd walked right into that one.

"I don't know," I said, sinking to the edge of the bed. "But I'm doing this, and you can't stop it. It's commanded by a freaking god, Mom. Who are we to argue?"

"You can't stop Ragnarok," she said. "I've seen it now. There's no stopping it. It's fate. Each god must do his part, but in the end, all must fulfill their destiny and doom."

"Then you should know that Bifrost has to be ready for the gods to cross," I said. "That only makes it more important for us to do our job now. Come on. They're waiting for us."

Downstairs, I sucked in a breath when I caught sight of Joaquin. I had known we were taking him with us since it was the only way to get rid of him aside from homicide, and we were teenagers, not freaking murderers. But seeing him still made me break out in a cold sweat. A shudder went through me, and I tried not to remember that night, the knife in his hand and his fingers in my hair, against my skin.

"Don't even look at her," Zeke said, grabbing Joaquin's arm like he was getting ready to manhandle him if he so much as stepped towards me.

I really didn't like the idea of riding all the way to Boston with him. He'd unsettled me all week, but no one wanted to risk letting him leave. Rosa didn't know how far her spell would carry, if it would last when she was away from him. He might disappear or come after one of us again.

I was pretty sure that I had let him know I wasn't some weakling he could push around, but I wasn't taking chances. The night of the attack, he'd gotten me at a vulnerable moment when I'd just had a huge fight with Xander, but it wouldn't happen again. He was a giant. Now that I knew it, I wouldn't trust him, no matter how funny and charming his human side might be.

"Ready?"

I jumped a mile as Eliot's hand brushed the small of my back. I glanced up at him, not moving to step away. He smiled down at me, his eyes so warm and sparkling the tension melted from me, and I found myself relaxing back against him. With his dark curls, glasses, and infectious smile, he was completely gorgeous. My eyes fell closed as his thumb made a slow circle on my lower back, and my legs started trembling for a whole new reason.

God, I needed to get a hold of myself. We were in the middle of something completely nerve-wracking, and yet one touch and I was imagining what his fingers would feel like if they slipped under my shirt and caressed my bare skin.

A shiver of longing went through me, and I opened my eyes. Eliot watched my face with keen interest, as if observing what his touch could do to a girl was a scientific experiment. But his thumb was doing something that was anything but clinical. It slowly trailed down my spine to my tailbone, and I drew a deep, shuddering breath. His eyes lit on my lips, and all I could think about was how his lips would feel like on mine. Would they consume me like Xander's, or ignite me like Zeke's? And how could I possibly go from never-been-kissed status to wanting to make out with every guy in the house?

I was so confused I wanted to turn and run out the door, to escape this chaos inside my head. When my mother's footsteps sounded on the stairs, Eliot whipped his hand away from me so fast you'd think he'd been burned. "See you at the car," he said, ducking past me and out the door.

My heart was still thudding when my mom reached the bottom of the stairs with her bag. We weren't sure exactly how this world-hopping worked, but we were prepared to be there a few days at least.

"What's wrong?" Mom asked when she saw me standing just inside the front door.

"Nothing. I'm fine."

Every time I lied to her, it became easier.

Outside, Neil waited in the Mercedes SUV. When I opened the door and saw Joaquin in the back seat, I balked.

"Hell no." Xander's growling voice sounded behind me, and I spun around to find him standing there with his arms crossed, glaring at his dad. "Gwen's not riding in a car with her attacker."

"It's okay." I swallowed past the swell of nerves building inside me. My head and heart and body were all pulling in different directions. "I'm not scared of Joaquin," I said softly, putting a hand on Xander's chest.

"No," he said, stepping between the Mercedes and me. "I don't care. There's not enough room for everyone anyway. You can ride in the other car with me."

We hadn't really planned out the car situation, since we'd been more worried about what happened when we got to Boston. Now, it seemed so silly that something so trivial could trip us up. Zeke got out of the Mercedes and went to the garage to get his own car. And although I'd told Xander I wasn't scared of Joaquin, when I saw him sitting in the back of Neil's car, unguarded, with an open doorway between us, my pulse raced. My chest warmed with gratitude that Xander had stepped in front of me. I gripped his jacket, pressing my face into his shoulder like we were riding on his bike, the cold air burning across my face, flying over a hill with the ocean blurring by across the dunes.

"Come on," he said, turning away from his father and Joaquin. His strong hand engulfed mine, and he led me to the garage and pushed me into the back seat of Zeke's waiting car with Peyton. I slid into the middle seat to make room for him. He leaned in, resting his fists on the seat, and pressed his lips to mine. My heart somersaulted, my veins liquifying in my chest. Before I could register what was happening, he pulled away.

"Aren't you coming with us?" I asked, my insides rearranging around the new ache when he stood and gazed down at me with hooded eyes.

"I don't trust Joaquin," he said. "I need to watch him."

I nodded, knowing it was stupid to feel like he was abandoning me when he walked away. I just wanted all of them with me all the time. But he was right. At least some of them had their brains still intact. Maybe because they'd all had this experience before with regular people. I felt small and ridiculous in the face of this huge desire that threatened to take me over. They knew how to function as normal human beings without letting their hormones rule them, while I didn't seem able to keep from being swept away every time we touched. It didn't seem fair. It wasn't a level playing field.

Even worse, what I'd said to my mom echoed back in my mind, clear and true as the sky. I didn't know if I was falling in love. I knew I wanted my stepsiblings, and it wasn't only because of the god. But I didn't know how to tell what part of it was the god, how much of it was just me having my first crush, and how much was being so overwhelmed by the presence of all these attractive guys that I couldn't choose which one I wanted most. And worst of all, I didn't know if any of them felt anything back except the pull of the god. What if we completed the task and Heimdall left us? Would they want anything to do with me?

The thought sent a pang of fear through me. I'd only just begun to be a part of their family, their inner circle. It still felt new and fragile, like something too good to be true. If it crumbled to nothing in my hands, I might not survive it.

"Damn," Peyton said after a long, awkward moment. "I'm going to have to get used to seeing you kiss my brothers, aren't I?"

I didn't know what to say. My face burned as I slid away from her, buckling into the other seat. She turned to look out the window, but Zeke twisted around in his seat, bracing his hand on the back of the passenger seat. "So you and Xander, huh? The bastard. I should have known."

I remembered the heat of Zeke's kiss the night before, how it had spread through my whole body, and how I'd never wanted to stop. How right it had felt. I felt safe with him, comfortable, admired. He made me feel good about myself in a way none of the others did.

"Xander doesn't even date," I said, turning to the window. "It's not like that."

"I don't know if I'd go that far," Zeke said. "He might hate girls, but he's never been one to discourage them from doing everything in their power to change his mind."

I glanced at Peyton, my heart twisting painfully. "He said he didn't—"

"Are you sure he didn't say that he doesn't hook up?" she asked. "Because everyone at school knows that. But yeah, I don't know if I'd say he doesn't date. He just does it more to punish girls than to actually enjoy their company."

All the joy and excitement of the moment with Xander had been dashed by her and Zeke's words. He'd kissed me—right in front of them. I should have been marveling in the miracle of that change. Instead, I was filled with guilt that I'd kissed him in front of Zeke, and trembling with insecurity that Peyton's assessment might be true of all girls. Was Xander just toying with me, leading me on because I was such an easy target? Punishing me because some other girl had hurt him?

Eliot slid into the front seat. "Let's go," he said, buckling in. "Bifrost is waiting."

No one spoke as we pulled out of the garage and followed the Mercedes down the long driveway. Finally, Peyton turned to me. "I'm sorry. I know that's not what you want to hear. I told you before. Xander's a complicated guy. And he's a wonderful brother. But he's no saint. You know that. Three days ago you hated him."

I pressed my nails into my palms, focusing on that pain rather than the ache in my throat. Would Xander go that far just to hurt me? I didn't think so. But I couldn't know that for sure.

"Why do I get the feeling I missed something?" Eliot asked, flipping down the visor and meeting my eyes in the mirror.

"Xander kissed Gwen," Peyton said.

"Was it hot?" Eliot asked with a grin. He didn't seem the slightest bit surprised or phased by that. He'd been the one who pushed me to smooth things over with Xander to begin with. Maybe he'd sensed that we were fighting the attraction between us all along.

But I wasn't as cool as Eliot. I turned to Peyton. "You forgot to mention that Joaquin also slobbered all over my face when I was tied to his chair."

"What?" she asked, her eyes widening.

"If you're going to broadcast the news every time I kiss a boy, you might as well keep track of them all."

Her mouth fell open, and I immediately regretted my words when she turned back to the window, her pink ponytail trembling as she bent her head.

Shit. I lay my head back against the seat and closed my eyes. I really did not want to start off a two-hour car ride like this.

"I'm sorry," I said.

"It's okay," she said, not turning from the window. "We're all a little tense."

I got the feeling it wasn't okay at all.

Chapter Six

Gwen

At last, we arrived in Boston. We were supposed to go to Mass General and poke around, with Neil throwing cash and his big name around to grant us access to different parts of the hospital. We'd go rent a hotel room and make the circle to call Heimdall if we couldn't find the entrance.

When we found it, one of us would go through for just a minute, look around, and come back to report what they'd seen. Neil had supplied us with backpacks filled with first-aid kits, water bottles, food rations, clothes, and a few camping items like flashlights, batteries, and compasses. We had no idea which world we'd step into, or what it would be like. Rosa, who had been in the dwarf world in her lifetime, would be our guide. She said she didn't know much about the other worlds, but she could read the rune stones and guide us to our missing pieces.

When we hit Boston traffic, I lost sight of Neil's car. I could feel the distance between us, anxiety gnawing at my insides like a rat was nibbling at my nerve endings. Joaquin had been playing nice for a week, but what if the spell wore off and he went all psycho again? Xander and Finn were in that car.

My mom was in that car. The realization jarred me that I'd been more worried about them than her. I'd thought about them first. For the first time in my life, my mom wasn't the foremost thought in my mind. Guilt churned inside me, but also resentment that I had to feel guilty for that. The Keens didn't spend all day thinking about their dad. They mostly thought about themselves and each other, from what I could tell.

I sat back in relief when Eliot said we were stopping to talk to them. Twenty minutes later, we pulled up in a mostly empty parking lot at Walden Pond. It was cold out, with low clouds hanging over the sky that hinted at snow. The window of their car slid down silently, and I had a second to marvel at how nice expensive cars were. The cars I'd spend most of my life in had squeaky window cranks, or automatic windows that leaked, got stuck, or didn't work at all.

Neil's face appeared in the window. When I'd first met him, I'd thought he was as posh and polished as his sleek black Mercedes. Since then, I'd started to see the cracks in his exterior, the strain all this had put on him.

"Finn thinks we should look here," he said.

"Why here?" Zeke asked out his open window.

Neil ran his hand through his dark hair. "He says he has a feeling about it."

"Good enough for me," Eliot said, unbuckling his seatbelt.

"Aren't you the one with the premonitions?" I asked.

"Anxiety," Eliot corrected, turning in his seat to smile at me. "Finn's hunches are always right."

"Wow," I said, biting back a smile of my own. "I figured you'd need a more scientific explanation."

"Hey, they're one hundred percent accurate so far. Just because I haven't found a logical explanation doesn't change the cold, hard facts."

"I thought we were going to the hospital," Zeke said to Neil.

"It won't hurt to check here first," Neil said. "The hole could be here, but they might have needed a fairly blank slate to inhabit a human, so they chose infants. We don't really know how it works."

"If we don't find anything here, we'll go to Mass General," Eliot said. He was already out of the car by the time he finished speaking. He pulled my door open and hauled me out, where I stumbled against his solid chest.

Sliding his arms around me, he lifted me off the ground and hugged me tightly. "Here we go."

I laughed and pushed away from him, starkly aware of the others eyeing us as they climbed out of the vehicles. He seemed much less concerned with what anyone thought. I hadn't yet mastered that skill.

"All right, psychic boy," Zeke said, throwing an arm around Finn. "Lead us to the rainbow bridge."

"I don't know if we should call it that," Eliot said. "Heimdall didn't seem to like it."

We donned our packs and started down a path towards the pond. The trees were bare and stark, and although we could hear traffic noises, it felt strangely removed from the city. Finn took the lead with Zeke close behind, and the rest of us fell into our usual order along the trail behind. Rosa and Neil brought up the rear, keeping Joaquin close. We had told our parents pretty much everything Heimdall had said—how we were pieces of him, that we had to find Bifrost and fix it, that we had to get rid of Joaquin. We'd left out his suggestion to murder Joaquin, but Mom was definitely keeping herself between us on the trail. She was possibly the only person on earth who trusted Joaquin less than I did.

While we walked along the edge of the pond, Finn scanned the trees intently as if looking for a sign. I slipped past the others and fell into step beside him.

"What are we looking for?" I asked.

"The biggest tree you've ever seen."

"I don't know about that," I said.

He gave me a small, close-lipped smile. "That's right. You've probably been to the Redwoods."

"Yep."

His fingers brushed mine and my chest squeezed, but he pulled back. Shoving his hands in his pockets, he frowned and studied the woods again.

"What's wrong?" I asked, dropping my voice so no one else could hear. I reached out to touch him but hesitated. He'd withdrawn, so that probably meant he didn't want to touch me. I just didn't know what I'd done.

"Nothing," he said. "I think this is it." He left the path, making his way to a huge tree looming over the pond.

"How do you know?" Peyton asked, wrapping her arms around herself. She looked up into the bare branches, biting at her lip nervously.

"I don't," Finn said, shrugging and stuffing his hands deeper into his pockets. "I'll climb it and see."

"No," Zeke said, dropping his backpack and stepping towards the tree. "I'll go first."

"So we're just going to climb a tree, and somewhere up there, we'll find a hole in the fabric of the universe?" I asked.

"I thought I was supposed to be the skeptic," Eliot said, sliding an arm around me as he gazed up at the tree.

"You're not doing a very good job," I said.

"Ouch," he said, squeezing my waist. I leaned against him, thankful to have someone to hold onto as vertigo swept over me. The tree was so tall. I really, really hoped the rip was not too far up the towering trunk. I didn't even like stairs.

Xander and Neil helped Zeke reach the first branch and he began climbing. "Be careful," I called.

"Don't worry. I'm just going to check it out," Zeke said. "I'll let you know if I find anything."

"What about me?" Joaquin asked. "Do I go last?"

"You do whatever we tell you to," Xander said, glowering at him.

Joaquin cringed under his murderous stare.

Suddenly, Peyton cried out. I turned to her. She'd covered her mouth, and her trembling finger pointed to the tree. I whipped around, ready to tell Zeke to watch out. But there was no Zeke.

I screamed, running to the trunk and scrambling for purchase. The pull in my chest to climb the tree overpowered even my terror of heights. Zeke was not on the ground. He was not in the tree. He was nowhere. He hadn't even said goodbye. I had to be with him, though—with all of them.

Xander's arm closed around my middle, and he pulled me back. "Hey, calm down," he said. "Finn was right, that's all. He'll be back in a minute."

He kept his arm around me, my back to his chest. The solid, hard beat of his heart comforted me somehow. He was here, real, alive. And so was I.

We all stood around staring up at the tree. Finally, Neil swore softly behind us.

"We'd better go get him," Eliot said.

"What if it's not safe?" Peyton asked, her eyes panicky. "What if he hasn't come back because he's..." She broke off, covering her face with both hands. Neil put his arms around her, and the rest of us exchanged sober glances.

"We can't just leave him," I said at last. "We have to go after him."

"It's the only way," Eliot said. "We have to fix the bridge together. Lift me up."

"We should say goodbye," I said, trying to keep my voice even but not doing a very good job. "We don't know anything about this world. What if we're gone a long time? What if time works different there?"

I turned to my mom, the immensity of what we were about to do crashing into me. What if I never saw her again?

"She's right," Peyton said, her voice trembling and tears in her eyes. She threw her arms around Neil and started blubbering a goodbye.

I wanted to say the right things to my mom, but I couldn't make the words come. There was so much to say. That I was sorry I'd been short with her lately. That I believed in her goodness, despite her choices that I didn't agree with. It all seemed so petty and insignificant now. She'd kept me alive. Did it really matter if we'd lived in a car or a mansion? Did it matter that I'd lived without human contact beyond my mom? Did it really matter that I hadn't had ballet lessons, birthday parties, or a boyfriend?

Whether it did or not, I hadn't. And that wouldn't change. What would change was the way my mother remembered me, the way I remembered her. I didn't want to carry guilt and regret with me into another world. I wrapped my arms around her and held her tightly.

"Gwen," she said, her voice choked.

"I know," I said. "Me, too."

We were not a family who lived on hugs and heartfelt confessions and conversations about feelings. But somehow, we understood each other deep down, under all that. I pulled away, and she took my face between her hands and looked at me like it was the last time she'd see me. A tear slipped from her eye. "We'll be here when you get back."

I nodded. Squaring my shoulders, I turned and stepped toward the tree. Joaquin leaned against the trunk, his feet crossed, watching us with an uncharacteristic frown on his face. "Must be nice," he muttered.

"What?"

"Family," Joaquin said.

I opened my mouth to say that he'd probably killed his own family, but then I shut it. That wasn't funny. At all.

He nodded at where Neil had engulfed Xander in a bear hug. I waited for Xander to pull away and tell his dad to do something unsavory to himself, but instead, he wrapped his arms around Neil. That gesture cut through my rising panic and sobered me. This was real. We were entering another world, and there was a chance not all of us would return.

Finn had his arms around Peyton, who was still crying. Only Eliot seemed excited instead of nervous. He came over to us, his face nearly bursting with anticipation. I didn't know how he could be so calm. My heart was racing, my breath coming so fast I felt faint.

"Give me a boost?" Eliot asked. Joaquin and Finn joined Neil, and they boosted him up. He looked down at us, then back up at the tree. "Bifrost, here I come," he said, and he started climbing hand over hand, without looking back. I fought the urge to call out to him, to tell him to stop, we couldn't do this. What if we came out in the middle of some crazy Viking battlefield?

"I'm next," Rosa said, stepping up. The guys boosted her into the tree. She was shorter and stouter than the others, but after a little scrabbling, she had hauled herself onto the branch. She looked down, gave a wave, and started after Eliot.

"Joaquin," Xander said.

"Can't I go last?"

"No. Now. I want to keep my sights on you." The tallest guys were left, boosting him up. By the time he'd reached the first branch, Eliot had disappeared. My throat got tighter and tighter as the others climbed higher. I'd lost two of my boys. I didn't even realize I thought of them that way until the words popped into my head. They were trickling away one by one. I bit back the cries that threatened to burst from my mouth. Now I understood how Mom could get so overwhelmed by what she saw in her visions that she ran screaming down the street, not caring what anyone thought—not seeing anyone around. I was barely holding myself from doing the same thing on the bank of Walden Pond.

"Gwen," Mom whispered, plucking at my sleeve. "You don't have to go."

"Mom." I wrapped my trembling, clammy hand arounds hers and held on as Peyton swung up onto the branch like a freaking acrobat. Maybe dance and cheer lessons would come in handy in the other worlds after all. At least she was strong and in shape. I'd spent most of my life sitting in a car. I really hoped that climbing a fifty-foot tree was the only endurance test I had to pass. The vertigo I had just looking up at it made my throat close off.

Despite my fear, there was no going back. It wasn't even an option.

Lena Mae Hill

"It's my turn," I said, squeezing Mom's hand, my heart lurching around in my chest like a bird beating itself against the bars of its cage.

"You'll be careful?"

I turned and gave her one last smile. My insides had turned liquid with fear, but I couldn't let her see it. I was good at calming her even while I was falling apart. "I'll be back, Mom," I said. "I promise."

I knew I shouldn't make that promise, but I also knew that I had to. We always kept our promises. If I couldn't keep this one, I'd die trying. And Mom needed my reassurance. She trusted my word more than anything else in this world.

As they lifted me up, I tried to find a bright side. Maybe this would be good for us both, to learn to live apart, to worry about ourselves instead of each other. She had a new husband to care for her, one who knew exactly how to help a sick woman. I realized when I reached the first branch that I hadn't said goodbye to him.

I looked down. He was watching from below.

"Thank you," I mouthed when our eyes met.

Neil gave me a tired smile, and then he turned to Finn. When his eyes left mine, I suddenly saw how far from the ground I was. My fingers clenched on the branch, and my head swam with dizziness. And then Finn's face appeared over the branch.

He must have seen the panic on mine because he didn't tell me to get off his branch. He climbed up beside me and rested a hand between my shoulder blades. "Always look up," he said softly. "We'll climb together."

"Got it," I breathed, my whole body shaking. "Only look where we're going, never where we've been."

"Exactly," he said. "One step at a time."

It was better looking up, if I didn't look all the way up. If I only focused on the next branch I had to grab, I could do it. Finn climbed right behind me, and when my foot missed a step and I gasped, he pushed it onto the branch before I could look down.

Soon, I couldn't find a branch, but the bark of the tree had gotten rougher, and I could grip the sections of it and pull myself up on them. The trunk seemed to be getting bigger as I climbed until I could no longer see around it. I looked up, only to see more branches, these ones with leaves. It seemed like I'd been climbing for hours.

"Xander?" I asked, feeling strangely blind not being able to glance behind me.

"I'm here," he said, his voice quiet but closer than I expected.

Without thinking, I searched him out. He was right below me, on the next branch. And below him…

My head swam, and my stomach lurched like I was going to vomit.

"Oh god," I gasped, gripping the tree and closing my eyes.

Finn's body slid up behind mine, pressing me to the trunk. "It's okay," he said quietly, his cheek against my ear. "You're okay."

They must have known. They'd looked down already. But when I'd glanced down, I hadn't seen my mom and Neil twenty feet below. I'd seen... nothing. Nothing but branches spinning around the trunk in an endless parade. And the trunk continuing into infinity, growing up through a bottomless abyss.

The world I knew was gone.

Chapter Seven

Gwen

I may have screamed. I threw my body against the tree trunk, gripping onto the branch with numb, frozen fingers. The emptiness of the world below had knocked a hole right through my stomach. I would never, ever let go. I'd puke if I tried. I hadn't noticed when the tree had changed. It had happened so gradually. It was inconceivably immense, the sections of bark as large as my face and the cracks in it as deep as my fingers. The trunk was so big I couldn't see around it. Fog swirled around us, as if we were climbing through clouds.

Finn's hands closed over the backs of mine. "One foot in front of the other," he murmured, his warm breath entering my ear. "Keep going."

"Where are we?" I whispered, my eyes still closed.

"I don't know," he said, drawing the backpack off my shoulders with careful fingers. "But I know the others are waiting."

"Waiting where?" I asked, an edge of hysteria entering my voice. I let him take my hands away just long enough to slip the pack off. Knowledge of the Norse worlds was Neil's specialty, but I'd done some research when I found out what we were. I knew enough that I had a sinking feeling about what had happened. We weren't in a tree on Walden Pond anymore. We were on Yggdrasil, the World Tree—a tree so tall it connected nine worlds, each as big as the human world that I'd known all my life.

The thought of how far I could fall right now blasted my brain right out of my head, leaving only a ball of primal fear.

"Don't think about it," Finn said, his voice a comforting lull. He handed my backpack down to Xander and faced toward me again. "Think about them waiting just ahead and me right here. Listen to my voice. Do you trust me?"

"Yes," I whispered, laying my head back against his shoulder.

"I'm going to move with you," he said. "Just follow my lead. Are you ready?"

I shook my head, just wanting to rest against him and let him carry me. I didn't know if I could ever unclench my fingers from around the branch.

"Well, get ready," Xander said below us. "Because we aren't alone."

My head snapped up when I heard what he'd heard—a flapping sound like canvas sails. "What is that?"

"Eliot will know," Finn said. The fog blinded us from anything farther than five feet along the branch.

"Okay," I said, my voice shaking. "I'm ready."

I'd never told a bigger lie in my life.

We started up, though Finn must have felt how weak I'd become, how useless I was. I wasn't ready for any of this. Heimdall had chosen wrong. I wasn't cut out to be a god. A freaking tree had defeated me. How was I supposed to face the things in other worlds? I wasn't brave. All I wanted was to turn around and run back to my mom. But I'd have to climb back down.

Down.

The thought made my stomach clench and my knees buckle. I gripped the branch in front of me, the bark craggy and cracked. The flapping sound rushed by again, along with a strange, hoarse cry, like some kind of seagull.

"Go," Finn said. "Left hand." His arm moved with mine, his hand closing around a chunk of bark above my hand. "Left foot, and push up."

I followed his directions, and our bodies scraped up the tree together. I focused on the heat of his limbs, his thigh pressing gently against the inside of mine, and his knee nestled behind mine. Suddenly, it was all I could think about. Out of habit, I started to push it down, to ignore the pull of his body. But then I changed my mind.

Maybe I could use this to my advantage. Most of the time, my irresistible attraction to them reared its head at the most inopportune times. Times like this. But if I could use it to get me up a tree as tall as nine freaking worlds, then I'd do it.

"Where's Eliot when you need him?" Xander grumbled as we started up again. I heard him, but my mind was far away. I was shutting down, my brain unable to take in the alien world around me. I let my body take over, focusing only on the warmth and strength of Finn's chest against my back, his arms around mine, his breath sweeping across my cheek. We climbed faster, leaving the seagull thing behind. When Finn spoke his quiet directives into my ear, sparkles rained down my body, making my skin burst into life like new buds in spring. Every cell in my body was a flower, blossoming under the warm sun of his attention.

We moved together in an addictive rhythm. His chest rested against my back, his hands following mine as if he'd pin them above my head, his chin brushing my neck as if he'd skim his lips against my skin at any moment. The warm murmur of his voice against my ear made my toes curl and a sigh escaped my lips.

We climbed and climbed and climbed. My legs and arms ached, my shoulders knotted, and my hands were scraped so raw that I was sure each step was the last I could take.

The fog around us faded into darkness, and soon I could barely see the handholds in front of me. My whole body was one big throb of pain.

A chattering noise jerked me out of my stupor and back to reality. Something shot past us, and I shrank back, suppressing a cry.

Xander cursed loudly.

"Is that Xander I hear swearing like a sailor?" said a voice from above. And even though I'd only known these guys for a few weeks, the familiarity of Zeke's voice made my knees threaten to cave from relief.

"Zeke," I called, so thrilled that I nearly forgot that something had just zipped past us in the darkness. I hurried upwards with renewed energy, my heart hammering.

A minute later, hands reached down for mine, and Zeke pulled me up into his arms. He stood on a branch at least ten feet across, and the others sat or stood clustered together, their flashlights lighting a circle around them.

Rosa knelt close to the trunk, a handful of carved stones in front of her knees. She didn't even look winded. My legs and arms were as rubbery as gummy worms. I was getting really tired of being physically inferior to everyone around me. I vowed to start a serious workout routine when I got home.

If I got home.

Eliot pulled off his backpack and handed me a water bottle before passing it around to the others. Xander set down my pack along with his.

"You got my bag," Zeke said, reaching for mine. "Thanks, bro."

"Unless you want to wear Peyton's yoga pants, I don't think you'll like what you find in there," I said.

"No one brought my bag?" Zeke asked. "You guys suck. I sacrificed my own safety, and you couldn't pick up my bag on the way?" He grinned to show he was kidding, but a sinking feeling settled over me. Not because he'd lost his few supplies—we'd share everything with him—but because we were practically kids. We couldn't even remember to pick up his bag. How were we supposed to save the human world?

"I'm kidding," Zeke said, snagging Peyton's flashlight and slugging her shoulder. "But I'm going to need one of these. And someone's going to have to share deodorant, or we're all going to pay for that one."

"Dude, your god can't even take care of your B.O." Joaquin said, slapping his knee with exaggerated laughter. "Classic."

"I consulted the runes," Rosa said. "This is the branch that takes us to Bifrost."

"I'm ready to get out of this tree," Zeke said, stretching his arms above his head. His triceps bulged against the cotton shirt hugging his skin.

"Do we just… jump?" I asked with a gulp. I peered off the branch into the darkness. The blackness diminished my fear some since I couldn't see the endless nothingness surrounding the tree on the way down.

"We could call a magical flying unicorn and see if it can give us a lift," Xander said. He smirked when I glared at him.

Nearby, the sound of something rattling the leaves made me nearly jump out of my skin. Zeke pulled me and Peyton close, huddling over us protectively.

Xander turned to Eliot. "Any idea what that is?"

Eliot shook his head. "Not until I see it."

"I don't think Gwen's gonna make it," Joaquin said. "She looks like she's about to pitch off into the abyss. You know, I bet a little giant juice could perk you up." He made a lewd gesture, and Xander pulled back like he was going to punch him.

Eliot grabbed Xander and pulled him back. "Ignore him. Let's go."

"I'll help you, Gwen," Zeke said. "I'll jump with you."

"She can do it," Xander said. "Don't baby her."

Just then, a shudder went through the tree. I swayed on my feet, and Zeke tightened his arms around us. I pressed my face into his muscled chest, solid and hot beneath my cheek. "What was that?" I whispered.

"I don't know. I can't see anything. It's too dark." A shiver went through Zeke's body. If this big hunk of a man was afraid, then I had every right to be terrified. He held me as gently as if I were a baby bird. I didn't want to be treated like an invalid, though. I wanted to be strong and ready, as capable as they were. I wanted to be brave.

"Okay," I said, drawing back from him. "Whatever's hanging around in this tree, it doesn't seem very friendly. If I have to jump, I'll jump."

My words sounded confident, but every part of me was screaming in rebellion at the thought of jumping. And then I made another mistake. As I stepped back, my foot hit my bag, and it tipped over. It tumbled down the branch and disappeared, just like that. My heart nearly stopped. Any of us could fall that easily, that fast. One second there, the next…

"We can share clothes," Peyton said, giving me a sympathetic smile.

I wanted to scream. I didn't care about stupid clothes. These people thought that mattered to me. They didn't know I'd spent weeks wearing the same clothes on the road. I'd left everything I owned a hundred times in my life when Mom had decided something had found our motel room or storage locker or even our car, and she hadn't wanted to go back to get whatever meager possessions we'd accumulated in that city.

I cared about *them*. I cared about getting through these tasks with our lives and our bodies intact. We hadn't even set foot into another world, and we'd already lost a third of our supplies. At this rate, we'd be eating each other by tomorrow.

"We need to go out onto the branch," Rosa said. "We will jump into a kind of limbo. It is not any world, but the space between worlds. That is where we'll find Bifrost."

The thought of jumping into nothingness made my heart nearly stop. But I wouldn't show it. I'd be strong and courageous like them. Those who still had packs picked them up, and we started off down the branch. If I kept my eyes on the branch in front of me and pretended that the darkness was just grass outside the path of the flashlight, it wasn't too bad. And it was a relief to use different muscles for a while.

As we walked, another tremor went through the tree and I flinched.

"Maybe it's the serpent that hangs out at Yggdrasil's roots," Eliot said. "It's supposed to shake the tree trying to knock it down."

My throat went dry, and I reached for his hand. "Right now?"

"Not right now," Eliot said. "That was just a tremor. We'll be okay."

"I'll carry you," Zeke said, scooping me up into his arms.

"I can walk," I said.

"I know," he said, giving me that dazzling grin. "But it's more fun to carry you."

"I'm as capable as anyone else here," I said, squirming out of his arms. I stood on tiptoes and gave his cheek a quick kiss. For a second, I felt brave. I'd kissed him, not the other way around. It felt more daring than climbing a tree into another world with a guy who had recently tried to kill me. I turned quickly and started forward again.

"If we were at home, I'd make Daddy charter a helicopter," Peyton said with a sigh.

"Sorry, Princess, your private jet isn't coming," Xander said. "It's jump or get picked off by whatever's taking stock of us."

"Jumping is just falling on purpose," I said. "Who would do that voluntarily?"

Suddenly, a bushy red animal streaked past us on the side of the branch.

"Gah," Zeke cried, yanking me back against him. Peyton, who was a few steps ahead, let out a little yelp.

"What was that?" I asked.

"Was it a rat?" Peyton asked. "Because I really don't like rats."

"Have you ever actually seen a rat?" I asked, trying to imagine their mansion being infested like the tiny studio apartment Mom had rented for cash one month. I spent most of my free time that month sweeping up rat droppings, plugging and re-plugging holes where they came in at night, and chasing them around with brooms hoping I wouldn't get bitten and contract rabies.

"Yes," Peyton said with a sour look in my direction. "I had to dissect one in biology."

"I think it was a squirrel," Eliot said.

"No, it was definitely a rat," Peyton said. "I had to cut open its slithery little tail." She shuddered dramatically to show how little she'd enjoyed that.

"Whatever's running around up here is not a rat," Eliot said.

"If that's a squirrel, I'm not sure it's better than a rat," Peyton said. "It looks like it ate all the other squirrels."

"Maybe they have squirrel steroids in this world," Zeke said.

Rosa, Joaquin, and Finn had gotten a little ahead of us, and my chest tugged at me to go up there, to get Finn. We should all be together. But my legs wanted nothing more than to collapse. We couldn't see the others up ahead, but I could hear Rosa's voice murmuring in the darkness.

"Let's catch up with the others," I said.

With a shiver, Peyton wrapped her arms around herself and picked up the pace. The tree trembled again, and I was grateful when Zeke twined his arm through mine and took my hand, lacing our fingers, so we were walking side by side, pressed together.

A second later, the giant red furball raced back towards us.

Chapter Eight

Gwen

This time, Peyton screamed. She pinwheeled her arms, stumbling backwards. Zeke and I grabbed for her at once, drawing her back into our embrace. I was struck by her softness, how small and insubstantial she felt compared to Zeke's rigid muscles. I slid an arm around her small, soft waist and pressed myself to her back, hoping somehow, our two small bodies could form a stronger, more formidable presence together.

The animal stopped and looked at us, its tail whipping back and forth. It was red and fluffy with a long, luxurious tail like a fox but furrier, bright black eyes, and a little twitching nose. My fear melted, and my fingers itched to reach out and pet it.

"Awww," I said.

"Gross," Peyton whispered, shivering against me.

"It's like a cute, fluffy bunny."

"It's probably rabid," she said. "That thing's big enough to rip my face off. It probably grew so big by eating human brains."

"Better hurry," it said. "The others think you're wasting time. Rosa's tired of hauling your slow butts around."

My brain balked at what I'd just heard, and I blinked a couple times at the others, who looked equally flabbergasted.

"Did anyone else hear that?" Xander asked. "Or do I need to see a shrink again?"

"No," I said slowly. "I think it just... spoke to us."

"Of course I spoke," the furry critter said. "Do I look like an idiot to you?"

"Are you Ratatoskr?" Eliot asked, ever the direct one.

"Call me Ratr," the squirrel said. "Messenger of the Great Ash. Would you like me to carry a message to your friends?"

"We should probably just catch up," Xander said. "The longer we stand around talking, the farther ahead they're getting."

"I don't like being separated from Finn," I said, glancing at the darkness ahead.

"Or Rosa," Peyton said. "She's the one with the runes that are supposed to get us through the Nine Worlds."

"I'll go check in and let them know you're coming," Ratr said. He turned and dashed off into the darkness.

"Be careful what you say around him," Eliot said. "He's known as being a gossip."

"We didn't say anything bad about anyone," I pointed out. "Not even Joaquin."

"Just… be careful," Eliot said, frowning.

"I think he's cute," I said. "And so what if he likes gossip? Doesn't everyone?"

"True," Peyton said, falling into step with Eliot a few paces ahead.

"Can I take him home?" I asked. "I feel like I'm in a Disney princess movie when he talks."

"I prefer *Beauty and the Beast*, where the little creatures are teacups," Peyton said.

Just then, Ratr raced back into sight. "They're not waiting," he said. "They said Gwen's weak. It's a miracle she can even go for five minutes. And they took bets on if Zeke was carrying you."

"What?" I asked, pulling up short. I felt like I'd been slapped. I mean, it was true. And it wasn't like they were being mean. Let's face it, I was no body builder. I'd been busy trying to survive for the past ten years, not worrying about my biceps.

"Ignore them," Zeke said, his hand slipping around my waist and giving me a squeeze. "You're doing great."

"Thanks," I said, but I knew he just said that to make me feel better. I wasn't doing great. I was so slow I'd kept most of the group behind. If something got one of us now, it was my fault. I'd be responsible for one of their deaths just because they'd stayed behind to protect me. And if it came to a fight, they all had more muscle. Sure, I could be a little scrappy, but endurance was not my strong point.

"Any message back to them?" Ratr asked after a short silence.

"Who said that?" I asked, forcing my aching legs to keep moving.

One more step. One more step.

"It doesn't matter," Eliot cut in. "Keep walking."

"I am walking," I snapped. "No one's carrying me."

"We're almost there," Eliot said, his voice low. "Don't let him get to you."

"It matters to me," I said. "Did Finn say it or did Joaquin? It makes a difference."

"Probably no one said it."

"Tell them to leave a mark where we should jump," I said to Ratr. "And that they don't have to wait."

"Happy to relay it," Ratr said, turning and scampering off down the branch, fluffy tail bouncing.

"Still want to take him home?" Peyton asked.

"You guys don't have to wait, either," I said. "I'll be along. I'm sorry I'm slowing you down."

"You're not," Peyton said, smiling at me over her shoulder. I hated the sympathy in her eyes, so close to pity. She knew it had gotten to me, hearing the truth so plainly.

"You're out of shape," Xander said bluntly. "No one is blaming you. Shut up and walk."

"I think what he means is that you should conserve your energy and not worry about gossip," Peyton said. "No one expects you to win a race."

Tears stung my eyes, and Zeke's arm tightened around me. "Dude, we're not leaving you here," he said.

"Let's get off before he comes back," I said.

"I'll get you off any time, babe," Zeke said, his fingers tickling my side.

"She's right," Xander said. "Let's find Rosa and jump. I don't want to hear more of what that thing has to say."

Zeke scooped me up, and this time I didn't protest. I was only slowing them down by refusing to be carried. I wrapped my arms around Zeke's neck, my legs around his waist. His hand spread across my bottom. I tried not to notice the warmth of it searing through my jeans. Resting my head on his shoulder, I let myself exhale, the tension easing out of my shaking limbs.

After a few minutes, I'd relaxed against him, and a different kind of tension began to build in my body. I inhaled his scent, like soap and something sharp and more animal than a girl. I breathed it in like I needed it to live as much as oxygen, sucking in lungfuls and letting it fill my body until I was dizzy with the smell of him. My hands played over the hard ridges of muscle in his back as he walked, aching to pull up his shirt and feel his bare skin under my palms. With each step he took, his body shifted slightly against mine, the friction increasing as it coiled into a tight fist of need inside me.

"Is this making you as crazy as it's making me?" Zeke murmured against my throat. His warm breath spilled over me like honey, sweet and golden.

"Looks like this is where we jump," Eliot said, his voice cutting through my daze. "They left a note."

I'd almost forgotten where we were, who was with us, everything but the perfect synchronization of our bodies. But when Zeke stopped walking, I drew back. "If you climb off me right now, I'm going to have an embarrassingly big problem," he muttered, holding me against him.

"What?" I asked.

For the first time since I'd met him, Zeke looked less than sure of himself. He cleared his throat, avoiding my eyes as he shifted slightly, so I could feel the problem he was talking about. Suddenly, I was the one embarrassed. Heat raged through my entire body, and I was intensely aware of the others around us. One of whom I had kissed, and who might not like that I felt this way about someone besides him.

"Here comes Ratr," Eliot said.

"I'm going to jump," Zeke said in my ear. "I don't need him knowing about this."

Before I had time to work up the proper amount of terror at the prospect, we were airborne. Or rather plummeting through the air at breakneck speed. I screamed, my arms and legs instinctively clutching Zeke. Seconds later, we slammed down on something soft and spongy. Zeke's strong body absorbed most of the impact, but pain drove a spike through one of my knees when we landed on it. We rolled over a few times, my body still wrapped around his. When at last we came to a stop, Zeke was cursing under his breath.

It was completely dark around us, but I could feel a dry, scratchy growth under us like moss. The night was hot, nothing like Boston this time of year. Suddenly, all the adrenaline inside me was spent, and my limbs went soft and shaky. A thrill of exhilaration went through me. We'd jumped, and I hadn't died. I was fine. More than fine. All the hunger of the past few minutes washed over me, and I wanted to share it with someone. With him.

"Are you okay?" I asked, my fingers exploring his shoulders, the blocky muscles of his pectorals that fit perfectly under my palms.

His hands fit over the backs of mine, stilling my groping fingers. "I admit I'm a little confused right now," he said, pressing my palm to his heart.

I could feel it hammering. I swallowed, trying to pull back, but he held my fingers in place. "Me, too," I whispered.

"Well, let me un-confuse you about one thing," he said, sitting up and pulling me close against him. My legs still straddled his hips, and our bodies locked together even tighter as we sat facing each other.

"About this?" I asked.

He sucked in a breath. "Yeah. I like you, Gwen. A whole lot more than I should since our parents are married."

My heart rose to my throat. "Me, too," I admitted.

A thud sounded close beside us, and I detached myself from Zeke and stood, guilt racing through me. The curses coming from out of the darkness told me it was Xander who had landed beside us. Xander, who had kissed me earlier this same day. Shame flooded through me, and I remembered the words of the girl at school.

God, she moves fast.

Was she right? Because I didn't think this was just the god. I wanted my stepbrothers, and not just one of them. I wanted them all. And it was seriously messing with my head.

Another thud sounded, then another.

"Well, this is going to be fun," said Peyton's voice out of the darkness.

"What?" I asked.

"Didn't Zeke tell you?" asked a voice from nearby. Finn's voice.

Shit. How long had he been there? He'd heard everything we said, all that passed between Zeke and me. He'd been sitting in the dark waiting for us. Now, I felt even worse than I had seconds before.

"Zeke's afraid of the dark," Peyton said, switching on her headlamp. She swung it around, taking stock of all six of us.

"Hey," Zeke said. "I didn't tell her your flaws."

"That's because I don't have any," Peyton said with a smug smile.

"Where are Rosa and Joaquin?" I asked.

"Maybe he was eaten by whatever was in that tree," Xander said, sounding a bit too happy at the prospect.

"But we need Rosa," I said, panic edging my voice. "She's our guide."

"I'll light a fire," Eliot's voice said, and his flashlight beam cut through the darkness. "They should see it and come find us."

I stood and called out, but Peyton shushed me. "What if there's something else out here that hears us and comes running?"

"What do you think is out there?" Zeke asked with a shiver.

Eliot pulled out some matches and tinder, and we gathered a few piles of moss and started a small fire. We seemed to have jumped out over a hill covered by lumpy, scratchy moss, which had cushioned our fall. I didn't want to think about what would have happened if we'd come out over a bunch of boulders.

"I'm going to see if there's firewood," Eliot said, standing and shining the light around.

"Don't go far," I said. "We don't know what's out here."

"I don't see a rainbow," Peyton said, pulling out her phone. "And I don't have service."

"Did you think you'd be able to phone home, E.T.?" Xander asked.

"No," Peyton said. "But it was worth a shot. And I wanted to take a picture of the rainbow."

"Dude, you can't take a picture of stuff here and bring it home," Zeke said.

"Why not?"

"I don't know," he said. "You just can't."

"Uh, guys," Eliot called from where he'd gone exploring with the flashlight.

"Did you find Rosa?" I asked, starting towards him.

"No," he called down. "But I think I figured out why it's so hot here."

"Somehow, I don't think he found a sauna," Peyton said with a sigh. She wiped her pink hair back from her sweaty forehead as we scrambled up a mossy incline and onto a stretch of bare stone. At the very top of the hill, the rock fell away into a sharp drop. Sheer stone cliffs formed canyon walls in front of us. Eliot stood at the edge of the drop, his flashlight pointed down into the chasm. Far below, we could see a river of darkness with veins of orange glowing along it.

"Is that... lava?" Zeke asked.

"Let's hope the volcano doesn't blow tonight," Xander said.

"It doesn't look like a volcano," Eliot said. "It's a river, not a lake inside a crater."

"Whatever," Peyton said. "I'll take it over the tree. That rat-squirrel was awful."

I swallowed, balling my hands inside my sleeves despite the heat. "Do you think... what if... Rosa and Joaquin went too far out on the branch and fell in there?"

Silence fell over the group as we contemplated the possibility. Joaquin was gone—but so was our guide. Without her rune stones, we had no map, no direction at all. Panic clawed at my ribcage from within, trying to tear its way out.

"Finn was with them," Eliot said. When we turned away from the canyon, I realized Finn hadn't come with us. He was sitting by himself next to the fire, his silhouette looking small and vulnerable.

"Let's go ask him," Xander said, striding back towards the fire.

"What's up with Finn?" I asked Eliot as we all started back.

To my surprise, he didn't come up with an answer right away. When he spoke, his voice was halting. "I'm not sure," he said. "I'll try to talk to him, but he's been acting weird since... since you showed up at our house, actually."

"What's he normally like?" I asked, guilt twisting in my chest again. I knew Finn didn't date—he'd told me he didn't even talk to girls. I wondered if this whole god bond thing was messing with his head like it was messing with mine. If he was having trouble knowing what was real and what was the product of sharing a deity.

"Like now, just not as much so," Eliot said with a crooked smile that made my heart skip.

He was so calm, so collected that it put me on edge. I couldn't figure out what was going on inside his brain that was always moving, always figuring out other people. I wanted to figure him out, but he sat back and observed like he never expected anyone to turn the microscope on him. I hadn't had a chance to delve past his surface at all.

"Where's Rosa?" Zeke asked as we reached the fire.

Finn's shoulders hunched over further. "I don't know what happened to her or Joaquin."

"What do you mean you don't know?" Xander demanded. "You were with them."

"That squirrel," Finn said. "It said some things to Rosa about the dwarves. She said she was going to check once we got here. But she never got here, as far as I know."

"How did that happen?" Peyton asked, planting a hand on her hip. Was she wondering which of us would betray the others, too?

Finn's bowed head and slumped shoulders didn't speak of betrayal, though. He looked defeated, as if he expected us to attack him.

"Maybe she stepped off at a different spot," I said, resting a hand on Finn's shoulder. "One that led to a different world."

"She must have," Eliot said. "Maybe she stepped off the other side or kept going. We don't know how it works. We saw the note, and we jumped. We're lucky we all ended up together."

"Maybe she took Joaquin back to the giant's world," Zeke said. "She was supposed to do that, too."

"She was also supposed to get us to Bifrost," I said, trying not to lose it.

"Let's just wait until morning and we can look around more," Zeke said. "She has the rune stones. She should be able to find her way back to us if we stay put."

Since we didn't really have any options without her, we agreed. We didn't know where we were going or how to get there without Rosa. We were all tired and sore, so we settled around the fire to eat the food in the remaining backpacks.

Eliot sat beside Finn and spoke in a low voice. I watched from the corner of my eye, not wanting to interrupt. Even though I didn't know what was going on with Finn, I felt like I understood him somehow. I knew turmoil. I didn't understand how someone could be so accepting of this, the way Eliot was. I also didn't know how to relate to someone so guarded, more guarded than Xander, who at least showed his emotions.

I found myself crawling across the distance between us, curling my body against Xander's side. He felt familiar and solid against me, the way he had the other night. Zeke slipped into the space on my other side, providing a safe border from whatever might be out there in the darkness. A deep sense of belonging settled into me. I closed my eyes, knowing that even in this foreign land, in another world, I had somewhere to belong with these five people around me.

Chapter Nine

Gwen

I woke to see the sky lightening above. Xander's lips were close to my ear, his warm breath tickling my neck. His long, dark eyelashes, the envy of any girl in the world, curled softly against his cheek, and his arm lay heavy across my middle. On my other side, Zeke slept, his blond hair picking up the morning light. He'd thrown a leg over mine, and his hand rested protectively on my lower belly.

For a moment, I absorbed this new feeling, the feeling of being cared for and watched over. It made me warm from my toes to the tip of my nose. I snuggled down, relishing the comfort of their bodies next to mine. It felt right like nothing in my life had ever felt. At last I had found the place I belonged, and it was right between these two people.

A scraping sound drew my attention, and I sat up, my mind sharpening as the night before crashed back in on me. I cast a glance around, searching for a sign of the two we'd lost. They were both gone. I didn't know how we'd make our way without Rosa. I'd read some books, and Eliot had definitely done his research, but that didn't mean we could save the freaking world. We were kids. Rosa was the adult with experience who was supposed to show us the way. Our parents would never have let us come here without her.

It wasn't Rosa who had made the sound that startled me. It was Finn, trudging up the incline where the rest of us had gone the night before, his hair loose around his shoulders. Casting a last look back at the sleeping boys beside me, I reluctantly untangled myself from their limbs and started after him.

My hands were swollen from the day before, my palms an angry red, and my knuckles aching from overuse. But in truth, I probably shouldn't even be able to move them today. When we'd fallen from the tree, Zeke's weight had landed on my knee, but it didn't even hurt today. The healing power of hosting a god seemed to have taken care of the worst parts of my injuries. I'd always been pretty healthy, never getting sick even though we didn't live in the best conditions. But this was much more than that. When

Joaquin had cut me, it had healed within an hour. Still, healing quickly seemed a high price to pay for having to endure this insanity.

Anxiety gripped my chest as I clambered up the incline after Finn. I didn't know what Eliot had said to him the night before or if it had helped. When I reached the top of the embankment, Finn was standing at the edge, looking down into the lava stream. Across it, on the far side of the huge chasm, we could just make out the shapes of a city in the sky, emerging from the darkness. Tall spires glinted faintly in the creeping dawn light, though we could barely distinguish the silhouettes of buildings shrouded in mist.

"So, this is what you were looking at last night," Finn said, his voice flat.

"Yeah." I stopped beside him, unsure of what to do with myself. Why had I followed him? Had I actually thought I could help him feel better? Eliot was the smooth talker, and if he couldn't do it, I certainly couldn't.

"No sign of the others," Finn said.

"It must have been really scary," I said. "Jumping into this world alone." I tried to imagine the fear of jumping into the dark by myself, without Zeke's protective arms. Falling, and landing in this strange, dark place. Sitting there alone, not knowing if or when anyone else would arrive. Wondering if I'd been tricked into jumping, and no one was coming.

Finn didn't answer, just stared down into the lava river. I crossed my arms and hunched my shoulders. I felt awkward next to him, clumsy and somehow extraneous.

"How long were you here by yourself?" I tried.

"Not that long," he said. "A while."

"Did Joaquin tell you to jump?" I whispered, my throat thick. If he'd somehow woken up, if he was under the giant's control again, he might be trying to separate us…or get rid of one of us.

"No," Finn said. "Rosa said it was the right place, and that rat…it said some things. I was a little mad, I guess. I wanted to get away from them all. So I jumped without waiting for her to explain more."

I didn't know what to say to that. I didn't know Finn well enough to know if that was normal for him. I didn't want to label him as the stereotypical moody, impulsive artist, even though he seemed that way. I'd already learned that people weren't that easy to label.

"You think Rosa went on to dump him in Jotunheim?" I asked. "Maybe the giant woke up, and she had to get him away from us."

"Yeah, maybe."

"What's going to happen to him?" I asked.

"I don't know," Finn said, shoving his hands in the pockets of his jeans. Hot air gusted up from below, blowing long tendrils of his hair from his face. "What's going to happen to any of us?"

"What if Heimdall doesn't leave us when we're done?" I asked, admitting my greatest fear in all this. I wanted to live my own life, to be normal. I could hardly do that with a god hitching a ride inside me. "He's been part of us since we were born. I don't know if we'll ever be done being gods."

Finn frowned. "And that means Joaquin's stuck as a giant forever, too, right?"

"I know he was your friend," I said. "I'm sorry if he's stuck in the giant world. But to be honest, I'm relieved he's gone. Even with the rune spell on him, he made me nervous. What if it wore off?"

"I was worried, too," Finn admitted said. "It's just... I know Joaquin. He's not violent. Once the giant was asleep, the real Joaquin felt terrible about what he did."

I bit my tongue, not wanting to remind him that his friend had been plenty violent the other day. Even though he'd been possessed, it was hard for me to completely forgive him like Finn had. I just wasn't that good.

"Well, they're gone now," I said at last.

"I'm sorry I didn't stick closer to them. I should have waited for you."

"What did Ratr say that upset you?" I asked. If it stung as much as what he'd said to me, I didn't blame Finn for not hanging around listening for a minute longer than he had to.

He shrugged, hunching his shoulders. "A lot of things. Like that you guys didn't trust me when I was with Joaquin, and that I was... different."

"We never said that."

"But it's true," he said.

I was tempted to reach for his hand, to comfort him the way I had at home. But I didn't know if he wanted my comfort now. Something had shifted between us yesterday, and I could feel it pressing into the space between us, unspoken words suffocating me. We'd shared an intimate experience when we were climbing, but instead of feeling closer, as I'd felt with Xander, all I felt was the sting of rejection as Finn pulled away and closed himself off from me. I wanted to shake it out of him, to make him talk to me about it. But I didn't even know how to talk to him about it, so how could I ask him to open up to me?

"No one blames you," I said at last. "Why are you so hard on yourself?"

He let out a laugh that was nothing more than a quick release of air. "I don't know. Maybe I learned it in church. We're all sinners, right?"

"Doesn't sound very fun to me."

"It's not supposed to be fun," he said. "It's a way to be better, to be accountable. But how can I be a good Christian if I'm part of some other god I don't even believe in?"

"I… I don't know," I said. "I'm the last person you should ask for advice. I've never set foot in a church in my life."

"What about what we want?" he said, turning his tormented gaze on me. "We didn't ask for this. Where is our free will in this whole situation?"

I wanted to make my own choices and live my own life as much as the rest of them, but complaining about it wouldn't help anything. All we could do was obey now and hope it was enough to satisfy Heimdall.

"Maybe we don't always get free will," I said. "Maybe sometimes we have to give that up to serve the greater good. If it's a choice between having free will and saving everyone in our world from being possessed by giants and turning into psycho killers, I'll be a god's puppet."

"I'd like to think we can do both."

"I don't know, Finn," I said. "I'm just working on the part where we fix the bridge so the gods can cross."

As we'd talked, the sky had grown brighter. At last, the sun hit the city on the in the sky. It was so high it appeared to be floating on clouds, with great spires of gold and silver almost blinding me when the light hit them. I drew a breath, moving instinctively towards Finn.

"We should wake the others," he said.

"Yeah." I hesitated, not sure how to say the things I wanted to say.

"You go," he said. "I'll stay here."

I turned to go, but then paused. It was like I could feel what was happening inside him. "You don't have to be separate from them," I said. "If you're different, it's because you make yourself that way."

"I know," he said, his back to me. "It's just... Everything is easy for them."

"You've had the same life they did."

"They're used to feeling this way," he said, his voice dropping.

My heart thudded. I'd been willing to walk away without finding out what was going on with him. All I had to do was ask. If only I knew when to push and when to leave him alone. Peyton would have known.

"Feeling this way about... girls?" I asked.

The second the words left my mouth I cringed. I sounded so desperate and naïve. Of course, he meant that. If he was like Zeke, he would have said yes, the way Zeke had last night. And I would have told him I felt the same. But Finn was not Zeke. He didn't say anything, and the longest, most awkward moment in the history of any of the world—of all Nine Worlds—followed. Then I turned and ran down the mossy slope, escaping the painful silence hanging in the air.

Eliot watched me arrive back at the campsite, breathless and squirming with discomfort. Why had I gone after Finn? I should have known I couldn't comfort him. I understood struggle, but I couldn't understand the complexities of his turmoil. For me, survival had always come first. I didn't have the luxury of moral dilemmas.

"He okay?" Eliot asked, watching me intently.

"Not really," I said, accepting a bottle of water that he held out to me. "Anyone here good in an existential crisis?"

Eliot laughed, which immediately settled my nerves. "First, we save the world. Then we deal with our internal crises. Sound good?"

I nodded, a smile tugging at my lips. "I was just thinking something along those lines."

The others were stirring around us, awakened by our conversation. Peyton sat up and stretched while Zeke and Xander blinked at each other and then scooted farther apart.

Eliot held out a hand, and I pulled him to his feet. "I'm a little worried that there's no sign of this bridge," he said. "Want to try calling Heimdall?"

"He said we couldn't call him in this world," Peyton said. "Where's Finn?"

"I guess Ratr upset him last night," I said, nodding towards the rim of the canyon.

When everyone was up, we headed up the hill towards Finn. Halfway there, the sun fell into the chasm below, and a roaring sound filled my ears like when the wave had knocked us off the beach. I looked up in time to see a giant arc of water rising from a cave in the wall of the canyon. It rose and rose, thousands of feet into the sky, a thundering river flowing not on the ground, but through the air.

"Holy mother of Heimdall," Zeke said, his jaw dropping.

"Holy nine mothers of Heimdall is more like it," Xander said.

"That's one crazy water slide," Peyton said. "Anyone pack an innertube?"

It was unlike anything I'd ever seen—a churning, wild thing, almost alive, seething its way through a huge swath of the sky. It was so incongruous with the shining city in the distance, which stood peaceful and idyllic like a picture of heaven.

Finn stood frozen on the rim of the canyon, his small frame dwarfed by the powerful torrent above. My eyes caught on his sad figure and I started running. "Finn," I called, racing towards him, afraid he'd be swept into the lava below.

The rest of the Keens followed as a stream of air rushed from the cliffs below and climbed the water like a shimmering mirage. Just before I reached Finn, a sound like a train barreled into us, and a wall of fire shot up the side of the air current, following the arc of the water. Three elements formed an arc from the base of the canyon wall to the shining city, just like Heimdall had described.

As the bridge roared through the sky, I could see why calling it a rainbow diminished it. Rainbows were pretty and sweet. This was terrifying in its power.

We stood in a line along the edge of the cliff, gaping at this thing we were supposed to fix. I didn't see how it needed fixing. It looked pretty intact to me.

"So we're going to cross that," I said slowly. "This should be easy."

"Yeah," Peyton said. "Especially since you can't swim."

"And I'm covered with burn scars, so I'm not that fond of fire," I pointed out.

"I guess you'll have to climb the air part," Eliot said.

"Lucky me, I'm afraid of heights," I said.

"No fucking way," Xander said. "You're not going on that, Gwen. No one here is. I'll go fix the damn bridge. You can stay here on solid ground."

"Bro, you really think we're going to let you go alone?" Zeke asked.

"I don't think anyone can go alone," I said. "Heimdall said we have to do it together. All nine of us."

"Then we'd better find the rest of our squad," Peyton said.

As if in answer, a roar sounded from below. The fire had spread along the lava turning it to a blazing river of fire. Halfway across, two people struggled through, trying to reach the other side as they burned alive.

The shock of the sight drove through me like an ice pick. But there was something else, too—an irresistible urge to save them. It dragged me a step closer, until my toes were hanging over the edge.

"Gwen," Eliot shouted, grabbing for me. "You can't save them."

"It's *them*," I screamed, shoving his hands away.

I turned back and looked down.

Down.

It all happened in seconds. They were at the bottom of an enormous canyon, two burning forms. And above them were hundreds of feet of sheer cliffs. The world swam before my eyes, and my knees gave way, and suddenly, I was pitching forward into the chasm of fire.

Chapter Ten

Gwen

I screamed like I'd never screamed before in my life. Not like when Zeke jumped from the tree with me the previous night. That had been a short fall. Not like when Joaquin had been torturing me, and I kept it inside my head, screaming for my siblings to come find me. This time, the scream tore from my throat, a primal, animal cry. I felt it, but I couldn't hear it over the roar of fire, wind, and water.

Thoughts and memories flashed through my mind. Heimdall saying we'd lose one as we gained another. I hadn't realized it could be me. I could be the loss. I could be the betrayer. I could be any of the members in the prophecy. I just happened to be the one plummeting to my death. Terror had frozen me, turned me to stone in midair, so I couldn't even flail or scream or think.

I remembered the last fire—the one that had taken our house and my father. I remembered before that, back when he'd carry me on his shoulders, holding onto my legs so I wouldn't fall. Scattered pieces of my life swirled by like bits of paper rising from a fire on a plume of smoke. My mother screaming about ravens. A tiger I'd seen in a forest where no tiger should live, how silent and still it had been as its golden eyes took me in. My mother saying it wasn't dangerous. Computers were dangerous. I remembered the gum wrapper blowing across the rest area where she told me she'd met Neil—on a computer.

I remembered my mother warning me these boys could hurt me, the heart-stopping tension in the air when Peyton pulled back from lining my lips with makeup, and the ravaging hunger in Xander's eyes before he kissed me. The certainty in Zeke's kiss, the knowledge that it was right. Finn's shy smile. Eliot's reckless one. The unbearable charge of being in the room with them. Then the fire swallowed me.

I slammed into something solid and... alive.

"You should not be here," shouted a guttural, foreign voice.

You think?

Fire blazed around us, and I smelled the singe of burnt hair as I made out the flaming man holding me in his arms.

"It's her," another voice shouted, a voice belonging to the other guy, visible through gaps in the dancing flame. "Get her out."

Fire licked at my skin, the heat pulsing over me in unbearable waves. I wanted to black out, to go away, to not feel my flesh cooking, and my skin bubbling. I screamed again, and again, and then my mouth was too scorched to go on. Hours could have passed or only minutes, but suddenly I was dunked into frigid water. It seethed around me, steaming and gurgling, forcing its way into my nostrils and down my throat like the wave that had claimed me on the beach the day of the wedding.

The wave hadn't killed me. The fall hadn't killed me. The fire hadn't killed me. But this water swallowed me, and at last I blinked out.

"Wake up."

I opened my eyes. Heimdall was there, my god, my savior, my tormentor.

"Help me."

"You must be strong," he said, his voice booming like thunder through the worlds.

"What if I'm not?" I asked. "Why did you choose me?"

"I entered nine weak mortal beings because they were nearby when I entered Midgard, but I have made each strong. You jumped into the river of fire to collect two of my pieces."

I probably shouldn't mention I hadn't jumped. I'd fallen, quite unwillingly.

"You are almost complete," Heimdall said. "You must find the last piece before the bridge goes out. It is fading even now."

"But how?"

"Trust your guides," he said, his image flickering.

"We lost our guide."

"You do not need outsiders," he said. "You only need to complete me. My pieces will take you to Jotunheim. All nine of you must blow the horn so that the gods may cross. You have trials ahead, but I will not appear again. I am with you always. I am your heart. You need not call me, for I am inside you. Just listen, and you will find me there. Do what you must to stay strong and united, and let nothing come between you."

Heimdall vanished, and I was back in my solid body, wet and shivering and burning all at once. A mouth was on mine, pushing air into my lungs.

"She tastes like golden honey," a deep voice said. A form swam above me, then clarified. I shoved him off, sitting up and spewing freezing water.

"I'd vomit, too," said the second man, laughing heartily as he slapped my back so hard I was sure a rib cracked. I stared down at my hands, my skin charred and blistered and swollen. I wanted to touch my face, which throbbed with the same unbearable pain as my hands, but I didn't dare.

We were in a damp, mossy cave with water dripping from the walls. A seething wall of water—the waters of Bifrost—blocked most of the mouth of the cave. Through a small gap at the edge, I could see the burning river.

All I could think to say was, "I'm alive." It came out as a rasping, tortured sob. The fire had been extinguished, but the exposed parts of my body screamed with raging pain, as if I were still burning.

"Yes, you are," said the guy who had been giving me mouth-to-mouth. They were both soaked, their clothing not much more than charred tatters hanging on their huge, muscular frames. Each of them stood at least seven feet tall, with long, wild blond hair and matching beards, though they didn't look much older than me.

"Are you... Vikings?" I asked, looking back and forth between them, willing my mind to work through the screen of pain.

"We're Thor," one of them said, his barrel chest swelling. "I'm also called Alvan and this is Valdan. We can heal your wounds."

I would have ripped off my skin and handed it over for the promise of relief. I nodded mutely, allowing Alvan to lay me gently on the cool, mossy stone floor. The huge men took up positions on either side of me, careful not to touch my throbbing skin. Their bodies were solid walls of muscle that would have made Zeke look child-sized. A flicker of fear went through me at the knowledge of my sheer helplessness, but I was in too much pain to worry about what they had planned. I needed help.

They locked arms over me, and a faint golden light began to emanate from their skin. Though they didn't touch me, I could feel heat of their bodies burning into me, drawing a scream from my throat. "It gets worse before it gets better," Alvan said. "We walk through the fire every day, and we're fine, healthy men, aren't we?"

I tried to say yes, but I wasn't sure if the words made it through my lips. I felt like my skin would peel off under the warmth of their sunny glow.

"Thor chose the most beautiful beings in the Nine Worlds," Valdan said. "We show our worthiness of his inhabitation by walking through the river of fire each morning, just as Thor did when he was in his true god form."

"As long as we stay together, we're a complete god, and we can't be harmed," Alvan said. "The closer you are to your other pieces, the faster you will heal, too. It doesn't work for all wounds, but it works for most. The water has begun to restore you already. Look, Valdan, her skin is healed by our presence."

"We are gods," Valdan said, as if reminding him. "They say human skin is like silk. I've never touched it before. Shall I?"

119

"Not now," I growled. The mere thought of anyone touching my seared skin made me want to start screaming and never stop.

Heimdall was singing inside me, though, saying yes, he wanted more. Anything that brought us closer was good: our parents marrying, being drawn to my stepsiblings, being healed by these two Viking gods. But then Finn's voice echoed in my mind asking if we could still have free will. Like a conscience, it hovered over me, telling me I was healed now, that I had no reason to still be so close to these strangers.

I sat up again, scooting from between the Viking gods. "I'm okay," I lied. Though my skin looked fine, inside I was raging with heat like a deadly fever. Speaking felt like glass grinding in my throat.

"Don't you want to get closer?" Valdan rumbled behind me. "That's our task as pieces of the gods. Alvan and I are twins. We share everything."

"Um, no."

"I can see how closeness might be achieved differently with a pretty human girl than with each other," Valdan said. "We are, after all, the god of fertility."

"You're also supposed to protect humans, aren't you?" I asked, standing on aching legs.

"We were protecting you," Alvan said. "We saved you from the fire."

"Thank you," I said, squeezing water out of the remains of my jacket. It promptly fell into lumps of sodden, scorched stuffing. "So, you're Thor. Just the two of you?"

"We are strong enough to hold the most illustrious god," Valdan said, hopping up and strutting in the firelight illuminating the cave.

The light of the fiery river behind him glimmered off his enormous, golden pectorals. Water trickled over his skin, carrying soot with it. I was momentarily awestruck by his physical perfection as I watched a droplet roll between the ridges of muscle that formed a V-shape on his lower abdomen. Swallowing hard, I pulled my eyes away from where the V dipped under the tattered band of whatever he'd been wearing on his bottom half.

"Wow," I said. "Though if you have to walk through fire every day, I'm glad all I got was a glowing guy who wants us to fix a bridge."

"Oh, we've got Heimdall, too," Alvan said. "That's why we saved you."

"So if I wasn't part of the same god as you, you'd have let me burn to death?"

"We can't save every bird and bug that falls into the river," Valdan said.

"I'm not a bug. I'm a human being."

Alvan waved my concern away as if the distinction wasn't worth noting. "You can thank us properly when you're up for it."

"Great job protecting humanity," I muttered. "I take it you're not human."

"Elves," Valdan said, throwing his shoulders back. He lifted his locks of wet hair to reveal a pointed ear ringed with intricately carved silver, gold, and bronze cuffs. "We've been visiting Bifrost for many years, ever since Thor manifested. Heimdall only recently awakened in us."

"When I joined the others," I said, halfway to myself.

"We've been waiting for your arrival," Alvan said. "Watching Bifrost. It grows weaker every day. We must save it quickly. The giants are gathering to fight us even now."

"Just when I thought we might catch a break." The pain of the fire remained, but my skin was only barely red where grotesque scars should have been. I slid my hand under my shirt, hoping I'd find skin as smooth as Peyton's where my old burns had scarred me. But the puckered, unfeeling skin remained.

"You have the other six, yes?" Valdan asked.

"Five," I admitted. "We're still missing one. And we kind of lost our dwarf guide to the Nine Worlds."

"We will guide you," Alvan said, puffing out his chest and planting his fists on his hips in a heroic pose.

I couldn't tell if he was joking or not, so I held back my laugh at his dramatics. "Cool," I said. "Now, how do we get out of this chasm of hell?"

"Oh no," Valdan said. "This is nothing like Helheim."

Alvan went to the cave mouth, stuck two fingers between his lips, and whistled so loud it shrieked up and down the canyon. "Our goats will bring the chariot around," he said. "I look forward to meeting Heimdall's other hosts."

Before I could ask if the word "goats" meant something different here, my question was answered by the appearance of two large, horned goats. Okay, then. If I were going to pick something to ferry the king of the gods around, I would have chosen a powerful stallion—or heck, why not a flying unicorn? But who was I to question the choice of a couple of smelly goats? They pulled a chariot as promised, and I was aching to rejoin my other parts.

I climbed into the chariot, and the two elves hopped in on either side of me. I lost track of which one was which since they looked exactly alike. One of them threw a massive arm around me while the other took the reins.

"I will hold you so you don't fall when we climb steeply," said the one whose arm surrounded my shoulders. Heimdall had told me to trust these guys, so I tried to relax against the mountain of muscle. Still, the elf's familiarity made me uncomfortable no matter how right Heimdall said it was. I wasn't ready to be touched by most humans, let alone freaking elves.

Elves.

My head swam with the insanity of it all. I wished I'd learned more about the Norse worlds before starting on this journey. I couldn't comprehend, let alone prepare for, the strangeness of it. It was enough to drive anyone over the edge. No wonder Mom had come unhinged.

The chariot banked sharply, the goats soaring into the air, and I clung onto the side of the chariot, squeezing my eyes closed as we rose higher and higher.

"You're safe, little human," the driver elf said, reaching back and patting my head in a strangely paternal gesture, considering he didn't look any older than Xander.

"I find myself drawn to you in a powerful way," the other one murmured in my ear.

"Don't worry," I said. "It's just the god."

A few minutes later, we touched down on the top of the cliff.

"Gwen," Xander said, running to the chariot and wrenching me from the elf's arms. "Who the hell are these guys?"

One of the elves leapt from the cart, his eyes flashing with excitement as if he'd been itching for a fight. Xander stepped towards him with menacing intent, but I threw my arms around him, clinging to his neck. After a moment, his tension eased, and his arms tentatively wrapped around me. "Are you all right?" he said into my hair, glaring over my head at the elves.

I nodded as a sob of relief built in my chest. I held it in, forcing him to take my weight so he wouldn't get himself killed by fighting two gigantic elves. They might be part of Heimdall, too, but that didn't mean we'd be best friends.

The elves introduced themselves to the group. Alvan had a tiny braid in the side of his wild mane, which was the only difference I could see. Valdan stroked Peyton's hair in wonder while Alvan pounded Zeke on the back so hard he winced.

"Dude, way to make everyone else in the world feel like crap about himself," Zeke said, openly admiring the elves' physical perfection.

"If I wasn't gay, I'd be all over that," Peyton said. "You boys are fine."

"They're also going to be our guides until we find Rosa again," I said. "We're almost complete. Only one more piece to go."

Peyton tightened her bubblegum-colored ponytail. "And if it just falls into our laps like these two, we should be back in time for next week's game."

"We saw these guys catch you," Eliot said. "We could tell they were our pieces. It's getting easier to sense each other, too. I could feel that you were okay when they took you behind the water." His words tumbled out, his eyes bright with excitement. I was pretty sure it had more to do with him geeking out on this Norse stuff than the fact that my clothes hung in blackened tatters that barely concealed anything.

"Did the water heal you?" Finn asked, watching me curiously. His eyes stayed locked on my face, never venturing south.

"Sort of." Though I was usually appalled by attention, especially to my scarred body, I found myself wishing he'd look at more of me. Wishing he would gawk the way Zeke was gawking. A strange energy was buzzing through me now that we were almost complete, urging me to do things that weren't exactly part of my usual run-and-hide routine. Giddy excitement built inside me when I looked around at our eight parts assembled at the end of Bifrost. I felt bold, almost invincible after surviving that fire. It was as if it had charged me instead of nearly killing me.

"We healed her," Valdan said, giving me a mischievous wink. "Elves have the magic touch."

"I feel like I'm still on fire," I admitted. "I think I'm partially cooked." My energy level might be at an all-time high, and my skin was intact, but I was definitely not all better. Just touching Xander hurt as if I had a sunburn all the way to my bones.

"You're scalding hot," Xander said, frowning at me.

"Can we get you in the water to lower your body temperature?" Eliot asked.

"She doesn't need the water," Alvan said. "She needs you. If you all pile on, she'll be healed in no time. Together, we're almost a complete god. That's powerful magic."

"The closer we get in every way, the stronger we'll be," Valdan said. "And I especially enjoy getting close with pretty humans."

Chapter Eleven

Gwen

We stood in a circle, falling into our usual pattern. I took one of Zeke's hands and one of Eliot's. Then Heimdall's words came back to me. "Heimdall's not coming," I reminded them. "I saw him when I blacked out. He won't visit us like this."

"But what if we need him?" Peyton asked.

"He said to trust our instincts when we feel him," I said. "He's not going to manifest outside us because he *is* us. We're supposed to listen to what's good for the whole, all of us together."

"You being well is good for all of us," Peyton said. "But how do we do it?"

"What is this?" Alvan said, gesturing to the circle. "You look like you're waiting for a table to fall between you. Get closer. We are one."

He herded us closer, Valdan circling to the other side of the group. Together, they squeezed us into a huddle, linking their hands around us. An awkward giggle forced its way through my lips when I felt bodies pressing against mine, and I was relieved when Peyton giggled, too. Zeke stepped in front of me and gripped my hips, eagerly pulling me against him.

"Ooh, boy," Peyton said. "Talk about family bonding."

I could feel the back of her hand against my bare thigh where my pants had burned away, and I pressed into her touch without thought. Finn was sandwiched in beside her, trying to give me space, even as the elves kept pressing us tighter. Xander's chest crushed my other shoulder almost painfully, his hips pressed to the side of mine. Eliot's chest rose and fell against my back, and a tremor shot across my skin when his fingers touched the bare skin of my waist.

"Good," Alvan said. "Lay your hands on her and give her your healing touch."

"I don't think I'm comfortable with this," Finn said.

"Me, neither," I said. Though I'd said it to make him feel better, it was true. But as our bodies jostled together, my reservations melted. The electric charge I'd felt when I touched one of them before was nothing compared to the roar of power building between us now. A moment of doubt ran through me. I was worried what this group contact would do if just being in a room together could cause a mini natural disaster. Was the earth going to open and swallow us whole? The lava turn into a volcano?

Xander's hands landed on my skin, one on my scarred belly and one flat across my back. I gasped, squirming at the intensity of the electricity it sent through me. My body was the volcano. As the heat of the fire dimmed within me, another kind of heat was building like molten ore under my surface. The pain faded, but something else took its place, a thirst like nothing I'd ever known. My skin shrieked, not with pain but with need.

I wanted their hands all over me, their bodies crushed against mine until I was nothing but a tiny lump of coal. I wanted them to squeeze so tightly they hardened me into a diamond. I could hardly breathe, but I didn't want to breathe, I wanted to explode into flame. My blood pulsed hot inside me, wanting to slip through my pores and into their bloodstream, to be absorbed by them.

Zeke's hips pushed into mine, and suddenly, something inside me burst. The release of pressure seemed to ignite the whole group, and a shimmering radiance swallowed us, as if we had become nothing but charged particles bumping together, our friction illuminating the world below.

For a minute, no one moved. We stood there in the warm glow of our own skin, our own god-bodies. Slowly,

Alvan nodded. "That's how it will be when all your pieces are together. You're better than mortal humans."

His words seemed to break the spell, and we separated, all of us retreating a few steps, not daring to make eye contact. Finn had his hands pushed deep in his pockets, and I realized he'd been that way the whole time. He hadn't been part of our bonding ritual. His skin wasn't glowing with an unearthly sheen, like he'd been brushed with gold dust. Instead, it was red, though I couldn't tell if he was embarrassed or angry.

When he stepped away from the group, I felt further from him than I ever had. My heart twisted, aching for him. Even though it was awkward to look at the others in that moment, I felt a closeness that hadn't been there before. We had all shared something, and he had chosen not to be part of it. I didn't know how to reach him, but I had to before it was too late. We had to do this together, but it was more than that. We had to feel a sense of unity.

"That was… intense," Zeke said after a minute. "I think I need some alone time, if you know what I mean."

"I think I need some Alej time," Peyton said with a strained laugh.

"You said the water in Bifrost is cold?" Xander asked.

Peyton sighed. "I'll go take a dip with you. Alej time is probably not going to happen today."

"You should have broken up with her," Eliot said quietly. He was as shiny as everyone else, but I regretted that my back had been to him when we were so close. I had missed his reaction, and now he watched us like specimens as usual. I wanted a chance to see what made him tick.

"What? Why?" Peyton asked, planting a hand on her hip and glaring at him.

"The same reason I stopped hanging out with Barb and them."

Peyton tossed her pink ponytail back. "And what reason is that?"

My heart started hammering, and I fought the urge to run down the hill towards our camp. I didn't want Eliot to say whatever he was going to say.

"Because you don't feel the same way about her that you feel about Gwen."

I felt like he'd slugged me in the chest. This wasn't supposed to be spoken aloud. It was the elephant in the room, something we all felt, but not something to just blurt out in front of everyone.

Peyton's mouth fell open and she scoffed. "Obviously. She's been my girlfriend for more than a year, and I just met Gwen, who also happens to be legally our sister, in case you forgot."

Ouch.

If my face got any hotter, I might ignite like the lava river. I felt not only exposed but rejected in front of everyone. I crossed my arms tightly over my chest, torn between wanting to snap back at Peyton and wanting to stay quiet so they kept their attention on her meltdown. I decided on the latter, since the only thing I could think to say to hurt her was that I didn't even like girls, and the truth was, I didn't know anymore.

"What's that river in Egypt called?" Xander said, smirking at Peyton.

"No matter how much you pretend when you're with her, Alejandra is not Gwen," Eliot said, frowning at Peyton. "It's not fair to anyone involved."

"You're the ones in denial," Peyton said. "What happens when we fix this bridge and go back home? You think any of this will matter? It's like a drunken party, and we're all going to sober up in a few days. Then who's going to feel stupid? Not me, that's who." Peyton turned and stomped off down the hill.

Which meant everyone was free to stand around awkwardly again, each of us avoiding eye contact. Was Peyton right? Would we regret giving in to our own desires and calling it Heimdall's fault? In a way, it was freeing. We could do this thing that wasn't allowed in our world, and we could blame the god in the end. It hadn't been our choice. We'd been compelled by something bigger. It didn't matter that we would have wanted it and enjoyed it for its own sake without any influence from the god at all. We didn't have to admit that part.

"You humans," Valdan said, shaking his shaggy head. "You share a beautiful experience, and you all want to run away and process your delicate feelings instead of treasuring it for the wonder that it is and then moving on to battle."

"What's she going on about, anyway?" Alvan said. "You humans think you're going home in a few days?"

"Well, yeah," I said. I was glad to change topics, but the way they were looking at each other, like they knew something we didn't, made my chest constrict. "Once we fix the bridge, Heimdall won't need us."

The elves exchanged a frown. "That's not how it works," Valdan said. "You were chosen to be part of a god. It's who you are. You can't walk away from that any more than you can walk away and leave your body behind."

My heart began to thud slow and hard inside my chest as dread clenched its fist around my heart.

"Why would you want to leave your god?" Alvan asked. "It's a great honor to be chosen. The greatest honor in all the Nine Worlds has been bestowed upon you."

"We were chosen at random," I said, trying to keep the hysteria out of my voice. "Heimdall came into Midgard, stumbled across six weak babies in the same place at the same time, and took up residence in us."

"I don't care if it's an honor or a curse," Xander said, eyeing me suspiciously, as if I'd made this happen. "I didn't sign up for forever."

"Neither did I," I cried, throwing my hands up.

"You have been part of it for your whole life, whether you knew it or not," Valdan said. "Heimdall has let you get soft, doing as you please. But now you have been given a quest. You must complete it. This is a great honor in itself."

"I'm with them," Zeke said, aiming a thumb at the elves. "Who wouldn't want to be a god?"

"What do you mean, we can't walk away?" Finn asked, moving back towards the group. "He can't force us to do his bidding."

"I don't think you understand this," Alvan said. "Heimdall isn't leaving you. He can't leave you. You're part god, just like you're part human. You'll be both for as long as you live. There's only one way out."

My breath came faster as my whole world shifted to accommodate this new knowledge. A feeling of doom settled into my bones, but it was as if I'd been waiting for this all along. Somewhere inside, I'd always known that I'd never get to be normal. That had always been nothing but a fantasy, too good to be true.

There was no normal for us. We would be this way forever. Inescapably drawn to each other, on-call in the Norse worlds every minute of our lives, never free to relax because at any time we could lose someone who was quite literally a part of us. We weren't just part of a god. He was part of us.

Chapter Twelve

Gwen

Until we had our last piece, we had no reason to hang out at Bifrost. We couldn't cross the bridge until all nine of us were together to form a complete god. Only the elves could cross before then, since they were already hosting an entire god. But we needed to bring Heimdall across from our side, which the elves explained as a kind of landing pad on the border of Midgard. It wasn't part of our earth, but it also wasn't part of any other world. It was a limbo that existed in the spaces between the worlds.

After some discussion, we settled on a new plan. With the flying goat chariot, our new elven guides were able to carry us into the branches of Yggdrasil. There, we hoped to find Rosa and then go on to find the ninth part of

Heimdall. The elves knew how to get to the dwarf world, where Finn said Rosa wanted to go after talking to Ratr, and to Jotunheim, the land of the giants. In my vision in the water, he had told me to go to follow the elves to Jotunheim, but the thought of entering a world populated by Joaquins made me shudder.

Alvan's words played in my head as we started up the trunk. *One way out.* Heimdall had told us we'd lose someone. Surely, Finn wasn't so opposed to hosting a god that he'd jump out of the world tree into the nothingness of between-worlds. Would he?

I glanced back at him. He stayed close today, not going ahead as he had the day before. If we ran into Ratr again, I wanted Finn with me. I would have avoided Yggdrasil altogether, but the elves said it was the only way to travel. Considering the lack of traffic, I took it that the relations between worlds were not super friendly.

Halfway through the day, the same sound we'd heard the night before came to us, like a canvas sail whipping in the wind. "We should get off the tree," Alvan yelled from ahead. "We can drop into Alfheim from here."

"The world of light elves," Eliot said from a few branches ahead. The flapping sound came again, this time closer.

"Please tell me there are no bats in this tree," Peyton squeaked.

136

"Are you afraid of all animals?" I asked, trying to distract myself from my own fear. It was bad enough that I couldn't look down without wanting to pitch forward and hurl. Now, there was something flying around that I couldn't look for, because if I did, I might see how far down the tree went and faint, and then I'd be the one they lost.

"Not all animals," Peyton said. "Kitties are cute. And pugs. And unicorns."

"Unicorns?" Finn asked behind me.

"Hey, if we can be in another freaking world, hosting some random Viking god, there could be unicorns. Don't even tell me you're not questioning what's real right now. Everything we've ever known is up for debate. Do you realize I didn't even know how old I was? That's like the most basic thing ever."

"What?" I asked, stopping to catch my breath for a second. Breathing and speaking had felt like torture when the elves had pulled me from the fire, but everything felt better now—better than it ever had. It was as if I could taste the fresh oxygen filling my lungs. The only thing I'd lost had been my clothes, and Peyton had supplied me with jeans, a cheer tee, and a light jacket from her pack.

"Yeah. Finn and Eliot were supposed to be a year older than me. Remember when Dad told us about being adopted? I was in the NICU the night you and the twins were born. I'm actually older than all of you. He lied to be about my age for my entire life."

Before I could answer, something shot out of the enormous leaves of the branch below us. It moved so fast I couldn't make out the head before it streaked past, but I could sure as hell see the slithering, serpentine body that blurred by, its skin glistening with sleek black scales. The body curved, still sliding by. It was as thick as a large man's torso and too long to see both ends at once.

Adrenaline punched through my veins so fast it nearly knocked me flat, and my breath froze in my lungs. I was too terrified to make a sound. I wasn't ready for this. We needed to go back, start over, prepare for something impossible.

"Holy mother of hell," Peyton shrieked, her face going white with terror as she gripped the tree.

Her fear shocked me out of my trance and I scrambled up beside her. "It's okay," I said. "Alvan and Valdan are getting us out of this tree. All we have to do is make it to the next branch."

Peyton closed her eyes and took a breath. "Promise?"

"I promise," I said, leaning forward and pressing my forehead to hers. I could smell her bubblegum lip gloss, and my mouth watered with inappropriate desires. "Come on. I'll climb with you."

Together, we made it the next ten feet and hauled ourselves onto a huge branch.

"Did you see the dragon?" Eliot asked, his eyes flashing with excitement.

"We saw it," Finn said grimly. His face had gone pale, and sweat had broken out along his lip. Selfishly, I had been so caught up in getting Peyton and me up the tree that I hadn't realized he was struggling.

"Finn, are you okay?" I asked, gripping his clammy fingers.

"Fine," he said, shaking his head. "I don't like…"

"He's scared of snakes, that's what," Peyton said from where she lay facedown on the branch, panting. "Like any sane person."

"We need to get off this branch," Valdan said, drawing a sword.

"Aren't you supposed to have a hammer?" Zeke asked.

"We can only wield Mjolnir together," Alvan said. "To protect you, it is better if one of us goes first and the other protects the rear."

The beating of wings approached again, stopping further conversation. Leaves tore, and suddenly, the snake shot towards us. This time, I did see it clearly. It was a reptilian thing sporting a fan around its neck like a giant lizard and burning eyes with pupils shaped like slits.

Finn crumpled to the branch, dragging me down with him. Peyton screamed. Xander cursed. Zeke delivered a punishing right hook to the creature's fist-sized eye. It screamed, a grinding bird-like wail, and flew off in the direction Zeke's blow had turned its head. The body slithered through the air, and I saw the source of the flapping sound. It had small, leathery wings that started about a third of the way down its body and ran most of its length to its tail. Its scales had a dull shine, like snake scales, but its eyes were intelligent.

"What did you do that for?" Eliot asked Zeke. "Now it's pissed."

"That's what they say to do if a shark attacks while you're surfing," Zeke said. "Punch it in the face."

"That was no shark," Xander said.

"A freaking dragon," I whispered, my gaze meeting Peyton's shocked one. Like before, the sheer weight of this crashed into me. This world wasn't going to be like ours. We were completely unprepared. Even with two elves to guide us and two gods between us, there were more things in these words than my mind could comprehend.

"Let's go," Alvan said. "Run!" He took off along the branch, and seconds later he disappeared into the leaves.

"You don't have to tell me twice," Peyton said, jumping to her feet.

The dragon was so big its body was unwieldy, and our only advantage was being smaller and quicker. It took much longer for it to slow and come back than for us to move.

"It's wrapping around the trunk," Eliot said. "It's going to bind us to the tree."

I ducked under the dragon's body, then dropped to my knees, turned back, and grabbed Finn's hand. "Come on," I said. "Look at the branch instead of the dragon and crawl forward. Follow my voice like I followed yours yesterday."

Finn nodded, his face now closer to green than white. He followed my instructions, though. Suddenly, the dragon's tail whipped by. I yanked Finn to his feet and took off after Peyton and Eliot, who had already ducked under the dragon and gone after Alvan.

"Don't look back," I yelled to Finn.

"Don't look down," he called back.

A hiccupping, hysterical laugh choked my throat as the wingbeats approached again. We were used to the human world, to our small terrors, and now a dragon literally circled us. It was like something out of a fairytale.

"It's coming back around," Xander said behind us. "Get down, and I'll hit it like Zeke did."

"I don't think that will work," I said. "It's too smart."

Before I could explain, its head burst through the foliage, its jaws stretched wide and long fangs gleaming. I threw myself onto the branch, yanking Finn down with me. Xander had produced a switchblade, and he dove under the dragon's head, twisting to slash at the underside of its jaw. Valdan leapt forward and impaled the dragon just behind its tapered head. Letting out a raspy screech of fury, the dragon slammed its body down on us. Its weight knocked the breath out of me. It slithered across us as it slowed.

Finn's hand went rigid in mine, and he let out a shuddering sob. I imagined living my worst nightmare, and I gripped his hand, trying to reassure him even as the reptilian skin slid across my face. My body ached and my ribs felt crushed, but I could breathe again. It was heavy, but we'd gotten away with nothing but a body slam. Digging my fingers into the crevices in the bark, I dragged myself forward.

Zeke rushed back and yanked me free of the dragon before turning to help Finn.

"It's slowing down," I said. "It's going to circle back."

"All I have is a knife," Xander said, his eyes meeting mine. Something passed between us—a knowledge that this was it. We'd never even made it into another world.

"Keep running," Valdan said, grabbing my hand. Zeke had his arm under Finn's and was running with him as Finn hobbled along. The dragon's weight must have hurt one of his legs. Xander leapt over the dragon and tore off down the branch with Valdan and me close behind. My side ached with every step, as if someone were punching me in the ribs.

"What happens when we get to the end of the branch?" Peyton called, looking back over her shoulder at us.

"We jump," Valdan shouted.

At the thought of jumping again, my stomach lurched and my knees gave way. Valdan stumbled, but he righted himself, scooped me up in his arms, and kept running. We were going full speed when the dragon's head burst from the fog and straight at us. Xander gave a hoarse cry and slashed at it with his switchblade, making a long, crimson gash in the black scales. But the momentum was already with it, and it couldn't stop even if it had tried. It streaked past him, slamming into Valdan and me.

Its fangs ripped through my jacket, slicing through my shoulder and down my arm. Pain rocketed through me, my whole body rigid with agony.

"Hel's army," Valdan cursed, wrenching me free of the curved fangs. I choked out a cry, my brain still too stunned with pain to comprehend what had happened.

Zeke ran back and grabbed me from Valdan's arms, savagely cursing the elf. He yanked me away and stumbled backwards. A look of pure terror flickered across his face. It took me a second to realize what was happening. As he lost his balance, he threw me onto the branch, away from him. I fell back, then shot up, my hands desperately swiping for him.

"No," I screamed as my fingertips brushed only air instead of his solid grasp. I lunged after him, but just like that, he was gone. One second his stunned face was looking into mine, and the next, there was only leaves and a swirling fog rising up from below. A cry tore from my throat, and I lurched after him, my mind screaming for me to save him even as my body seemed to be moving through sluggish lava. My chest and arm were on fire, my blood turning to molten iron that would burn me alive from the inside out.

"Don't jump," Xander yelled, his arm whipping around my waist. He fell backwards onto the rough bark with me in his arms, horror choking my throat.

"Zeke," I screamed, ignoring my own pain.

"I know," Xander said, sitting up and sliding me off his lap. His face was pale, all his usual bravado replaced with bleak realization. "Killing yourself won't save him."

"But we can't just... we can't..." A hiccupping sob engulfed me. When Heimdall had said we'd lose someone in another world, I'd believed him. The reality of it, the weight of it, only hit me the moment it came true, though. I should have watched Zeke closer, kept him closer. I should have held him tighter. I should have told him I loved him, given him more. I should have given them all more. They could be gone any second.

Xander wrapped his arms around me, burying his face in my shoulder. Peyton collapsed beside us. Eliot stood back, his excitement gone, and his face pale with shock. Finn was slumped over a few feet away, his face in his hands. This was what it meant to lose one of us. We were supposed to be finding more pieces, to assemble all nine members. Now, we were down one more.

IGNITE

Chapter Thirteen

Peyton

My brother was gone. I couldn't comprehend it. I mean, I had grown up with all of them, but I'd always been closest to Zeke. He was my protector, my comfort, my other half. We were more like twins than the brothers who were supposed to be twins. I should be crying, screaming, leaping to my death after him. But I was so numb, I couldn't believe it was real. Nothing was real. This was all one big, bizarre nightmare, and I was going to wake up beside Alejandra and shake her awake, and we'd panic and giggle as she got dressed and ran out to get home before dawn, when her mom would come to her room to wake her.

"It's coming back," a voice said, breaking into my daze. I looked up to see Valdan hovering, his sword at the ready.

"What are you doing here if you're not going to kill it?" Gwen asked. By the accusing tone in her voice, I guessed she was thinking what I was. Why hadn't it been him? Which was horrible because he was a part of us, too. But he wasn't Zeke.

He was a stranger, not the brother who had carried me two miles down the beach when I was eleven and I'd been thrown by a wave and dislocated my shoulder. He wasn't the boy who had driven me home the first time I got puking drunk, who held my hair back half the night. And okay, maybe Zeke had made fun of me for it, but that's what big brothers did. They also snuck their little sister into the house and up to bed so their parents never found out. They cheered harder than anyone when you made the cheer team, and shared the depths of their despair on the bus ride home from losing a big game. They lied and said it was going to be okay when your mom was dying because that's what you needed to hear to keep from breaking.

Valdan was just some giant elf with ridiculous muscles. He wouldn't stand up for me when Joaquin asked me to make out with my girlfriend at a party so he could watch.

"I must get a killing hit," Valdan said in his thick accent. With his blond hair whipping around him and his eyes intent, he looked more like a Viking than ever. "One by one, it will pick you off if I don't."

"Where's Alvan?" I asked, bolting upright. "Isn't he supposed to be guarding us in front?"

He shook his head. "You're too slow. He's probably in Alfheim by now."

"We need Heimdall," Gwen blurted. She swayed on her feet, staring down without comprehension at the blood soaking her torn jacket. She looked as if she'd forgotten that the dragon had bitten her until that moment. To be honest, I had, too. She was still here. Still alive. Zeke wasn't.

"We are Heimdall," I said. "He told us he wasn't coming back, remember? He's just a voice in the sky, anyway." I realized as I said it that those were the words Alejandra used to talk about god, and in that moment, she seemed as far away as she was—a different world, a different life, different rules. Eliot had been right. I could never share my life with her. This secret would sit between us, pushing us apart until we were so far apart we couldn't see each other past it.

"Maybe we can pin its wings," Xander said, climbing to his feet.

"With your little pocket knife?" I asked. "Gwen's bitten. She can't run. Finn's hurt, Zeke's gone…" I trailed off, starting to hyperventilate.

"I can kill it," Valdan thundered, his massive chest puffed out with indignation.

Suddenly, the dragon's head burst through the fog again. At the same moment, a cracking sound came from above, and a girl leapt from the clouds and landed squarely on the dragon's head, pinning it to the branch with a long silver blade.

I let out a little yelp of surprise. Okay, it was more like a shriek of terror.

"And that's how you pin a dragon," the girl said in a thick accent that was vaguely German but not exactly. She sounded like the elven twins, but she stood astride the dragon's head like some kind of badass Buffy the Dragon Slayer.

"Who are you?" I choked.

"A silly little sticker like yours will only anger it," she said to Xander. "Not to mention it's like trying to kill a goat with a toothpick."

"I was going to kill it," Valdan said.

"Sure you were," she said. "Nice try, muscle-head."

Venom spurted from the dragon's fangs, and its furious red eyes moved so fast they vibrated in their sockets.

"Is it dying?" I whispered, my fingers tangling with Gwen's.

"Don't look at its eyes," the girl snapped. "It will hypnotize you." She had brown hair and wore brown leather from head to toe. But damn. She kept her feet like a pirate standing on deck of her ship, rocking with the tree branch that swayed as the dragon seethed.

"Zeke," I said, scrambling to hold on as the branch bucked. "We lost our brother. He fell."

"Oh, him?" she said.

"Did you see him?" I asked, wanting to grab the girl and shake her. I leapt to my feet, my fear forgotten in the face of my anguish.

"Yes, he was falling, like you said."

"And you just left him?" I screamed.

The girl glanced up, clapping her thumb and fingers together in a gesture that would have meant excessive talking if someone in our world had used it. A second later, a huge, feathery creature landed on the branch beside us. I couldn't tell if it was a bird or a dragon, and at that moment, I really didn't care. My brother was sitting on its back.

"Zeke," Gwen cried, lurching to her feet. She grabbed her wounded shoulder, and that's when I saw angry red streaks rising up the side of her neck to her face.

"Dude, I rode a *dragon*," Zeke crowed, sliding off the creature and landing beside her. His brow creased with concern when he saw her condition. Blood had soaked the sleeve of her jacket.

"Cool," she whispered. She swayed on her feet, then stumbled forward, and collapsed into his arms.

"Gwen," I cried, leaping forward.

"She was bitten?" the girl asked, still standing over the writhing dragon's body.

"Yes," I said. "Can you help?"

"Yes, but let's get out of this tree. You think the dragons are bad, wait until you meet the squirrels."

Squirrels? Was this girl off her rocker? That gossipy rat was nothing compared to this snake dragon.

Eliot, however, didn't seem to share my skepticism.

"Ratatoskr," he said. "We met him already. I'm Eliot."

"Gracelyn," she said, tossing her brown hair back. I caught a glimpse of pointed ears and an intricately carved silver cuff right below the tip. So, she was an elf.

I wanted to roll my eyes at my brother because of course Eliot would introduce himself to the girl first, but even my snark had deserted me. "This might be the first time I've ever said these words, but can we please save the talking for later?"

"That is a first," Xander muttered, putting up his blade. "But I couldn't agree more."

"My steed can only hold two, maybe three of us at once," Gracelyn said. "I can take the two girls at the same time. I'll come back for the rest of you. Or you can jump like an elf. They're smart like that."

Gracelyn had a directness about her that made it hard to tell if she was a badass or a bitch. I decided to give her the benefit of the doubt. I had no idea what we'd encounter in these worlds, and I was just glad she was human...ish.

"Why should we trust you with our sisters?" Xander asked. "I'd be more comfortable going with Gwen."

"Altheim is our home," Valdan said. "You will be safe."

"Yeah," Zeke pointed out. "She saved me."

"I don't like it," Xander said.

Gracelyn smirked and stepped over the dragon, which had ceased flailing and gone still. "You think you can protect her better than an elven knight in training?"

"Nope," I said. "He doesn't think that at all. Do you, Xander?"

Xander glared.

"The longer we stand here, the farther the venom will spread," Gracelyn said. "But if you want to continue arguing, it's up to you." She braced her feet and yanked her silver blade from the dragon. Its limp body hung draped over the wide branch, black blood trickling down the crevices in the bark from where she'd impaled it.

"If there's something worse than a giant flying anaconda up here, I don't even want to know," I said, heading for the grey-blue bird-dragon thing.

"The rest of you, wait here or run to the end of the branch and jump," Gracelyn said. "I patrol the branches over our world. There's no more dragons around right now."

She leapt onto the back of her mount and wrapped her thighs around its long neck. It kind of reminded me of the flying dog-dragon thing in *The Neverending Story*, one of the many eighties movies I'd watched with Alej. It was kind of our thing. Thinking about her at home, wondering what she was doing, made my chest squeeze. She was probably just getting up and around, maybe taking the dogs for a run on the beach with her mom. The normalcy of it was so far removed it seemed like a sad, sweet dream from childhood.

Zeke helped me up behind Gracelyn, and Xander placed Gwen gently in my arms. Zeke leaned down and kissed the top of my head. "I'll be right behind you," he said. "But I'm kinda jealous you get to ride this thing, and I have to fall again. That was not fun."

I threw my arms around him and gave him a quick squeeze. "It didn't kill you the first time."

"Because an elf caught me."

"And she wouldn't have done that if she was just going to tell you to jump to your death now," I said. "Now go. Remember to tuck and roll."

Before he could answer, the beast we were on began to flap its huge, feathery wings. I held onto Gwen with one arm and dug my fingers into the creature's pelt with the other. Now that I was on it, I could tell that it didn't have feathers at all, but some kind of fur. Each hair was like the barb of a feather with tiny barbules off the side that were soft as silk. But though it might have been as fuzzy as goose down, the beast was no kitten. I could feel its powerful muscles as it flexed its wings, beating them harder and harder until at last it lurched forward off the branch.

I screamed as we dropped, swallowing the sound as we swooped forward, the air rushing against my cheeks. It was a million times more exhilarating than riding Xander's motorcycle. I whooped as the creature banked to one side, riding a current.

"What is this?" I yelled.

"It's a dragon," Gracelyn said over her shoulder, turning so I could hear her. "Every knight has to train and tame their dragons before they get their knighthood."

"Girls can be knights here?"

"Of course," she said, sounding perplexed. "My mother was one of the greatest knights Alfheim has ever known."

We swooped down, and my eyes blurred as the wind dried them. Then tears wet them, clearing my vision. I blinked at the world coming into focus below. In the distance, I could see jutting mountains and twisting spires of green and brown poking up to the clouds. As we got closer, huge white craters marked the flatland. Directly below us were welcoming green meadows, rivers and lakes, and small brown buildings with large round water tanks attached.

"Does everyone here have a pet dragon?" I asked nervously as we sped towards the ground.

"They are not pets," Gracelyn said. "And not everyone has one."

"I didn't know there were dragons in the Norse worlds," I said. "My dad may have overlooked that small detail."

"You don't have dragons?"

I snorted. "In movies."

"What is that?"

"Um… like stories that people act out."

"I like those," Gracelyn said, smiling. I guessed she was our age, maybe a little older. I hadn't really come to terms with being a year older than I'd always thought. Every time I started to get mad at Dad, though, something more important came along and stole my focus. How could I care about my age when I was riding a blue dragon with an elven knight, and my stepsister lay poisoned in my arms?

"Dragons have always been in the Nine Worlds," Gracelyn said. "We have stories, too. They have been in this world for… maybe five hundred years. If your stories are from the time when humans visited the other worlds, they're far out of date. That's nearly two thousand years ago."

My brain balked at that thought, but I managed a small laugh. "I guess things have changed a lot then. Eliot's not going to like that."

"Is your world the same as it was two thousand years ago?"

"We're officially and completely ignorant," I said.

"That's obvious."

"To be fair, we know nothing of these worlds, so even if we'd planned to stay, we had no way to prepare for any of these things. We don't have giants or dragons in Midgard, so of course we have no weapons to fight them."

"In the flatlands, you'll mostly want to watch for rebels," she said. "Dark elves and dwarves raid occasionally. Giants come around from time to time."

"Oh," I said faintly. "Is that all?"

"There are animals, too," she said. "But don't worry. They are more afraid of you than you are of them."

A laugh escaped me, but I managed to hold in the edge of hysteria. "We say that in our world, too."

"Then why are you afraid?"

"I'm not really good with wild animals," I said. "The only animal we have to fear in Cape Cod are sharks."

The dragon touched down, and I slid off its back, giving it a pet on its soft fur. Gracelyn hopped down, her supple leather boots landing silently in the soft brown dirt of the yard where we'd landed. Instead of green grass lawns and cement roads, they had green grass all around and soft dirt yards and roads.

Three tall men ran from the nearest building, moving in step with such precision that it was hard to believe they weren't all part of the same being. I opened my mouth to protest when they scooped up Gwen, but they'd already turned away, whisking her inside without deviating a single step from each other.

"My brothers," Gracelyn explained. "Go inside. I'm going to check Yggdrasil for stray humans in need of rescue."

"Does that happen a lot?" I asked. "Rescuing humans?"

"No," she said. "But I doubt your people can figure out their way down."

She spoke in a throaty language to her dragon and trotted off towards an outbuilding while I turned back to the one where her brothers had taken Gwen. It was a tall, round building with a steeply pointed, thatched roof that looked sort of like a five-story wooden teepee. The door stood open and I hurried inside.

The three elf guys stood back from an enormous hanging bed where Gwen lay. The thin stuffing from my jacket was coming out in wisps, each one painted red from her blood. But worse than the blood were the crimson streaks now covering most of her face like the rays of a sunset.

"Are you going to help her or just stand there watching her die?" I asked, running to the bed.

"Our apothecarian is on the way," one of them said. "But she's definitely going to die."

"Jerk," I muttered as I turned to the bed and took Gwen's hand. It was the same unnatural red as her neck and face.

A few minutes later, the doctor arrived pulling a small carriage. He was about my size, with deep brown skin and a topknot of shiny black hair. He looked no older than me. Unlike the other elves I'd met, his pointed ears were unadorned with jewelry. I wondered if that meant he hadn't won any awards at his job or something. I wasn't sure I wanted a high-school aged elf operating on my stepsister who also happened to be a permanent part of me.

"You're the doctor?" I asked.

"I am a healer," he said, his voice so low and rumbly I did a doubletake. He pulled out various bags and pouches from his cart, which looked kind of like a baby carriage that you pulled behind instead of pushing in front of you.

"What are you doing?" I asked when he pulled out a pointy blade.

"We must see the puncture marks to know if she has time," he said.

I helped him remove Gwen's jacket and shirt, averting my eyes when she was exposed. I couldn't miss the red hue of her skin though, the streaks painting halfway down her abdomen, where they mixed with the burn scars twisting across her middle.

One of the fangs had torn a slash down her arm. The other was a clean puncture, a circle as big as a marble and swollen as big as a fist under her skin. The edges of the wound, where her skin was torn, had turned an alien shade of green. From that a rainbow of color spiraled out, blue, purple, and finally, the angry red that had crept across most of her top half.

"These burns," the doctor rumbled. "From a fire giant, yes?"

"Yes," I said, nodding as tears filled my eyes. I swiped them away. "What can I do to help?"

"We need to pack the puncture wounds with dragon moss," he said, removing handfuls of packed green moss from a pouch. "It draws out the venom. It might be enough."

I bit back my disgust at the thought of shoving moss into the gaping holes in Gwen's shoulder and down the gash on her arm. In our world, the sight of blood made me faint. You couldn't have paid me to touch someone's wound. My reaction to it wasn't any different here, but I was different. Reality was different.

The doctor got to work, so I swallowed hard and reached for the mossy stuff. It was dry and spongy, and the slight smell of a swamp rose from it. I gulped again, and then took a pinch and gently pressed it to the wound on Gwen's arm. I didn't even tremble, let alone faint. After seeing what lay beyond our small human world, I could never go back to the simple life I'd lived—and loved— before finding out what I really was. I didn't even know the name for it. Godling? Demigod? God-human hybrid?

"She's fortunate the tooth split her skin," the apothecarian said. "The venom there is near the surface and will be easy to draw out. This other one..."

Just then the door burst open, and my four brothers stood there, all of them stripped to the waist and dripping wet.

"What happened?" I asked.

"Your chauffer failed to mention that the opening to this world is over a lake," Xander said, stomping to the bed. The others gathered around, exchanging glances and staring down at Gwen's inflamed skin.

"The doctor doesn't know if she'll make it," I said.

"No crying," Zeke said. "She's going to be fine. Gods don't die."

"What if they do?" I asked, my throat so tight I had to choke out the words.

"Heimdall doesn't, though," Eliot said. "He's there at the end."

"You're gods?" the doctor asked, drawing back.

"We're *a* god," Eliot said.

"All of you?"

The door opened, and Gracelyn appeared with our elven twins.

"And them," Xander growled, his brows drawing together.

"In that case," the doctor said, tying up his pouch. "Leave the moss in place to draw out the venom, but it's your bond that will heal her. If all your pieces are together, it should not take long."

"What if they're not?" I asked.

"Longer," the doctor said. "But she might live yet."

"How long?" Eliot asked.

"A few moons," the guy said with a shrug.

We looked at each other.

"This will be enjoyable," Alvan said. "I look forward to being close again."

I turned to Gracelyn. "Is there somewhere we can stay? We can pay you... somehow. I'm sure."

"There's an empty lodge three stops down. Just move in."

"From living on the Cape to squatting," I said. "Sounds about right."

"We'll take it," Zeke said. "If no one minds."

Gracelyn shrugged. "No one lives there. It's yours while you stay."

I didn't really understand elf rules, but it sounded like a good place to start getting Gwen healthy again. I wasn't sure what exactly was required to heal one of our pieces from a dragon's bite, but if it was anything like healing her burn injury, I didn't want an audience.

Zeke bent and scooped up Gwen, cradling her body against his chest. "If this doesn't work, we're getting out of here and going home," he said.

But all I could think about were Heimdall's instructions. We were on a quest, and we couldn't leave until it was complete. Not even when we lost one of our members. A heavy emptiness settled into my belly at the realization. We weren't going home anytime soon.

Chapter Fourteen

Gwen

When my eyelids fluttered open, I found myself staring into a pair of intense brown eyes. For a second, neither of us moved. I didn't know where I was, or who I was, or what had happened. It was only me and this other person, this person I belonged to and who belonged to me. I knew that, if nothing else.

"Eliot," I whispered, raising my fingers to his throat. I hadn't even realized I knew his name until I said it. And I knew him. My voice sounded scratchy and strange to my own ears, but his was familiar when he spoke.

"Are you really awake?" he asked, his face breaking into a smile that warmed my body right down to the tips of my toes. "I must be dreaming."

"I'm awake," I said. "What happened? Where am I?"

"You were bitten by a dragon," he said, stroking my hair behind my ear. It all came rushing back—the tree, losing Rosa, finding the elves, losing Zeke. The relief of finding him, again, and how everything had changed in that moment. I'd known what he meant to me, and what they all meant to me. I'd known how silly it was to keep pushing them away, worrying about what other people would think. I had sworn I would never do that again. And then, before I could act on anything I'd realized, I'd blacked out.

Now I was waking up, remembering. I felt as if I were coming back to life. The tip of Eliot's finger circled the back of my ear, slowing as it moved down the side of my neck. A shiver went through me, and Eliot's eyes flickered with some knowledge. He shifted forward almost imperceptibly, his gaze dropping to my lips. He swallowed, his fingers finding the hollow of my throat. In his eyes, I saw everything he'd never shown me before—a vulnerability and hunger that matched my own.

I'd caught him unguarded when he thought we were alone and I was sleeping. I wasn't going to miss the chance to see past his defenses. Leaning in, I let my lips touch his full, red ones. I'd waited for this kiss, wanted this kiss, since the moment we'd met in the hallway at Neil's, and I'd admired his lips. They were soft and plump, warm against mine, and tasting faintly of peppermint. Instead of taking control of the kiss and showing me his superior experience, he pulled back. I wanted to scream with frustration.

"Gwen…" he said, his eyes searching mine. "Are you feeling okay?" His eyes cleared and took on their usual intensity, studying me like I was something to analyze. I didn't want to be analyzed. Just before collapsing from the dragon bite, I'd realized that I'd held back too much for too long. That I hadn't given Zeke or any of the others enough. I didn't want those regrets any longer. I wanted to lose control, to dive into this and embrace it, embrace them all.

"I'm okay now," I whispered. I'd wasted too much time, and I'd woken with an urgency to make up for it. I slid my arm around his neck, drawing him in, pressing my lips to his. After a second's hesitation, he melted against me, returning the kiss. When my tongue touched his, a sound came from deep within him, something primal and helpless. His hands moved up my back gently, palming my shoulder blades and drawing my chest to his. My skin ached for his, and I pressed myself against him, gripping his face between my hands. I pressed in deeper, wanting the taste of him in a way I didn't understand. My tongue caressed his, exploring his mouth, moving in rhythm with his.

My body throbbed with a knowledge that I couldn't back up with experience. It knew what it wanted, knew what to do. I arched against him, my hands fisting in his shirt, my back arching under his hands. Hooking my leg over his, I pulled him closer, wanting every inch of him pressed into me. His hands slid down my hips, drawing them against his slowly.

Turning my face to deepen the kiss, I drank in the complexity of his mouth. It wasn't just peppermint, it was mint leaves growing in the sun on a hot summer day, warm and lazy, but brittle as a snap of frost.

It wasn't enough. I wanted more of him, more of his mouth, more of his body. I slid my hands under his shirt, marveling at the softness of his skin, the animal heat of it. His muscles tightened under my touch, coiling with a power waiting to be unleashed inside me. I gasped into his mouth when I felt the strain of his hardness inside his jeans. Everything in my body screamed with a need to drag him closer still, to devour him, absorb him, and become one and the same person.

"Wait," he said, pulling away at last. "God, Gwen... Is this what you want? Right now?"

"Yes," I said without hesitation. There was nothing to wait for, no one I wanted more than him, nothing that could be more right.

I tried to kiss him again, but Eliot responded tentatively. When I pulled back, his breath swept over my lips, cool with mint, and my own thoughts began to clear. Suddenly I realized I had no idea where I was or how I'd gotten here.

"My breath must be horrible," I said, covering my mouth with the tips of my fingers.

"It's not."

"My mouth tastes like a swamp."

"Okay, maybe it's a little mossy," he said with a grin. "But trust me when I say that guys do not care about that when a girl is kissing them."

"Is that Gwen?" Peyton's voice asked behind me. "Gwen's awake!"

It sounded like footfalls all over the house started racing my way. Xander was suddenly there, sliding onto the bed behind me. He wrapped an arm around my waist and drew me hard against him, inhaling deeply. "If you ever do that again, I swear I'll kill you myself."

"What did I do?"

"You almost died," Xander said against the back of my neck. A shiver worked its way through me, and I pressed back against him, remembering a few nights ago when he'd kissed me. God, and kissed me and kissed me.

Zeke arrived, sliding onto the narrow space of the bed behind Eliot. Eliot's body pressed even more tightly against mine as Xander's pinned me from behind, and a shudder of longing passed through me. Zeke leaned over me and smiled, his blue eyes crinkling at the corners. "You're back," he said, stroking my cheek. "Thank all the gods in Asgard."

I remembered his kiss, too, under the bleachers. The heat of it, the confidence, the simplicity. I remembered everything before the tree. And the insanity that had happened since, fantastical things out of my mother's visions, like a child's nightmare.

Suddenly, all I wanted was to feel like I'd felt under the bleachers when Zeke kissed me. Safe and simple and pretty, and like it all made perfect sense. Without thinking, I closed my eyes and lifted my lips to his palm.

"She woke up alive," Eliot said. "In every way."

Heat rushed to my cheeks, and I fought the urge to bury my face in the blankets, wishing for once he wouldn't be so blunt.

"What were you doing that woke her up?" Finn asked from the doorway.

"I wasn't doing anything," Eliot said, his voice tight. "I was watching her sleep."

Peyton slid onto the top of the bed, pulling my head into her lap. "You have no idea how worried we've been."

"Is everyone okay?" I asked, pushing up from the bed. An ache throbbed down my arm. "Where are the elves?"

Peyton gave me a funny look. "They're fine. Everyone is fine but you."

I peeled back the blanket covering me and looked down at my arm. A green, lumpy scar resembling the ridge along a crocodile's back ran from my shoulder to my elbow. Disgust filled me, and I shoved it back under the blankets, my breath coming short. If I'd thought my burn scars were bad, they looked like a joke now. A joke that could be easily hidden.

"What… happened?" I asked, my voice coming out strangled. "How long have I been out?"

I caught the glance they exchanged, though Peyton quickly hid her concern and gave me a bright smile. "You got really lucky," she said. "The elf doctor said almost no one lives if they don't get help, like, the second they get bit. But we've been here making the circle, sleeping in this bed with you, and trying to be with you as much as we can. That's what Heimdall said to do, right? To be close. We weren't sure if it would work when you were unconscious, but the elves said it would help."

I pushed up, and the blanket fell away from my hideously deformed arm again, but I didn't hide it this time. It wasn't a wound. It was a scar. "How long?"

"A few months," Zeke said.

I could barely choke out the word. "What?"

"Three months," Eliot said, his voice quiet but firm.

"My mom," I cried. My heart slammed in my chest so hard I thought it would stop. My fingers gripped the blankets as if letting go would send me spinning off into some crazy universe where there were nine worlds instead of one. I closed my eyes, trying to make sense of my reality all over again.

"I know," Peyton said. "But we can't do anything about it."

I tried to imagine my mother living without me for three months. Not knowing what had happened to me. I'd disappeared and never come back. She'd be more than devasted. She'd be broken, destroyed by it.

"We have to go back," I said, throwing off the blankets.

"Heimdall said we couldn't go back until we fixed Bifrost," Finn said quietly.

"What about school?"

"We couldn't go back even if we tried," Xander said. "Maybe ever, but definitely not now. This is bigger than graduation."

"But it's your real life," I said, panic clinging to my words. I needed my mom. I needed to know she was okay.

"We couldn't just leave you here in Alfheim," Zeke said. "School will still be there when we get back."

"There's no medicine in Midgard to fix a dragon's bite," Eliot said. "Let alone try to explain it."

"It's not so bad here," Peyton said. "If you don't care about personal space or possessions."

I tried to imagine the Keens, who had grown up with everything they could ever want, not caring about possessions. Then again when I thought about it, none of them seemed really attached to their things except Xander and his bike. He wouldn't like the personal space issue, either. I found his hand and squeezed, knowing how much he'd sacrificed to stay with us. He squeezed back, leaning his head against my arm.

"We need to get back," I said. "So how do we make it happen?"

"We can learn more about the other worlds in Alfheim," Eliot said. "In case we end up stranded in one of them next time."

"Okay, elven wannabe," Xander said. "We all know you're enamored with the elven princess."

My stomach dropped. I'd just been making out with him. "Elven princess?"

Eliot's ears went red, and he grinned and plucked at his hair, which was getting longer and a little wild. "She's not a princess. She's a future knight."

Peyton rolled her eyes. "You're not an elf, Eliot."

"I know that," he said.

God, I wanted to smack myself. Was he really in love with someone else? Not that I was one to talk. But what we had, all of us together, was special. And she was an outsider. I noticed Eliot was wearing a brown linen shirt with laces in the front. Had he left his shirt at her house? An unexpectedly fierce flare of jealousy streaked up my spine, and I climbed out of bed. My knees gave way, and Zeke rushed to catch me.

"Give it a minute," Eliot said, leaping to my side, all concern now. "You haven't walked in three months."

"I'm fine," I said through gritted teeth. My legs felt like rubber bands, but I forced my feet to hold me. "I want to go back now. We can make a plan at home, and come back better prepared. Heimdall can't object to us preparing, and we can see our parents."

Peyton put a hand on her hip and rolled her eyes. "Heimdall doesn't care about our human activities, about school, or anything we left behind. We can't go back until we've done our job."

As I looked around, I saw they were all wearing at least one elven garment. Peyton was clad from head to toe in leather. "Are you all training to be dragon slayers?"

Peyton snorted. "Not even."

"Elves don't really understand the concept of ownership," Zeke said. "It's cool sometimes, like when no one was sleeping in this house, so they let us just have it. But not as cool when they take your clothes while you're sleeping, or come in and lie down and sleep beside you."

It was hard to come to terms with the fact I'd been sleeping for three months. Mom had been home with just Neil, someone who didn't know her quirks and ticks. And my stepsiblings had been here, learning about the elves, waiting for me. Sleeping in the bed beside me. The thought made me feel both vulnerable and loved at once. Then worry struck me, and I crossed my arms over my chest.

"Who's been feeding me? Bathing me?"

"The doctor gave us something to put on your tongue that you could swallow in your sleep," Xander said quietly. "We all fed you." The way his eyes fixed on me made my insides tremble.

"I bathed you," Peyton said. "We could have let an elf do it, but it didn't seem right."

I nodded, not sure how I felt about that. I'd have to think about it later.

"Okay," I said, nodding. "I obviously missed a lot, so I'm going to need you to fill me in. But first, I could really use a toothbrush and a cheeseburger, preferably in that order."

"Yeah, um, they don't eat meat here," Zeke said. "It's a major problem."

"If we have to finish our mission to go home, then let's do it," I said. "Now that I'm awake, let's find the missing pieces and get this over with."

Chapter Fifteen

Gwen

As we ate, the others filled me in on their time in Alfheim. Valdan and Alvan were usually around, but they had gone to Bifrost to do their daily trek across the river of fire just before I woke up.

"Did Rosa find us?" I asked.

Xander frowned and shook his head. "No."

"Joaquin did, though," Peyton said. "Lucky us."

My heart lurched. "Wait, Joaquin came back without Rosa?"

"He says she took him to Jotunheim," Eliot said. "But he didn't want to stay, so he came back to find us."

"He just keeps turning up," Peyton said. "Like a bad penny, as they say."

"But where is Rosa?"

"We don't know," Xander said. "She never came back."

"She's in the Jotunheim," Finn said.

I turned to him. He was so quiet I'd almost forgotten his presence. At home, he'd been quiet, too, but he'd seemed peaceful and chill. Here, he was…faded. Like a shadow of himself. "The giant world?" I asked. "Why is she there?"

He shrugged and poked at his food, some kind of potato patty. I remembered Eliot saying that Finn's hunches were never wrong. I just hoped Rosa wasn't stuck there, or that Joaquin hadn't killed her. I didn't know why else she wouldn't come to find us.

We'd just have to find her. We decided to leave the elf world and join Alvan and Valdan at Bifrost first. The more of our pieces we had together, the better, and they were our guides now that Rosa was gone. They knew their way around Yggdrasil and at least a couple other worlds. While in the elven world, the Keens had made friends with the elves, and not just the ones who shared our god. Eliot had even learned a bit of their language and trained to fight with them.

"It's like being in a video game," he said with a dopey grin. "I like to geek out on their weapons."

"And their elven maidens," I said, trying to sound like it didn't bother me. I had no claim to him, no right to be possessive when my own heart belonged to all the Keens, not just him. But as usual, my jealous streak wouldn't listen to reason.

"You're the only maiden I'm thinking about," he said, grinning at me across the small wooden table where we'd crowded to eat. They elves had directed them to an empty lodging, which was a tall, round building with one room on each floor like all elven lodges. It had a pointed roof and was six floors in total, though it was much simpler than the Keen's three-story mansion. The elves with families stayed in the same dwelling every night, but those who were unattached just wandered into whatever lodging and slept with whoever was in that home. To them, it was impossible to own a place, and they couldn't conceive of kicking someone out.

"Gracelyn says when we stopped interacting with the other worlds, it was literally the year seven A.D. Nothing about Midgard is the same, besides that it's inhabited by humans. Almost nothing we know about the other eight worlds will be accurate now, either."

I bit my tongue and didn't ask if that was his girlfriend. I knew I was being petty. I'd been passed out for three months—of course their lives had changed. Eliot had always had multiple girlfriends to satisfy his needs. I couldn't expect him to go without just because I couldn't give him what he needed.

"Did the dragon die?" I asked.

"That one did," Eliot said. "Gracelyn killed it."

"There are more," Zeke said. "They circle the tree in this world."

As we left the house to go find Alvan and Valdan so they could guide us to the last piece of Heimdall, I noticed that most of the backpacks were gone. Apparently, random elves had taken off with nearly everything we owned. In place of backpacks, my stepsiblings carried swords of different varieties.

"The elves say they're peaceful people, but they really like their weapons," Zeke explained. "I guess they're peaceful until someone invades."

"Their way of life is worth defending," Eliot said.

"Too bad you didn't find the missing piece while I was sleeping," I muttered. "Are you sure you haven't felt a pull towards any of the other elves?"

"Eliot feels a pull towards anything with two X chromosomes," Peyton said.

"Shut up, Peyton," he said, laughing and throwing an arm around her. "I could say the same for you."

I'd always felt like a bit of an outsider with the Keens, and it had only gotten worse here. At home, I'd expected it—they'd grown up together for most of their lives. They had a long, shared history and a million little secrets. They had lived a life of luxury while I'd basically lived in a bubble full of crazy. Of course I'd feel different. But after I'd arrived, all the strange things that had happened had involved all of us. I'd been a part of it.

In Alfheim, they'd had three months of experiences that didn't involve me, three months to learn about something so foreign and strange that it must have bonded them together even more. And despite their efforts, holding my hands and sleeping in the bed with me, I hadn't been part of any of it. I was still brand new to this.

When we stepped outside, the sun was hanging low and lazy over the fields nearby, sending up a warm green smell. I could hear the clank of metal somewhere nearby, and the smell of bread and frying onions filled the air. A few kids ran up and grabbed onto my brothers, greeting them by name.

"Wow," I said to Peyton. "Is there anywhere you aren't popular?"

Three guys appeared between the dwellings, so perfectly in step that I had to stare.

"Great," Peyton said, rolling her eyes. "These guys."

"Peyton," one of them called. "Where are you going?"

"Can we help you with anything?" the second one said.

"Have you eaten?" They ran up and circled Peyton, jostling me out of the way.

Finn steadied me, slipping an arm around my waist and giving me a quick squeeze. It was exactly what I needed, someone who made me feel like I belonged, like I was still part of this. And even though he only made me feel like I was part of something with him, part of being an outsider, I welcomed the sensation. A wave of gratitude swelled in me, and I reached to put my arm around him at the same moment he pulled away.

"Sorry," I said. "I didn't mean—"

"It's okay," he said. "Those are Gracelyn's brothers. Apparently, brothers here are very…"

"In step?"

"Yeah," he said with a small smile.

"They should go to our world," I said. "The minute they stepped into it, a boy band's choreographer would latch onto them and make them stars."

"The pointy ears might be a problem."

"It could be their signature look."

An awkward silence fell between us as more elves joined our parade, their chatter magnifying our lack of conversation.

"I have to tell you something," Finn said at last, touching my elbow to slow me.

My heart started thudding in my chest. I tugged my hands into the sleeves of my shirt, a long-sleeved cheer tee Peyton must have put on me.

"When you were sleeping I… I kissed you."

"What?" I asked, my eyes widening in surprise.

"You looked so beautiful lying there," he said. "So innocent. Like Sleeping Beauty. I thought maybe… it's stupid. I'm not the one who could have woken you up." He shoved his hands in his pockets and scowled.

"What do you mean?"

"If one of us is closest to you, it isn't me."

"Well, kissing a girl while she's sleeping probably isn't the best way to foster closeness."

His head hung lower. "I know. I'm sorry."

I thought about it for a minute, then nodded. "It's okay. I would have tried anything to wake you if I'd been in your place."

He looked at me sideways. "You're not angry?"

"As long as no one did anything else to me," I said, slipping my hand into his.

"No," Finn said, shaking his head vehemently. "Someone was always watching you."

"And Finn," I said as some more elves ran out to join the procession. "I feel as close to you as anyone else."

"Thanks," he said, but he didn't look like he believed it.

"I'd be closer if you'd let me," I said.

"I can't do what you and the others do to be close," he said, a troubled look on his face.

I could feel my cheeks warming as a mixture of outrage and shame swept through me.

"Maybe that's how things are outside Midgard," Finn said. "But I don't belong outside Midgard. I'm not part of these other worlds, and I don't want to be. Nothing we're doing feels right to me."

"You could just talk to me," I said, swallowing the sting of his words.

While we walked, every elf under the age of thirty came out to fangirl over my siblings. A tall, wiry guy with blond hair slicked back behind his pointed ears interrupted us, taking my free hand. "You've awoken," he said. "Have you found our village to your liking?"

"Um…it's okay," I said, pulling my hand away as delicately as I could. As soon as I'd extricated it from his, another elf appeared, this one with long brown hair and ivory skin.

"Is there anything you require, beautiful human?" he asked, taking my hand.

I wasn't sure how to respond to that. When I saw two girls hanging on Xander's arm, I decided I'd had enough of Alfheim in my short time here. "Do you know the way out of here?" I asked.

"Such a beautiful human should never make a perilous journey without an elven escort," another elf said, crowding in beside us. One of them had pushed himself between Finn and me, breaking our hold.

"Such lovely hair," another said, pulling a clip from my hair. "I stopped by to see you each day while you slept."

I wasn't used to so much attention. In my life, attention had always been a bad thing. Attention meant that my mom was having a breakdown, or the cops were eyeing us, and we needed to disappear. But I couldn't disappear here, with all these elves crowding around.

Casting a glance over the group, I found my stepbrothers as surrounded by adoring fans as I was. They looked much more comfortable with the attention. I'd never been fawned over in my life, and I wasn't very comfortable with it. Zeke cut through the cluster of elves and stood beside me, his shoulders stiff.

"We will supply you with a trained knight to escort you on your journey," someone said.

"We'll be fine with Gracelyn," Zeke said, taking my hand and smiling down at me with a warmth that made my heart flip in my chest.

There was some argument about which knight would take us to the World Tree, and which ones would provide the steeds to carry us. We arrived at a pristine lake, the surface reflecting the deep blue sky above, as well as the towering trees around it. A guy handed me a dagger for protection on my journey, and a snow-haired elf draped an arm over my shoulder and pointed to the water. "See that branch that extends over the water?"

I nodded, aware of Zeke's body stiffening beside me when the elf touched me.

"If you look above, you'll find the other trees that are reflected in the water," said the guy with white hair. "Only Yggdrasil casts a reflection without being seen in Alfheim."

Just then, a huge, snakelike head emerged from the water. I shrank against Zeke, stifling a cry and involuntarily grasping my scarred arm.

"It's just a water serpent," said a vaguely familiar voice behind me. I turned to find the girl who had killed the dragon in the tree. Gracelyn. She strode past us, and a rush of memory overwhelmed me—not only had she killed the dragon that bit me, she'd saved Zeke.

"Thank you," I blurted, hurrying to match Gracelyn's stride.

"Nothing to thank me for," she said. "They rarely leave the water, and they don't eat land creatures."

"I mean, thank you for saving Zeke," I said.

"We like humans," she said with a shrug.

"I noticed."

"The dragons will carry you up," she said.

"What?" I asked, looking around in alarm as I heard a flapping sound coming closer.

"How do you think you got down?"

"Didn't you kill it?"

"These are more civilized dragons," she said, smirking. Still, I shrank back when they arrived, each of them swooping over us. They were all different, from scaly to furry, but they were huge and could easily rip my head off if they were so inclined.

A hand slid around my waist, flattening against my stomach. "I'll ride with you," Xander said in my ear. "It'll be like riding my bike, but you get me from the back this time."

A shiver swept through me and I leaned back against his muscled chest, raising my arm to circle his neck. "Xander."

He inhaled, slow and deep, his fingers tightening on my hips. "I missed you."

"Me, too." I closed my eyes, my knees going soft and heat coiling through me. I didn't know how it was possible to want him so much and want someone else, too. When I was with Xander, I couldn't imagine feeling like this about anyone else. And yet, the way I felt for the others was just as real. I decided to simply focus on this right now, the way I'd focused on Finn to get me up the tree.

"Ready?" Xander asked.

I opened my eyes to see a scaly brown thing beside me, its nostrils smoking slightly. "Is there another way up?"

"No," Xander said, throwing a leg over the dragon's back and settling himself on it as easily as he would a horse. He looked so damn good in a pair of brown leather pants. I kept my eyes fixed on him and took his hand, ignoring the deadly creature under us as I climbed on. Its scales were hot and dry under me, its body much wider than Xander's bike. Its sides rose and fell with each slow breath.

"Do you really know how to ride this thing?" I asked as I seated myself in front of him.

"I didn't have anything else to do for the last three months," he said. "Except watch you sleep."

"Sorry to bore you," I muttered.

"Not a bit." I could hear the smirk in his voice as he added, "Sometimes you talk in your sleep."

"No, I don't."

"Yeah," he said. "You do."

I elbowed him, glad he couldn't see my red face. "What did I say?"

"Only that you were madly in love."

"I did not," I protested.

"You don't have to hide your feelings," he said. "It's obvious."

I started to protest, but before I could, he slapped the dragon's shoulder and uttered a word in a language I'd never heard. The dragon began to flap its huge, leathery wings, and my voice left me. I squeezed my eyes closed, holding back a scream. I really, really did not like traveling this way. Or by tree. Or by bridge.

My stomach lurched sickeningly when the dragon lifted up, and I could feel its powerful wings beating as it climbed through the air.

When I was back on earth, I was going to build myself a home in a cave.

"Open your eyes," Xander said, his arms tight around me.

"No way in hell," I yelled over the noise of the wind rushing in my ears.

"Come on, Gwen," he said. "Rationally, you know that you're not falling. I'm holding onto you." His voice lowered, his chin rasping against my ear as his warm breath swept over my skin. "I won't let you go."

"I can't," I said, my nails digging into the corded muscles of his forearm gripping my middle.

"You can," he said. "I'm right here. I won't let you fall." One of his hands slid down, palming my hip, while the other stayed wrapped around my middle.

"Promise?" I asked, my voice coming out more breathless than I liked.

"I promise," he murmured into my ear, sending heat rushing through my body. Every inch of me was pressed against him, burning against him.

I cracked my eyes open and saw the lake below. My fingers clenched around Xander's arm, the breath knocked out of me.

"Don't close your eyes," he commanded. "You don't want to miss this."

I did want to miss it. I was frozen in terror, as if the ground below would rush up and swallow me at any moment. Xander's hand moved up from my belly to my chest, then slid up the front of my neck, pulling my chin straight.

"Look," he growled. "It won't kill you. If you can't face this, how are you going to cross a bridge through the sky?"

I wanted to say that I wasn't. No fucking way. He'd have to do it with the others while my feet remained on solid ground. But I couldn't do that. He was right. This wasn't going to kill me, and if I didn't look it in the eye and overcome it, the rest of this trip was going to be impossible. I forced my eyes open, digging my nails into Xander. If he was going to make me face this, I was going to show him how much it terrified me. I wouldn't let him off easy.

My nails broke through his skin, marking him. Tears blurred my eyes, running silently down my cheeks. But I would not look away. The dragon rose sharply, and I choked back a sob of terror. I wasn't falling. I wasn't dying. It didn't even hurt.

But it felt as if my spine was being lifted out of my body.

"Are your eyes open?" Xander purred into my ear, his breath hot in the hollow of my shoulder.

"I hate you," I said, my voice shaking. I turned, reaching behind me to grip the back of his head as I pulled his mouth to mine. I opened for him. Fisting his hair as tightly as I could, I pulled him in deeper, arching back against him and devouring him hungrily as we climbed higher. Wisps of cloud brushed my cheek, icy and soft, as his warm tongue entered my mouth. He sighed, his grip tightening on my hip, his hardness swelling against the softness of my bottom.

I lost myself in his kiss, in the feeling of his hard body wanting, *demanding*, mine. I let my hands come loose from their death grip, distracted by how much I wanted to touch him, to feel more than just his forearm. His muscled thighs, the back of his neck, the curves of his ears, and the angles of his knees. At last, I felt us lurch to a stop. I gasped, pulling away. My lips were throbbing with want, with the bruising force of our kiss. My head spun, my core clenching with need.

With a smirk, Xander hopped off and held out a hand to me. "That wasn't so bad, was it?"

"What was that?" I asked. "Just an act to make me forget my fear?"

"It worked, didn't it?"

"I don't get it," I said, throwing my hands up. "What is with you? First you treat me like shit, and I get why you did that. But then you opened up to me, and I thought that meant something. I thought we had an understanding. Then you turn around and tell me you want to pretend nothing happened. I tried to be cool with that. Then you kissed me in front of everyone in the car, which isn't exactly hiding it. Now you kiss me and then immediately act all smug about it?" As I spoke, I scrambled off the dragon, ignoring his hand. I wanted to recover whatever dignity I had left, if any.

Xander arched an eyebrow. "You kissed me."

"You kissed me back like you meant it. But let me guess. Now you're going to tell me it was just pretend, and I should forget all about it."

Xander hooked his thumbs in his pockets and watched me with those cool, piercing blue eyes. "Are you done?"

I swallowed and forced myself to meet his eyes. "Yes."

"I've had a lot of time to think about it," he said as the dragon swooped off the branch and disappeared into the foliage below.

"About us?" I pressed. I wanted answers. I couldn't stand not knowing. I was attracted to the others, but I had something deeper with Finn and Xander. Finn was the first one who really opened up and talked to me, and now he'd pulled away. I couldn't let Xander do the same thing. Though it had taken him a while to come around, we'd formed a deeper connection that night he'd shared his past with me. Despite what he'd said the next morning, it was a big deal.

"What do you want, Gwen?" He stepped forward, pressing my back to the tree. "You want me to tell you how special you are? Of course you are. You want me to tell you how much I want you? You know I do."

My hands gripped his biceps, warm and trembling with the tension between us. "Then what?" I asked.

"We have a job to do," he said. "Then all this is over. When we've found the missing piece and fixed the bridge, we can figure out what we want to do. But I don't want to mess it up with my own selfishness."

"Selfishness?"

"If we're together, it might not be good for all of us, as a group," he said.

"What does that mean?"

Xander pulled me in, resting his hand on my lower back and pressing gently against me. He dropped his forehead to mine and closed his eyes. "I'm not the only one who feels this way about you," he said. "And I'm not going to fight my brothers for you."

"You don't have to," I whispered. "We can all—" My words were interrupted by a loud flapping sound and Xander stepped back. Another dragon landed, this one depositing Zeke and Peyton onto the branch.

"That never gets old," Zeke said, hopping off and lifting Peyton down. She smiled, but her gaze was shrewd as she surveyed Xander and me standing too close, unspoken words hanging between us.

I turned away and touched my lips, checking for swelling from the pressure of our kiss.

A minute later, Eliot and Finn arrived. I looked from one to another. My head was reeling from all this, and not just the danger. Finn had kissed me while I was asleep, and I knew that would be a big deal for him. He wouldn't kiss just anyone. He'd told me he didn't even talk to girls. And Xander had kissed me again. Just thinking about it made my heart race. I wanted more.

A few months ago, I'd never even touched a boy, and now I'd kissed three. And they were brothers. That was probably not good. Xander was right. Once we'd fixed Bifrost, we could worry about the attraction thing.

At least he'd had the sense to put a stop to it. I didn't think Zeke would stop anything, and I doubted Eliot would, either. They were used to getting girls, to sleeping with girls.

The thought made my heart skip. I *wanted*. But I didn't know if I was ready for that, though my body said I was. I could barely hold a conversation with a boy, and yet, I was constantly in a state of heightened arousal for whichever one I was with. It was too confusing, too much. I didn't want to think about any of it right now. It made me want to get in a car and drive far away, where no one could find me.

But there were no cars here.

No sooner had we gathered on the branch than a rustle sounded in the leaves.

"What now?" Peyton asked, throwing her leather-clad arms up.

A second later, a giant, red squirrel appeared from below the branch. "Greetings," he said. "I bring a message from your giant."

I relaxed. "It's just Ratr."

A grunting sound came from below, and the next second, a grinning face with floppy blond hair hanging over his forehead appeared over the edge of the branch. "Here you are," Joaquin said, heaving himself up to join us. "I thought I'd lost you for good."

Chapter Sixteen

Gwen

"See," Peyton said. "Bad penny."

I fought the urge to shrink away from Joaquin. Instead, I faced him squarely. "What happened when Rosa took you back to your world?"

"Dude, my world is the same as yours," he said. "I'm human, remember? I don't know any more about all this than you do. The only difference is that you have a whole mess of boyfriends to help you along, and I'm by myself."

"Poor Joaquin," Ratr said in his squeaky little voice.

"Cry me a river," Peyton said to Joaquin. "You spent as many nights alone in Alfheim as we did. None."

He grinned and held up both hands. "Hey, I can't help it that human wang is like catnip to elven maidens."

"And I can't help it that I look like a leather-clad warrior princess, but that doesn't mean that I am one. Just like you being away from us doesn't mean that you've been lonely."

"He is, though," Ratr said.

"Shut up, squirrel-brain," Joaquin said.

"We've treated you more than fairly, considering," Eliot said to Joaquin.

"Yeah," Peyton said. "It's probably time you headed home, Giant Boy."

"Dude, how many times do I have to apologize for trying to murder Gwen when I was possessed? It wasn't me."

"Can I push him off?" Xander asked.

"Ooh, this is getting good," Ratr said, plopping his fat squirrel butt down on the branch to watch.

"Where is Rosa?" I asked, crossing my arms and glaring at him.

"You won't get that answer out of him," Zeke said.

"Because I don't know," Joaquin said, throwing up his hands. "She took me to Jotunheim and tried to dump me there, but I got back on Yggdrasil and came to find you."

"How?" I asked, narrowing my eyes.

"Ratr," he said with his big goofy grin.

"No one knows Yggdrasil like me," Ratr said.

"And you left Rosa in Jotunheim," I said to Joaquin.

"Dude, I didn't hurt your fat lady dwarf. She's the one who kidnapped me and tried to ditch me. You can't blame me for running away."

"How long were you in Alfheim with us?" I asked, shuddering at the thought of Joaquin finding me unconscious.

"I've been everywhere, dude," he said. "I've gotten lost so many times. At least you have some elves to show you around. I'm on my own."

"A real tragedy," Ratr said. "Nothing lonelier than an outcast giant."

"If you've been everywhere, you can't be having too much trouble," I pointed out.

"We can't leave him in Alfheim," Eliot said. "They don't want a giant, either."

I turned to Joaquin. "Considering you tried to murder me, give me one good reason we should let you follow us around?"

"You might need me at some point," Joaquin said. "When your little boys aren't enough for you, you might need a real giant."

I considered for a moment. "What giant are you?"

"I told you. I'm Loki."

"He's Loki," Ratr confirmed.

Eliot's eyes brightened. "Really? Gwen didn't tell us that."

"Yeah, so what?" Joaquin said.

"Can you get us into Jotunheim?" I asked. Heimdall had said the elves would guide us there, so we had to assume he wanted us to go there to get his last piece. It might be wise to travel with a giant inside their world.

"Maybe I can," Joaquin said, eyeing me.

"He can," Ratr said.

"I guess the sleep spell wore off then," I said. "You're the giant now. Or you're just a human, and we're supposed to take pity on you? Make up your mind. You can't be both."

"Oooh, she got you," Ratr squeaked.

Joaquin grinned that too-big smile. "But I am both. I'm Joaquin, and I'm Loki."

"All of him? You're hosting a complete giant?"

"So what if I am? It's better to hang out in a tiny human body than go back to being in my original giant form, bound in chains with acid dripping into my eyes."

"It's a pretty harsh punishment," Eliot agreed. "I always thought it was excessive."

"Exactly," Joaquin crowed in his surfer dude tone. He held out a hand and waited for Eliot to high-five him.

"Now you're friends with him?" I asked.

Eliot shrugged. "I mean… Loki's pretty cool."

"He tried to kill me."

"Why are we even talking about this?" Xander cut in. "This guy is a psycho who hurt Gwen. We push him off and go get our elves."

"I'm not going to hurt anyone," Joaquin said. "Okay, I admit I hurt Gwen, but it was under duress. Now that you're already here, there's no reason for me to hurt any of you. You already made it."

"But we haven't completed our mission," I said. "So, you have the same reason to stop us as before."

"Actually, I don't," he said. "See, if you didn't get out of Midgard, I could stay in this form, chasing you around, and maybe wreaking a little havoc. But now I actually need you to succeed, so we can all go back to Midgard."

"We're not taking a giant back home," Zeke said. "You killed all our parents."

Everyone froze for a second, staring at Joaquin like they'd forgotten that. Zeke had been the only one old enough to have a few memories of his real parents, like I had of Dad.

"He's right," Xander said. "You killed Mom, too, didn't you?"

"Dude, your mom killed herself," Joaquin said. "You can't blame me for that."

"What?" I asked, drawing back from the Keens and flattening against the wall of the tree's trunk. "I thought your mom had cancer."

They all looked at me with identical blank expressions.

"Awk-ward," Ratr muttered.

"What made you think that?" Peyton asked after a long moment.

"You said she was sick for a long time."

"She was," Xander said quietly. "But not that kind of sick."

"Mentally," Zeke said. "Like your—ow!" He broke off when Peyton punched him in the ribs. "What?"

"No, it's okay," I said, taking a steadying breath. "Like my mom. That's what you were going to say. You're right. My mom is sick."

"Awww, how sad," Ratr said.

"She's sick, and I need to get back to her," I said, balling my hands into fists. "It's been too long already. Let's go." I turned and started down the trunk of the tree.

Climbing down was at least twice as scary as climbing up, but either Xander's lesson had worked, or I was getting used to it because I didn't completely lose my shit.

"At least you know she's with someone who has experience with this kind of thing," Peyton said, climbing beside me. "Dad will look out for her while you're gone."

"But your mom died while he was looking out for her, right?" Ratr asked, scampering along beside us.

"Get lost, fancy rat," Peyton said.

But his words stuck in my head. Neil might have been great with her mom, but not great enough to prevent her suicide.

"I thought you knew," Peyton said when I didn't speak. "I'm sorry. I would have told you. I figured Dad told your mom, and she told you."

"I thought one of the others told you," Xander said. "Since you barely spoke to me the first month you were here."

"That must have driven you crazy," Ratr said.

"It wasn't a month," I said.

"Don't be mad," Eliot said. "I thought that's why you brought your mom there. So that Dad could help her, and you didn't have to take care of her on your own anymore."

"That's a heavy burden," Ratr said.

"Why would I do that?" I asked. "I didn't know anything about your dad."

"But your mom doesn't like hospitals," he said. "Dad offered to help when I found her online."

"And she didn't even tell her own daughter," Ratr said. "She must not trust you."

I sighed. "I'm not mad at any of you. I just left my mom, though. What if…"

"What if she ends her life, too?" Ratr asked.

"If you don't shut up, I'm going to pin you to the tree and skin you," Xander said.

"He's just a cute little squirrel," Joaquin said, grinning.

"You're next," Xander said. "I can't stop you from following us around, but if you touch anyone in this family, I will fucking end you."

"Whoa, whoa, what did I do? I'm helping you get into Jotunheim, remember?"

"I don't like you," Xander said. "I don't care if you're the flunky surf rat or the giant. You messed with the wrong family."

"Dad talked to her about what she was seeing when they spoke online," Eliot said to me as we left the others arguing. "She said she wanted to be with someone who understood. He understands, Gwen. That's what she needed. She's not going anywhere."

"Thanks," I said. "But I need to get back to her."

"I know," he said. "We'll get you back. Whatever it takes, whatever you need… We'll do it."

"Why?" I asked, pausing to wipe my hair back from my forehead. "Your dad took us in and took care of us. He married my crazy mom. And you're rich. We had nothing. We brought nothing to your family but trouble."

"You brought you," he said.

"What does that mean?"

"It means we needed you," he said. "You might not see it because you didn't know us before. But you brought us together. And not just as a god."

We both reached for the same handhold at once, pausing before Eliot slid his hand behind mine and curled my fingers around the chink in the bark. He gave me a quick smile and then stepped down again, watching his feet.

"What you said to Peyton that day," I said after a minute. "Before the dragon attack. Do you even remember?"

"Sure, I remember."

"Why'd you say that?"

"I just didn't think she was being honest with anyone."

"And dumping your girlfriends was honest?"

"I was always honest with them," he said. "Just because I don't believe in monogamy doesn't mean I'm a cheater or dishonest."

"Then how was dating them dishonest?"

"Because I like you more."

I nearly missed the handhold I'd been reaching for. I wasn't expecting him to be so forward. My heart leapt to my throat, and I could hardly speak. "You do?"

"Of course," he said. "It's okay if you didn't notice. I don't have all the baggage that Xander has or all the muscles Zeke does. I'm used to being overlooked at first."

"Don't even pretend you're shy."

"Shy? No way," he said with a grin. "Patient? Definitely."

"So what are you waiting for now?"

"To win you over with my sparkling personality and subtle charm."

I snorted. "Wow. Very subtle."

"That, or I can just make sure to be there next time you wake up," he said. "Then I can win you over with my superior bedroom skills."

Face flaming, I studied the tree in search of the perfect hold.

"I'm kidding," Eliot said, his voice right in my ear.

I jumped, not having seen him lean close. "How was I supposed to know?" I muttered. "I've never done anything, and you're all…"

He smiled and shook his head. "I just turned sixteen, Gwen. Finn's never even had a girlfriend. Xander hasn't hooked up with anyone in years. You're not that far behind us, believe it or not."

"I'm going with not," I said. "You're all way more experienced than me."

"I'd be happy to help you catch up," he said, biting his bottom lip to hold back a grin.

"I'm sure you would," I said, trying to laugh with him, though my heart was thumping inside my chest. I wanted him to be serious. "Is that the line you give all virgins, or am I special?"

"You are special," he said, his smile dropping away. "Yeah, I have a past. But I saw how special you were the moment you ran into me in the hall the first time. That's why I broke it off with the other girls."

"But you don't believe in monogamy, so why dump them?"

"Maybe I could be taught."

"Yeah, well…I'm not sure that I could."

"Because you like both my brothers."

"And you," I admitted. "I'm sorry. I've never even had one boyfriend, and now I want six at once. It's ridiculous. I'm sure it's just the god thing."

He didn't answer for a minute, and my insides got all squirmy and wrong. I'd admitted the truth, but of course he would think I was greedy, or worse, slutty. I opened my mouth, trying to find a way to take it back, but he spoke before I could.

"I don't see anything wrong with it," he said, stepping off the tree onto a branch. The others were a ways above, so I stepped off with him to wait.

"You don't think I'm crazy?"

"To want six boyfriends? Yeah, that's certifiable. The foot odor alone could kill you."

"Oh."

"Again, kidding," he said, tugging at my sleeve playfully. "Lighten up."

I forced a laugh. "I'll try."

"I don't blame you," he said. "It's natural to be attracted to multiple people. And after all that time shut up in a car, of course you're going to want to indulge in the things you missed."

"Thanks," I said, feeling suddenly shy at being observed that way. I tucked my hands into my sleeves and leaned back against the tree.

"I won't lie, I've had fun with it," Eliot said, taking the spot beside me and pressing his shoulder into mine. "But right now, there's only one person I'm interested in. Maybe one day, you'll feel the same."

"And if I don't?"

He crossed his arms and stared out at the leaves on the branch while I admired the bulge of his biceps inside his shirt. "I don't know how it would work back in our world," he said. "It would be hard to keep it secret, and if people found out, they'd give you hell. But if we found a way to make it work, then…why not?"

"You're okay with that?"

"Are you asking me to be your boyfriend?"

"No," I said quickly, my face scorching hot.

"Damn," he said. "So close."

"It's not…I didn't mean…"

"Are you waiting for Xander to ask you first? Or Zeke?"

"What? No. I'm not waiting for anyone."

He pushed off the tree and turned to face me, resting his hands on my shoulders. "Then…can I be one of your six boyfriends?"

My heart stammered in my chest, and I bit back a smile. "I thought you were patient."

"Was that a no?"

"No," I said, letting the smile creep across my lips.

Eliot's hands slid up to my throat, lifting my chin with his thumbs as he stepped closer. "Was it a yes?"

"It might have been." My fingers hooked into his belt loops, tugging his slender hips closer to mine.

"Then say yes," he whispered, his lips curving into a smile, his nose brushing mine.

A warm shiver went through my body, and I let my smile join his. "Yes."

Chapter Seventeen

Eliot

I wasn't usually keen on public displays of affection, but with Gwen I didn't care who saw us. I'd wanted to kiss those plump, cherry lips since the moment I saw her in the hallway at home. I'd have done it right there if she hadn't looked so lost and confused, like she needed someone to take her hand and show her the way. I wanted to show her the way.

"This is really starting to feel like *déjà vous*," Peyton said. "I've lost track of how many times I've walked in on someone kissing Gwen."

"I think someone's jealous," Zeke teased.

I pulled away slowly, unable to keep the smile off my face. I didn't want to stop kissing Gwen—ever. I'd always thought it would take a miracle to make me choose one girl and forget all the others. There were three billion girls in the world. It was illogical to think I'd be happy with only one. But I was starting to believe in miracles.

With Gwen around, I couldn't think about another girl. Now that I'd kissed her, it had gotten even worse. I was on my way to becoming that pathetic guy chasing a girl around asking if he could carry her books and rub her shoulders. Actually, both those things sounded pretty good right now, which just went to show what a cliché I'd become. And I didn't even care.

"Hey, if there's any openings left in the Kissing Gwen Club, I'll join," Joaquin said.

Xander's eye twitched like he might explode.

I just smiled and stepped away from Gwen. Nothing could ruin my mood right now. I wasn't in the Kissing Gwen Club. I was in the Gwen's Boyfriend Club. But I didn't say anything. I liked that we had a little secret no one else knew just yet. Of course I'd tell my brothers soon, since we shared everything. We'd even shared the fact that we'd all kissed our stepsister. I liked that we were all in it together, like a dirty little secret from our world.

But for the moment, I had something with only Gwen. When we turned to go on, I smiled at her, and she gave me a quick, shy grin before ducking her head. It was the cutest thing I'd ever seen. I was officially smitten.

We followed the others down until we reached the branch leading to the foot of Bifrost, and then we jumped.

I held one of Gwen's hands while Zeke held the other, and we tumbled onto the mossy ground below. Bifrost rose above, but it had grown duller in our absence. The water was a murky jade green instead of clear as emerald. The flames only flickered, and the air current was all but invisible.

"What's happening?" Peyton asked when she landed. "Is this the beginning of Bifrost falling apart?"

We could hear shouts from far off, which definitely meant the water in Bifrost wasn't as wild as it had been the last time when we could only hear each other if we were standing close together.

"The elves?" Gwen asked, starting up the hill.

With a shrug to the others, I followed. At the top of the cliff where it smoothed to stone, we stopped. Far below, on the other side of the river of fire, stood a clamoring group of people. At first I thought they were human, but after a few minutes of watching, I knew different. Some of them had strong elven builds. I searched for our elves among the group, but I couldn't find them.

And then a giant loomed up from the bottom of the canyon. I stifled an exclamation of surprise. Okay, and maybe fear, too. This wasn't Joaquin being infested. This was a literal giant. The thing was enormous, at least fifty feet tall, with fissures of fire in its blackened skin. This was what Joaquin had inside him? I glanced over to find him standing on the rim of the rock, his face taut with excitement.

Then I spotted the two figures on our side of the river, where they'd taken Gwen when they pulled her from the fire. Our elves stood across from the crowd, shaking their fists like they thought they were evenly matched with this fire giant.

"We have to help them," Gwen said, turning to us as if we had answers.

"How?" Peyton asked. "They look like they're provoking that giant."

"We have to get them up here," I said. "We're all stronger together. You saw how strong we were last time we were here."

"Is that your word for extra horny?" Zeke asked.

Gwen gave him a warning look. "They have Thor's chariot. If we can get them up here, we can save them from that fire giant."

I was impressed that she'd taken the time to learn about the Norse worlds before we came, even if most of the information we had was thousands of years out of date. At least the setup of the Nine Worlds was the same—one giant tree that extended through the cosmos, with nine home worlds off the various branches and roots. We'd been to only two—Midgard and Alfheim. I was dying to see what the other seven were like, but if we didn't save our elven pieces, they couldn't show us where to go.

"Link hands," I said. "They'll feel that we're here, and maybe we can get them out."

Gwen's small hand slipped into mine, and I tried not to let it distract me as I reached for Finn with my free hand. A moment later, we'd completed our usual circle. It felt perfect with six. The other three might be part of Heimdall, but they weren't a part of our family. Gwen might have been different from us, but somehow, she just…fit. She made us better, made us good again. She had brought back the closeness that had faded after Mom died and Xander got weird and Dad got depressed.

"It's working," Peyton said. "I feel it. Do you guys feel it?"

I did. The charge wasn't anything like when we'd all hugged on Gwen to heal her, but it was stronger than when we'd done this at home. Instead of using all the power to make Heimdall appear, it stayed within us. But this place seemed to handle it better—wherever this place was. We were in some strange in-between, like when we were in Yggdrasil. We stood at the end of the bridge leading from Midgard to Asgard, the world of the gods that we'd seen in the sky the morning of our arrival. But we weren't inside either world.

Suddenly, the pair of horned goats we'd seen the last time charged along the sandy riverbank towards the twins, the chariot behind them.

"Whoa," I said.

"Come on, come on," Gwen muttered, her fingers tightening around mine. "Get in the chariot, you stupid Viking maniacs."

"Thor is known for slaughtering everyone in a dining hall when he gets pissed," I reminded her. "I think he's the 'fight now, ask questions never' type."

"Well, we're not," she said as they waved the goats away. "Let's go get them."

A minute later, the two goats trampled the moss behind us and skidded to a stop with the chariot in tow. "Whoa," I said again, looking sideways at Gwen.

"Get in," she said, hopping in without hesitation. Apparently, this trip was curing her fear of heights pretty quickly.

"Wait, we're going down there to fight a fire giant?" Peyton asked. "That sounds cool and everything, but so does, you know. Living."

"If we want to get back home, we've got to do whatever it takes to get the elves and stay with them," Gwen said. "And I plan on getting home."

A look I hadn't seen before came into her face as her jaw tightened in determination. Peyton had pushed the right button, found the one thing Gwen wouldn't be timid about. She'd never back down when it came to her mom.

I got in the chariot. The others followed, except Joaquin. Xander pushed him back when he tried to climb in. "Don't even think about it," he said.

I felt sorry for Joaquin, but I got over it by thinking about what he'd done to Gwen. The goats started forward and moments later we were dropping towards the canyon floor. I hadn't gotten to see this before, and I leaned forward to watch the walls rise beside us. At the top, they were pale sandstone, but as we descended, they turned dark, as if the heat had charred the rock itself. Near the bank of the lava river, the sheer stone walls were pitch black.

"Did you call the goats?" I asked Gwen as we rushed towards the river of fire below.

"What?" Gwen asked.

"You said we needed the goats, and they came," I said, pushing up my glasses and studying her. "Did you call them somehow?"

"I—I don't know," she said, pulling her hand from mine. "I was calling to them in my head, I guess."

"Cool," I said. "Maybe you have some kind of gift from Heimdall."

"So Finn can find the World Tree from anywhere on earth, and you can feel when I'm in trouble. As my superpower, I get a psychic connection with goats."

"Duck," Peyton shrieked.

"Not ducks," Zeke said. "Goats."

Xander shoved him to the floor, leaping on top of him. The rest of us ducked pretty well ourselves. A ball of flaming lava hurtled by, exploding into a shower of red-hot stones when it hit the canyon wall. The fire giant had spotted us. With a roar, it bent and scooped up another handful of molten lava.

"Oh my God, we're all going to die," Peyton wailed, throwing herself down beside Gwen and me.

"We're not going to die," Zeke said from behind us.

He couldn't know that, but I didn't correct him. In that moment, I was more inclined to agree with Peyton. She closed her eyes, gripping Gwen's hand as they lay face to face on the chariot floor, only inches apart. I hovered over them, not really wanting to be splattered by hot lava, but figuring it was the gallant thing to do.

Xander let out a strangled cry and swore savagely.

"You get hit?" I asked.

"Just a flesh wound," he growled through clenched teeth.

With a thud the chariot landed, and we all tumbled out. From below, the canyon was even more impressive. The river bubbled and churned, steam hissing from it. Beneath the water of the bridge, I felt like we were inside the world's most insane aquarium. Unfortunately, I didn't have much time to observe and enjoy because a fifty-foot fire giant was tossing lava our way.

"Get the elves," Gwen shouted, leaping from the chariot and racing for them. It would have been funny watching her pint-sized figure try to wrestle a couple of seven-foot musclemen into a chariot if it weren't for, again, the lava flinging going on.

"We need to get out of here," Peyton yelled as one of the goats began leaping around and bleating piteously, its hair burning.

"Stay here and make sure they don't run off with the carriage," Zeke yelled, and then he was running across the sand with Xander and me.

"We have to go right now," Gwen yelled at the elven twins.

"We've fought giants before," Alvan yelled back. "We don't run from them. The moment Bifrost falls, they'll invade Midgard."

"If you die, Bifrost will fall," I said. "Let's go. We can come back when we have all nine pieces."

I grabbed Valdan's arm, and Zeke grabbed the other, and we started dragging him towards the chariot. Gwen and Xander had gotten Alvan, and together the six of us sprinted for the waiting goats. My group reached the chariot and leapt in, ducking molten projectiles. Alvan roared in pain and fell just steps from the two goats. Across the river, the crowd had grown louder, cheering and jeering so raucously I didn't at first realize what had gotten them so riled. When I spotted the spear jutting from Alvan's thigh, I understood. Someone in the crowd of giants and other creatures had impaled one of our guides.

Before I could move, Zeke had leapt out and helped drag him into the chariot.

"Go," Valdan roared, and the goats charged off down the sand. I didn't know how two fat goats could haul six humans and two gigantic elves, but since they could also fly, I decided that human logic didn't govern this particular situation. Not to mention that they didn't even have wings.

When they took off into the air, I breathed a small sigh of relief. We weren't out of reach of the fire giant yet, but at least the gathering on the bank couldn't spear us.

"Um, guys?" Peyton said in a tiny voice. I knew that voice. It said she was barely holding it together, and she might go into hysterics at the slightest provocation.

"What's up?" Zeke asked, twisting around to see her.

"I know we're in the middle of a really not-fun version of Hot Lava, and one of you has literally been impaled, but there's something wrong with Finn."

Chapter Eighteen

Gwen

F inn. Shit. I'd been so busy getting everyone in the chariot that I hadn't even noticed he'd never gotten out to help us. In the chaos, I'd heard someone tell Peyton to watch the goats, but Finn…

When I turned, he was slumped over in his seat, his eyes glazed with a strange glassiness that drove a spike of ice through my ribs. A wave of *déjà vous* swept over me as I studied his face. I'd seen that look before. God, it was so familiar.

"Did he get hit?" Eliot asked, scrambling over the seat.

"No," Peyton cried. "I was watching. He was fine, and then he just…" She broke off, hiccupping and burying her face in his limp shoulder.

Finn's face was like…Mom's. I slipped over the seat, leaving Valdan in the front with Zeke and Alvan. They knew how to fly the chariot better than any of us, not to mention how to pull spears out of people. I knew how to tend to other kinds of wounds. I knelt at Finn's feet, reaching up to take his face between my hands.

"Finn," I said quietly. "Can you hear me?"

Nothing.

We touched down on the mossy plain above the canyon, just long enough for Valdan to grab Joaquin and toss him into the chariot with us.

"Are you fucking kidding me?" Xander growled.

"We need a giant for Jotunheim," Valdan said, taking off again before any of us could argue.

Joaquin grinned up at us from the floor. "It's so nice to be included."

"Don't speak," Xander said, putting a boot down on Joaquin's throat.

"Okay, okay," Joaquin, said. "Jeez, you don't have to rip out my jugular."

"You're still speaking."

"Maybe we can find Rosa, too," I said. "If she left Joaquin there, maybe she's still there."

"That would explain why she never came back," Zeke said.

"And this asshole is going to show us exactly where she is," Xander snarled at Joaquin. He took his foot off Joaquin's neck but remained hovering over him.

"Can we focus on the real problem here?" Peyton asked. She wrapped her arms around Finn and started rocking back and forth. "I knew he wasn't okay. He's been going along since we left home, but it's like he's not all here. I think he left half of himself back in Midgard."

"I tried to include him in training with the elves," Eliot said. "But he did it half-heartedly, if I could get him to go at all."

"He's not good at change," Peyton sniffed.

"He's not good at most things," Joaquin said. Even with hiccups and tear-stained cheeks, Peyton managed to glare so fiercely that his expression immediately turned defensive. He took in the scowling faces of the Keen siblings. "What? It's true. He doesn't try to fit in. He doesn't talk, he's not interested in sports, he's not all tech-geek like Eliot…"

"He talks to me," I said quietly.

"To us," Eliot said. "He's a misfit, that's all. As his twin, it's my duty to make sure that's not a problem. And it's not."

"Okay, okay," Joaquin said, sitting up. "Not saying it is."

"Then what are you saying?"

"Nothing," Xander said. "Because if he does, I'm tossing him from this flying chariot, and he can go back to his eternal punishment."

"I'm just saying," Joaquin said, actually looking earnest for once. "Maybe this isn't the place for him. Maybe it's too much."

"It's too much for all of us," I said, turning back to Finn.

"You think he died of fright?" Peyton asked, her face stricken.

"He's not dead," I said, pressing my fingertips to the side of his neck. "His pulse is fine. My mom does this. He'll come around."

"When?" Peyton asked, her voice rising towards hysteria. "What if we get attacked by dragons, or lava guys, or whatever the fuck is next."

Everyone stared at her. Even Zeke stuck his head over the seat and gaped. "Did you just…cuss?"

"So?"

"You never say *fuck*," Xander said.

"I also never wear freaking leather from head to toe— and by the way, when we get home, we will never speak of this again—or ride dragons, or gossip with squirrels."

"Then you don't do nearly enough drugs," Joaquin said, smirking.

Xander reached out and grabbed Joaquin by the throat. "Shut. Up."

"You do them, too," Joaquin croaked.

I turned away. "Xander does drugs?" I whispered.

"Are you actually surprised by that?" Peyton asked. "Come on, Gwen. You're not that naïve."

Stung, I turned all my focus on Finn, watching his eyes for signs that he was coming out of it. For once, I was not the person freaking out the worst, but it didn't make me feel better. If anything, I wished I could trade places with Finn and save him from the fear and pain that had sent him into this state.

Eliot's hand landed gently on my thigh.

"Finn's not a tough guy, but he's stronger than people give him credit for," he said. "He'll be okay."

I swallowed the lump in my throat and nodded. "I know he will."

"He's stayed strong in his convictions, and that's not the easiest thing to do when you're a guy," Eliot said with a grin. "Especially when your convictions tell you not to even *want* a girl."

"Sexist," Peyton said, rolling her eyes. "Girls have just as much trouble controlling themselves as guys. We're all hormonal, not just you."

"You might have hormones, but you're not a Keen male," he said. "You don't have quite the number of temptations."

"You're right, ten girls don't line up hoping to warm my bed every night," Peyton said.

"And if they did, and you turned your back on them all in favor of celibacy, I'd say you were strong, too," Eliot said.

I stroked Finn's hair back, feeling a rush of warmth for him. Around all the others, I felt inadequate for not having any sexual experience. But not Finn. Finn was different.

"Has this ever happened before?" I asked.

"No," Peyton said. "I mean, he might zone out at inopportune times, but nothing like this. He's spacy for sure, but I always thought it was an artist thing…"

"It's a Finn thing," Joaquin said. We all glared. "What? He's my friend. You think I don't know him as well as the rest of you?"

"Not that you deserve his friendship," Peyton said. "But yes, he's very forgiving. He sees the best in everyone. Even you."

Eliot squeezed his brother's shoulder. "He never managed to find a social group where he really fit, but he does fine when he has something to do, like art or surfing. He has friends."

"Even friends who probably only picked him out because he's in our family," Xander said, glaring daggers at Joaquin. "Don't believe this clown. He's friends with Finn because he was trying to pick off a piece of our god, and Finn was the weakest link."

I looked up, startled. "Until I came along."

Just then, the chariot started descending rapidly.

"Hold on tight," Valdan said. "We're about to enter Jotunheim, land of the giants."

My stomach bottomed out and my heartbeat quickened. I gripped the seat, trying not to pass out. I would not be the weakest link anymore. I would be brave, even when I felt like fleeing in terror. This was no time for cowardice—it was time to find our missing piece.

Chapter Nineteen

Gwen

Instead of taking us through Yggdrasil, Thor's goats flew us straight into Jotunheim. We came through the mists of between-worlds and descended into a dark green forest. As soon as we touched down, Finn's head snapped up. I was so relieved I couldn't do anything but throw my arms around his neck and hang there like a leech. He made a strange noise in his throat, a mixture of pain and startled laughter.

"Are you okay?" I asked, pulling back.

"You're kneeling on my toe."

"Oh," I said, scrambling backwards. "I'm sorry."

"It's okay," he said, glancing around at the thick forest surrounding us. "Where are we?"

"In Jotunheim," Alvan said.

Xander cleared his throat. "The better question is where the hell have you been?"

"First we must heal Alvan," Valdan said. "Then we can talk and walk."

We gathered around Alvan, who still had the spear protruding five feet into the air from his thigh. He was conscious, and I couldn't imagine how much pain he was in, but his face showed nothing. Remembering the last time we'd healed someone, I was hesitant to get close to Alvan. It had been powerful, and it felt good—too good—but there was an intimacy about it that I didn't know how to share with a stranger.

But I would be brave, like he was. I would do what had to be done. Find our missing piece. Fix Bifrost. Go home.

Alvan sat down on a large stone and gripped the spear. "I did not want to pull it out and lose blood before," he said. "I'll pull it out once you are all touching me, and it should heal quickly."

"Okay," I said. "We can do that."

"Closer," Valdan said, herding us toward Alvan. Apparently, he didn't just want us to put a hand on his shoulder. He wanted us to put as much of ourselves onto him as possible.

Alvan reached up and wrapped a massive arm around my waist, pulling me down on his lap. "Don't be afraid," he said. "I am part of you. I wouldn't hurt you any more than I'd hurt myself."

"That would be more convincing if you didn't voluntarily walk through a river of fire every day," I said, but I didn't pull away. I leaned back against his broad chest, resting my head on his heart.

"Help me pull out the spear."

"That's going a little far," I said, my breath coming faster as the others pressed in on us and the crackling electricity of our nearness built inside me. Peyton knelt beside us and leaned her head on my thigh, sending a current of heat traveling upwards. Xander's belt was inches from my cheek. Suddenly, all I could think about was moving my head a bit, brushing against the front of his pants. How could I make that look like an accident?

Oh, that's right, you can't. There's no way to make that look like an accident.

"Xander, too," I said. "He got hit with lava."

"I'm fine," he said.

"Shut up and stop being proud," Peyton said. "We can get you both at once. We're all here."

I slid my arm around Xander's thigh, relishing his sharp inhalation. Pulling him close, I drew on the godlike force inside that had become easier to separate from my human essence. My body sang unbearably as Alvan wrapped my hand around the hilt of the spear, his palm covering my entire hand. He was breathing hard, his chest heaving under my head. I could tell the contact with all of us was affecting him much the same way it had affected me the last time. I gripped the shaft of the spear, my head swimming.

"Now," he said, giving a mighty yank. He let out a roar as the spear ripped free of his flesh. Blood splattered across Peyton and me. I should have been disgusted, but instead, I found myself wanting to dance in the rain of his blood. Alvan's hand, still wrapped around mine, pressed my palm down on the wound, and he sucked in a loud, shuddering breath.

I sighed with pleasure at the warm wetness under my hand, at the hard contours of his body shifting under mine, and Xander's thigh pressed to the side of my chest, his fingers on the crown of my head. Again, I felt the completeness of this circle and the gaping absence of one member. The glow of Heimdall's energy filled us, radiating from us the way it had radiated from him. This was my family, my being, my purpose. In this moment, nothing mattered but being with them, being one with them. We'd almost achieved completion.

At last, Alvan sighed and released me. My ribs ached from his crushing hold, but I didn't care. The moment had been worth it, and we'd succeeded. Though my hand was sticky from Alvan's blood, the wound on his leg was nothing more than a puckered line.

"Dude, that's how you heal each other?" Joaquin said, a cat-that-ate-the-canary grin on his face. "I want to be part of a god. I'm totally jealous now."

The way he looked at us made me remember that I was human, and things were different in the human world. Suddenly, the shine within me dulled, replaced by a wave of shame.

"Are we okay in this world?" Eliot asked, seeming to collect himself before the rest of us. Actually, I wasn't sure Eliot ever lost control. It might not be possible for him, though he somehow achieved the same glow as the rest of us. Even Finn had a slight shine this time, though it was nothing compared to Alvan. The elf lounged on his perch, his eyes dazed with satisfaction, his skin glowing so brightly it hurt to look at him.

"Depends," Joaquin said. "Some giants are friendly to humans and gods. Some aren't."

"We should make our trip here as brief as possible," Alvan said. "In general, giants do not appreciate other creatures coming into their world uninvited."

"Just like humans don't," Eliot said. He scanned the towering evergreen trees around us, his eyes bright with interest. It didn't look too much different from our world. Though I wasn't sure we had the exact species of fir, a forest was a forest. The sun shone brightly, but a chill filled the air around us. Shivering, I crossed my arms and hugged myself. I halfway expected a frost giant to come bursting out of the woods at any moment.

"How do we find one of our pieces here?" I asked, glancing nervously at the towering trees. "If it's as big as earth, it could take a lifetime to find the last piece in our world, let alone in a strange world we know nothing about."

"If we meet one of ours, something weird will happen," Peyton said. "Like when we met. Or we'll feel a pull towards them like we feel towards each other."

"I don't feel the exact same pull towards all of you," Finn said quietly, his eyes on me. He'd been watching without saying much since he woke.

"True," Peyton said. "Sometimes, I feel the pull to strangle one of you, but I figure that's the sibling bond, not the god bond."

"Let's get going," Joaquin said, nodding towards the woods. "You don't want to be a giant's dinner."

"How do we know we can trust you?" Peyton asked, chewing on the end of her pink ponytail.

"I'm a friendly giant," Joaquin said with a devilish grin. "Most of the time."

"It's true," Eliot said. "Loki is usually helpful to gods and humans."

"That'll have to be good enough," I said. "We don't have Rosa here to lead us."

"Oh, so you'll believe him, but you don't believe it when I tell you myself?" Joaquin said, throwing his hands in the air.

"He didn't lure me to his apartment, tie me to a chair, and hold a knife to my throat."

Joaquin paused, giving me a chagrinned smile. "Fair enough."

"So where did you leave Rosa?" I asked.

"She's that way," Finn said, pointing into the woods.

"There's a friendly giant's house that way, too," Joaquin said. "Otherwise, it's anyone's guess who might find us trespassing in the night."

We took off through the woods in our usual formation, with the addition of Alvan and Joaquin in front and Valdan behind. The sky was still light beyond the dense canopy of trees, but it wouldn't last forever. We needed to get moving if we wanted to make it somewhere safe—as safe as we could get in the giant world.

The forest floor was thick with needles that had fallen from the trees, making our footsteps eerily silent. Every time a gust of wind whispered through the trees, I jumped at the shadows playing over the forest floor. I thought of all the times Mom had uprooted our lives in fear of these beings finding us, and a shiver worked its way through me. I'd spent my life running from giants, and now I practically provoking them.

To distract myself, I fell back and slid my hand inside Finn's elbow. A sigh of relief ran through my blood, and an instant calm settled over me. This was right. I needed more of him, more closeness, more of our god bond. He was blocking it, though. I could still feel his resistance to being part of us. But there were other ways of being close besides the physical.

"Are you okay?" I asked quietly.

"I don't know."

"Yeah, what happened back there?" Peyton asked, whirling to face us, a hand on her hip. "You're not going to shrug your way out of this one, Finnigan Keen."

I gave his arm a reassuring squeeze. "You can tell us. We're all in this, Finn, and it could be important. What did you see?"

He shook his head, starting forward through the woods again. Peyton fell into step beside us, hooking her hand around his other arm. "I thought you were dead," she said. "I turned into a blubbering mess."

"Sucks to be the weakest link, doesn't it?" Joaquin said from ahead.

Finn stiffened, but I leaned my head against his shoulder for a second. "Just tell us."

"The bridge," he said after a minute. "I saw the bridge... go out."

I forced myself not to react, though I wanted to shake him and ask how he couldn't see that the vision was a warning. It was so obvious. Or maybe only obvious to someone who had grown up with my mother and then learned that what she'd seen and feared was real.

"Has that happened before?" I asked.

He hesitated a long moment before answering. "Yeah. Sometimes."

"What?" Peyton squawked, her voice echoing through the silent forest. "And you didn't tell us?"

"You all know now," he said. "It's never happened like that before. It's always been while I was painting. When you get into the zone and you're not thinking. I'd snap out of it and...there it was." He gestured with both hands, as if the vision might appear in the air in front of us.

"What sort of things?" Eliot asked.

Finn shrugged again, his shoulders hunched towards his ears. I could tell he liked the attention about as much as I usually did. "I don't know. Ragnarok, I guess."

"And the opening to Yggdrasil. This could be incredibly useful," Eliot said. "Maybe you can find Rosa and our missing piece."

He chattered on, musing about what Finn's gift could do for us. Even though Finn didn't like the attention, I could tell he was relieved. We knew now, and we believed him. I wondered if I'd been more involved with Mom, if I'd believed her instead of indulging her, if she would have done better. If I'd understood that it was real, I could have helped her in the ways she needed.

I couldn't change that now, but I could make sure Finn shared his burden with all of us. It wasn't his alone. It was all of ours. If it hurt him, it hurt us. And maybe Eliot was right. Some good could come of it, just like his "anxiety" helped us. Maybe we all had gifts, and they only helped if we used them for the good of the group. If we kept them inside, they could hurt us, the way they'd hurt Mom and the way Finn's isolating himself hurt us.

Finally after several hours of walking, we reached a house that was at least three times as big as the Keen's mansion. The door towered thirty feet high and at least ten feet wide. It didn't look like a mansion, though. More like a regular house had been blown up to ridiculous proportions.

"I'm not going in there," I said. "No way."

Just then, the earth trembled under our feet. I grabbed Peyton's hand, and she grabbed for her dagger.

"Don't fight them," Joaquin said. "If you attack, they will crush you. If you're polite, they might help."

"Might?" Xander growled, stepping toward Joaquin.

"They'll give us a safe place to stay for the night," Joaquin offered as the ground trembled again. The trees parted, and a giant stepped through. She was about thirty feet tall, and to my relief, not made of molten rock. Though she was humanoid, she wasn't exactly like an oversized human. More like an oversized toddler with a tiny head, sturdy legs and arms, and a thick body.

"Humans," she rumbled from above. I cringed back against Alvan, who slid an arm around me and squeezed me tightly. He'd looked like a giant to me when I'd met him, but now, he seemed all too human and vulnerable.

"Are those barnacles on her knees?" Peyton whispered.

The door behind us burst open, and a smaller giant, this one only about fifteen feet tall, came bounding out. Peyton screamed, leaping behind Valdan. Alvan ripped his sword free, pushing me behind him and standing tall. I dug my fingers into his leather vest, squeezing my eyes closed. I thought I'd throw up from fear. This was it. Joaquin had led us into a trap.

"Please don't eat them, Mammy," cried a guttural, booming voice. I opened my eyes to see that the little giant had scooped up Finn, Eliot, and Zeke and held them to her chest.

"We're not humans," Joaquin said. "I'm a giant and they're gods."

The big giant plucked Joaquin from the ground and dangled him in front of her bulbous nose. "You're a giant?" she asked, then threw back her head and laughed. Joaquin's body looked pathetically scrawny hanging by the back of his shirt thirty feet in the air.

"Loki, in fact," Joaquin said.

That sobered her up. Her log-sized eyebrows drew together, and she brought Joaquin so close that her eyes crossed. "How do I know you won't trick me?"

"That's exactly what we were thinking," I blurted before I knew what I was doing. This giant didn't seem overly friendly to me.

Suddenly, the small giant dropped the three Keens she was holding and wrapped a thick hand around me, lifting me in one fist and studying my face while I gripped her fingers, hoping she wouldn't drop me from ten feet in the air, as she had the others. Luckily, none of them seemed to be seriously injured. They were all standing close with the group, watching. Finn was rubbing his shoulder.

"There's girl humans, too," the fifteen-foot giant said to the one she'd called Mammy. "And this one has pink hair!" She plucked Peyton from the group, holding us up for her mother to see. "Can I keep them?"

"I don't know," Mammy said. "What have you come for, humans?"

"We just want a safe place to stay," Zeke said. "Joaquin said your house was welcoming to humans. Please don't eat us."

"Can't he let Eliot do the talking?" Peyton hissed at me. The girl giant had clutched us to her chest, letting our legs dangle. Her thick arm held me so tight I couldn't even draw a breath to answer. After being in Yggdrasil, it didn't seem so high, but looking down still made my stomach drop. The giant was three times our height, and she had lifted us easily, like oversized dolls.

"We're looking for a missing piece of our god, and we were told he was in Jotunheim," Eliot said. "We are not here to trick you, and we would be happy to repay your hospitality in whatever way we are able."

"Thank all the gods in Asgard," Peyton sighed.

I remembered thinking Eliot must be awkward and shy. Now here he was, the spokesperson for us. Because who else but Peyton could do that, and she was currently being clutched to the bosom of a baby giant.

"Can I play with them?" the little giant asked. "Can I, Mammy? Can I?"

I cringed to think of what her play would entail. It was slightly better than being eaten, but that didn't mean it wasn't deadly.

"You won't steal from us?" Mammy asked.

"Never," Peyton said in a rush. "And we'll play with your lovely daughter, keep her entertained. When was the last time you had a night off to kick back and relax? Maybe have a glass of wine?"

She'd probably need a tankard of wine, but whatever. As long as we weren't on the menu. I prayed Peyton's negotiating skills would be enough. Maybe women were overworked and tired in all worlds, and that would actually work here. Mammy scratched her head and squinted at the sky.

"I'm an excellent babysitter," Peyton said. "I have references back in Midgard who would testify to it. And your daughter seems like such a beautiful, charming girl."

Those were not the words I'd have used to describe the giant holding us hostage, but I kept my mouth shut. I'd already brought attention to myself and look where it had gotten me.

"Are you vegan?" Mammy asked.

That was an odd question, but considering Heimdall said he was born from nine mothers, I didn't question it. I was learning that things in other worlds didn't have to make sense to my human mind.

"No," Zeke said. "We love meat. Maybe not man-meat, but we're all about some cheeseburgers."

"I don't know cheeseburgers," Mammy said in her slow, thick voice. "But the last guest that came through these parts tried to convince me of the health benefits of being vegan. I think he was trying to trick me into starvation."

I saw Eliot raise an eyebrow at Xander. "When was this?" he asked.

I wondered if we were all thinking the same thing. Could it be our missing piece?

"Oh, I don't know," Mammy said, lumbering towards the door. The others scrambled out of her way. "Perhaps on Freya's day."

"Friday," Eliot said. "Did he happen to be looking for the rest of Heimdall?"

"He didn't say," Mammy said. "But if you're only missing one part, he should find his way to you if you stay in one place. He will be drawn to your strong bond." She stopped at the door and squinted down at us, then shook her head. "No, you must not have a strong bond. I didn't know you were a god until you told me."

"We're working on it," I said. In truth, I wasn't sure how well we were doing. Now that we'd healed Alvan, I felt a bond with him I hadn't before. One I didn't share with Valdan or even Finn. But the group seemed to be always at odds.

"I suppose I could feed you and put you up for the night," Mammy said at last. "As long as you aren't picky."

"Not picky," Zeke said. "I'll eat anything."

"He's not kidding," Peyton said.

"So I can keep them?" the girl giant asked.

"You can play with them until they leave, Aud," Mammy said, stepping inside the huge door, still holding Joaquin in front of her. "Except for this one. I don't trust Loki with my child."

"Yay, dollies!" Aud said, thrusting us into the air above her head. I heaved when she turned me upside down.

Shuffling Peyton into the crook of her arm where she held me, she grabbed both elves by their blond locks and dragged them inside. They were half as tall as her, but she handled them like two big dolls—awkwardly but without care. The others followed as she pounded across a wooden floor and up a flight of stairs. The elves bumped on every step.

"Alvan," I cried, reaching for him, though he was dangling from Aud's other hand. He and Valdan got their feet under them at last, and Aud held them upright so their heads never hit. Knowing they weren't in immediate danger of concussion eased my distress. The guys were all boosting each other up. Each step was three or four feet high, and by the time we reached the top, even the giant was panting.

Aud dropped the elves and carried us along a hallway and into a room that was strewn with acorns, feathers, rocks, and bones.

"Future hoarder," Peyton whispered as Aud thumped back down the hall, leaving us alone.

"I hope those aren't human bones," I said, shuddering.

"Should we make a run for it?" she asked.

"How?" The windowsill was a few feet above our heads, but since we were on the second floor, I didn't like our chances. This wasn't like jumping from Yggdrasil and landing in another world. This was like jumping fifty feet and landing on rocks.

Before we'd figured out anything, Aud was back with an armload of Keens. She dumped them onto the floor, and they all tumbled over each other and scrambled to their feet. "Now, we can play," Aud said, thrusting her fist into the air.

"Okay, but first let's set some ground rules," Peyton said, putting a hand on her hip and standing up to the kid like she wasn't a pint-sized cheerleader facing a giant.

The giant stuck out one cracked, pitted lip. "I don't like rules."

"We're living things, and we don't like being thrown around," Peyton said. "Think of us as your precious dolls. You wouldn't hurt them, would you? Then they'd break, and you couldn't play with them anymore. So, you have to be careful with us."

I bit my lip, waiting for Aud's answer. Peyton seemed so calm, but it was all I could do to keep it together and not freak out like my mother. I tried to take courage from her, to be brave like she was. After all, this giant wasn't really that big. Her bedroom was no bigger than the Keen's foyer, including the height of the ceilings. I was almost up to Aud's hip, which meant I'd be toddler-sized to this toddler giant. Sure, she could pick us up and drag us around, but it wasn't like she'd accidentally step on us and crush us to death. And she seemed pretty fond of humans. I had to hand it to Joaquin—he hadn't led us into a trap.

This time.

Aud rolled her eyes up and squinted at the ceiling, her expression so much like her mother's that it would have been comical if we weren't negotiating for our safety and our lives. "Okay," she said after a minute. "I'll be careful. Can we play dress up?"

"I thought you'd never ask," Peyton said, clapping her hands. "Please, gods, tell me you have something that isn't leather."

Chapter Twenty

Gwen

A ud had a number of dress-up clothes, which she spared no alteration to make fit us. After chopping up a red satin skirt, she wrapped pieces of it around me and Peyton while the guys waited in the hall at Peyton's request. I averted my eyes as the giant wrapped a piece of satin around her, pulling it over one shoulder and tucking the end under Peyton's arm.

"There's enough for one more dress," Aud mused, stepping out into the hall and searching along the line of guys, her thick finger tapping her lower lip.

"How about you," she said, plucking Finn from where he sat with the others.

"How about not," Finn said with a frown, squirming in her grasp.

"But I want to make another dress," Aud said, her voice rising.

"And you can," Peyton said, racing into the hall to intervene. "Just…maybe Finn needs a nap right now. Plus, look at that one right there. Look at that pretty blond hair, just like a girl." She pointed to Valdan, who looked startled.

"But his hair is messy," Aud said. I flinched at the volume in her whiny voice.

"You could comb it," Peyton said. "Won't that be fun? You can style everyone's hair."

"I don't like you," Aud said to Finn, dropping him to the floor. His knees clattered onto the hardwood, and he crouched on all fours for a second, his head down. I ran toward him, but Aud snatched me up before I could reach his side. After dragging himself up, Finn stood and took a deep breath, dusted himself off, and shuffled towards the stairs.

"You're a bad human," Aud yelled after him. She scowled fiercely at me. "The rest of you are good humans, right?"

"Right," Peyton said quickly. "We all want to play with you. Want to comb my pink hair?"

Aud set me down and picked up Valdan with both hands, holding him out in front of her. "I'll comb your hair first. You need it."

"Okay," Valdan said, shaking his wild mane around his shoulders. "I look good in a dress. You'll see."

"Someone needs to do something about that boy," Peyton said, grabbing my hand and dragging me back into the room. She began to tuck and pin the piece of satin the giant had wrapped around me. It just fit around my body once, so that the top overlapped a bit, but the skirt only stayed closed if I stood still. The edges barely met, so the moment I took a step, my leg emerged from the open seam.

"I assume you mean Finn, not Valdan," I said.

"Of course I mean Finn. He's going to get us killed."

"He's having a hard time," I said, feeling instantly defensive of him. "He's not used to a world where the gods don't give him free will."

"And we are?" Peyton asked, circling around me to tie a strip of ribbon around my waist. "We all stepped into an alien world. I'm doing everything I can to be a giant's doll instead of her meal."

"Hopefully, he feels like he just exercised his free will," I said, longing to go after him, but not wanting to piss off a cranky giant toddler. Peyton had asserted herself with Aud, but we were all walking on eggshells.

"He's the reason we aren't as connected as we should be," Peyton said, holding out her arms so I could adjust her dress in a more flattering way. "Xander's right—Finn's the weak link. The giant said we don't even look like a god. We're all bonding and he's refusing. I'm all about free will, but not if it's going to hurt all of you."

"Yeah," I said, my fingers slowing as my knuckles brushed her bare shoulder blades. Like everyone, I'd rather have things go my way. I hadn't wanted to give up the life I'd barely gotten a taste of before being called away. But when the world was in danger, when my mom was in danger, what choice did I have? Exercising free will then would have been so selfish I couldn't comprehend it. And I couldn't have sent my new siblings into this without me simply because I didn't want to go.

"Gwen?" Peyton whispered. I realized I'd stopped working on her dress while I thought. My fingertips lingered on the skin between her shoulder blades. Skin that was lit with that unearthly golden sheen below a lock of pink hair that had come loose from her ponytail and skimmed across her back. An overwhelming urge to lean forward and press my lips to her skin sprang up inside me.

I pulled back, staring at the golden shine on my fingertips, too. Tucking them into a fold in my dress, I stepped away. "You're all good," I said. "It looks great on you."

Peyton turned, her eyes widening as she took me in all at once, no longer focusing on the deficiencies in my dress. Now, she was looking at me, wrapped in the fabric with a swath tied around my waist like a sash. She swallowed before giving a quick nod. "You, too."

A pair of leather pants dropped to the floor at our feet. For a second, neither of us moved. Then we looked up to see Aud had finished with Valdan's hair and stripped off his leathers. "Wow," Peyton said. "That is one beautiful man. Elf. Whatever."

I swallowed before tearing my eyes from his taut, muscular body. "Let's give him privacy."

"I don't think he minds the attention," Peyton said as Valdan gave a lazy wave, making no move to cover himself. My eyes wandered from the smooth, round muscles of his deltoids across the bulge of his pecs and down his taut abs to his narrow hips. I gulped, my heart stuttering in my chest as Aud swathed his powerful thighs in a band of red satin.

Peyton sighed. "Okay, show's over. I guess we can give him privacy now."

Stifling our giggles, we ran out into the hall, our fingers linking. When we'd recovered ourselves, we found Zeke, Xander, Eliot, and Alvan staring at us with identical expressions of wonder and hunger. No, not at us. At me.

I swallowed and scratched at my bare wrists, wanting some sleeves to pull my hands into, somewhere to hide. I felt so exposed with my arms bare, my hideous green scar on display. The air swept across my leg as it emerged from the fabric with every step I took. I was tempted to hold the ends of the fabric closed so my leg wouldn't be visible, but I stopped myself. Their eyes warmed me like the sun shining on my bare skin.

"Any chance you can take that home?" Zeke asked when I sat down between him and Xander.

"Any chance I can take that off?" Alvan asked.

My knee slid from the cut in the fabric that fell in a slippery pool around my feet. For a second, we all stared at my bare leg. Zeke reached over, touching his knuckle to my skin. He hesitated, his blue eyes meeting mine, a question hanging between us. I bit my lip, waiting as he slid his knuckle up the outside of my thigh, leaving a line of shine in his wake.

"Whoa," he said, staring at my thigh. "We're turning golden."

"Yeah," I breathed, aching for more of his touch, for more of his hands on my skin, sending shooting stars racing up my thigh.

"I wonder if we'd turn gold everywhere," he said.

"Please tell me you're not talking about your penis right now," Peyton said, rolling her eyes.

"Hey, it's a legit question," Zeke said. "Don't tell me no one else is wondering the same thing."

"That's a big no for me," Peyton said.

"I can't help it if I'm curious about my new godlike powers," Zeke said. "Maybe I'm, like, magically enhanced."

"Like any of you need it," I muttered.

"What?" Eliot asked, leaning forward to peer at me around Alvan's shoulder. If the grin on his face was evidence, he'd obviously heard what I said.

"You're *all* magically enhanced," I said. "Look at you. It's probably not a coincidence that your entire family is freaking gorgeous, even though you don't share the same genes."

"*Our* entire family," Xander said quietly. "That includes you, Gwen."

"I'm not really…I mean, our parents just got married."

He took my chin and turned my face towards him. "You're fucking beautiful."

I started to pull away, the itch to draw my hands inside the sleeves I no longer wore overwhelming me. I needed to get out of this dress, to put on a hoodie where I could hide, where eyes would stop caressing my skin and igniting it into flames of desire.

"Thanks," I whispered, cutting my eyes to the floor.

Xander tightened his grip, his fingers digging into my jaw, squeezing my face into a ridiculous pout. "Just looking at your lips makes me hard," he said. "If I hadn't taken a vow of celibacy, you'd be flat on your back on the floor right now."

My breath escaped me in a little puff, and Xander leaned forward, taking my lower lip between his teeth and teasing it gently with his tongue.

"Can I watch?" Alvan asked.

I pulled away and after a second, Xander released me, his eyes smoldering with lust as they raked over me.

"Damn," Zeke said. "Is it wrong that I find it really hot that my brother just made out with my stepsister?"

I tugged my dress closed to cover my leg and stared down at my knees. "What if… there are different rules outside our world? Being too rigid, holding on too tight to what we've always known, will make us go crazy."

For a long moment, no one spoke. At last, I raised my eyes. Eliot's gaze met mine, and something passed between us, a sudden understanding. "Like Finn," he said.

"Like Finn," I agreed. "I mean, we all know there's no such thing as giants, and talking squirrels, and elves. That's ridiculous. And yet, here we are."

"Because there's no such things in our world," Eliot said, motioning with animated gestures. "Midgard's views of what's possible, what's real, only apply to Midgard. If we refuse to believe what's right in front of us, if we cling to our old views, including what's right and wrong, we can't function in the other worlds."

"Exactly," I said, relieved that he'd known what I meant. "And as hard as it is for us to believe, it's harder for Finn, because he's not experiencing what we are. When we've been close together and that god-fire turns us gold, it's not in him."

"That makes sense," Eliot said. "We can believe it's real, and we're not losing our minds because we're experiencing it firsthand. But he's not. He's seen some of it, Ratr and the elves, but being in our god form helps us to accept it. Now, we see that we're not completely human, either. We don't expect everything to be as it was. We don't see it through fully human eyes. But he does."

For a moment, we all sat in silence. The spell was broken when Valdan stepped out into the hall, his body swathed in red satin, his blond hair combed into golden waves.

Xander clapped his hands, and Zeke wolf whistled. I couldn't help but smile, too.

"Give us a twirl," Peyton called.

Valdan executed a perfect turn, then strutted over to join us without an ounce of self-consciousness. "I told you I looked good in a dress."

His thighs strained against the fabric, which hugged his muscular backside—and the rest of him—in all the right places. I decided our world was sadly lacking in men wearing dresses.

I pulled my eyes away as Aud's footsteps approached.

"Finn's inability to let go of his attachment to Midgard is costing us all. But it's costing him much more," I said quickly.

"Should I go talk to him?" Peyton asked, turning to Zeke. "Or should Eliot?"

"No," I said. "I will."

They all stared at me, and I felt my face warm. I was grateful that the little giant appeared then and I didn't have to explain. Now that I'd experienced more of this god stuff, I thought I was figuring it out. The god-fire inside Finn had not been lit, but I could ignite it. I was sure I could put the light of Heimdall inside him and bring him to life with me. I could make him one of us and wake him from the gloom that had engulfed him since we arrived. But I didn't want to promise the others anything until I tried. I didn't know for sure if it would work without all of us, or if Finn would accept one person's touch more than the group as a whole.

I had to try, though.

Chapter Twenty-One

Gwen

The greasy, smoky aroma of grilled meat greeted us as we walked into the giant's dining room. It was really a great hall with a long table about twice as tall as us. Long benches lined either side of the table, and when Aud lifted us onto them, we could just reach the table when standing.

"I feel so dainty," said Joaquin, who was already at the table with Finn.

"I'm sorry I don't have more chairs for humans," Mammy said in her thick voice. "I only made one when the last guest was here. My husband does not like humans as we do."

"Except for dinner," Aud said cheerfully, picking up her meat and chomping into it.

"It's okay," Peyton said. "We don't mind standing. I eat standing up all the time at home."

"You do?"

"Sure," she said. "Usually walking around, too."

"I don't understand," Mammy said. "Don't you like to eat with others?"

"Of course," Eliot said. "We're honored to share your table. Sometimes in our world, we're in a hurry to get places, so we take our food with us. But this is much better."

"Oh," Mammy said, taking a seat at the head of the table. "You're not in a hurry tonight, though. Your missing piece will come here, yes?"

I exchanged a glance with Peyton. "We hope so."

None of us moved to take the seat she'd placed on top of the bench, making a chair high enough for a human. After a second, Joaquin said, "That's such a lovely seat you've made. I'd hate to see it go to waste."

"The guest of honor should sit there," Zeke said. "Gwen."

I shrank back beside Xander, not wanting to be on that pedestal. "What? I'm not the guest of honor."

"You're the hottest female here," Joaquin said. "Well, Peyton's hot, but she doesn't count as a female. Am I right or am I right?"

"I will cut you," Peyton said, hefting the knife beside her plate, which was approximately the size of her arm.

"Whoa, whoa, no need to get stabbity," he said. "I just thought we'd all enjoy getting an eyeful while we eat. Right, guys?"

"I think Valdan should get to sit there," I said. "He's obviously sacrificed a lot to get so pretty for us tonight."

With a bow, Valdan approached and climbed up into the chair, which was a bit like a crude lifeguard stand. Once the seating was settled, we turned to our food. I wasn't sure what we were eating, and I didn't think I wanted to know. I poked at the meat with my giant fork.

"Wow, this is amazing," Zeke said, shoveling in a bite with his hand. "You don't mind if I eat with my hands, right? I mean, this fork looks awesome, but my mouth is too small. I wish I could fit that much in at once."

"How inconsiderate of me," Mammy said, setting down her fork. "We will all eat with our hands!" She tore off a limb of the meat, the cartilage ripping with a grinding pop, and began to gnaw at the bone.

"It is good," Peyton said, pretending to put some in her mouth. "What is this? I need the recipe."

I was glad I wasn't alone in my trepidation. I'd definitely eaten my share of questionable food. I'd dug through Dumpsters so we wouldn't starve when Mom couldn't find a job. But I wasn't keen on the idea that I might be eating human flesh.

"It's a water buffalo," Mammy said. "My husband took it down himself."

"He must be a great hunter," Eliot said. "And very brave."

"He is," Aud said, juices running down her chin as she crunched on some gristle. "He's hunting horned bulls right now."

"Maybe he can take me on his next hunting expedition," Zeke said. "I wouldn't mind learning how to catch a buffalo."

Mammy frowned. "If you catch him in the right mood. If you don't, he might use you for targets." She laughed deep in her belly, her sturdy body shaking.

"Glad she finds that so amusing," Peyton muttered.

"Come, have some mead," Mammy said, sloshing amber liquid into huge chalices. She held up hers and said, "Hear, hear. To my honored human guests. We get so few of you nowadays. I remember when humans used to be more common, but it has been more than a thousand years." She thrust her cup into the air, then turned it up and drained the whole thing before setting it down with a thud that shook the table.

"I thought she'd never ask," Xander muttered, accepting the giant cup and sucking down a huge amount.

"Is that beer?" I asked, taking it from him when he passed it over.

He gave me a wicked grin and wiped his mouth with the back of his hand. "What's the matter, Gwen? Afraid you'll do something you regret?"

"I'm afraid we all might," I said, taking a small mouthful and handing it to Peyton.

"Here's to nights you wish you could remember in the morning," Joaquin said when it was his turn, chugging for a long minute.

We praised Mammy's mead, though I tried not to drink too much. I'd never had a drink in my life, and I hadn't expected my first time getting drunk to be at a giant's table, but pretty soon, the bench seemed to be swaying under my feet.

"Don't tell me you're already drunk," Xander said, his arm circling my waist from behind.

"Why not?" I asked, leaning into him just enough to feel his hips against mine.

He drew in a slow breath, his fingers tightening just above my hip. "I don't want you to think I'm taking advantage of you."

"You couldn't if you tried," I said. "All the alcohol in the world can't make me want you more than I do when I'm sober."

"You are drunk," he said with a soft chuckle, sending shivers all the way to my toes. He nuzzled my ear, and my entire body burned with a fire that had nothing to do with the god inside us. I closed my eyes, melting back against him.

His fingers traced teasing circles just inside my hipbone, landing right on my ticklish spot. A giggle burst from my lips, and I opened my eyes to find Peyton frowning at us.

"This little girl is up past her bedtime," Xander said. "She might need a cold shower, too."

I stiffened at his condescending tone. If not for the evidence I felt pressed hard against me, I might have been humiliated by the ease with which he seemed to turn his desire on and off. But his body couldn't fake it so easily. His body betrayed his desire and the power I had to ignite it.

"You can put her to bed in the guest room," Mammy said, lumbering up from the table. "The rest of you can keep feasting." She scooped us into her arm and thudded up the stairs. "The guest room should fit all nine of you, you're so tiny," she said, setting us down in a doorway. "There's a bath in the next room I had set up for Aud, but she hasn't used it yet. I made a ladder for the last tiny guest."

"Thank you for your hospitality," I said. I wondered if she was aware that I was almost the same age as Xander and not a kid, or if his comment had made her think I was a child. Maybe our size had thrown her off. She didn't seem too bright. Or maybe, like I'd said earlier, the rules were different here. She could be used to guests drinking too much and being hauled off to bed. And in this world, they might not even have the concept of stepbrothers. In the stories I'd read, gods weren't opposed to marrying their own sisters and daughters, so I didn't think they'd bat an eye at our relationship.

Mammy left us alone, her footsteps shaking the house as she trod downstairs. For a long moment, Xander and I stood listening to her rejoin the others. Then he pulled me into his arms, ducking to skim his mouth along my jawline as I circled his neck with my arms. His hand found its way into the cut in my dress, sliding up the back of my thigh and pulling me firmly against him.

"I've been thinking about doing this all night," he murmured into my neck. His hot breath melted over my skin, and I strained up, exposing my throat to his lips. His mouth played over my skin, sending tendrils of heat spiraling down into my core.

"I've been thinking about it for longer," I said. "But we never get a moment alone."

"I don't care anymore," he said, his teeth raking across my collarbone. "I don't care what any of them think, what anyone does. You're mine, Gwen. I don't care if the whole Nine Worlds know it."

"And you're mine," I said. "You're all mine."

His hand fisted in my hair, drawing my head back, and his mouth found mine at last. His kiss was rough and tasted of mead and desperation. I opened my lips, moaning into his kiss, my body charged with need. He answered me with a rumbling growl deep in his throat. His hand tightened in my hair and his tongue forced its way into my mouth.

My knees went out from under me, and Xander caught my weight, pinning my hips against his. Wrapping my legs around him, I locked my ankles behind him and let his hands support my weight. My own hands had a purpose at last, slipping under his shirt and massaging his hot skin and sleek muscles.

Xander stumbled forward, carrying me. At last, he broke away.

"Fuck, Gwen," he said. "What are you doing to me?"

"I'm not… What does that mean?" I asked, narrowing my eyes.

"It means you're making it really fucking hard to stop myself." He set me down, and I realized he'd carried me into the bathroom, where a ten-foot tall wooden tub stood waiting.

"But you stopped," I said. "The better question is what are you doing to me? Getting me all hot so you can laugh at me and tell me I need a cold bath?"

I turned away, hot tears stinging my eyes. Xander's arms slid around me, one pinning my hips to his and the other snaking inside my dress again. "I'm the one who needs a cold bath," he whispered, dropping his head against my bare shoulder. "I can't seem to stop touching you."

"If nothing can stop you, then don't stop."

"It doesn't matter if you'd feel the same when you're sober," he said, his hand sliding up the tender skin of my inner thigh, sending gold dust sparkling through my blood.

"You're not sober. I'm not sober. I wouldn't be able to be gentle with you right now."

"I didn't ask for gentleness," I gasped, dropping my head back against his shoulder.

He pushed me forward against the ladder leaning against the tub. I gripped the rungs as he gathered my hair, his hot lips finding the pulse at the side of my throat. I squirmed against his other hand, needing his touch on more than my thigh. His teeth tugged gently at my earlobe. "That's the problem," he whispered, his fingers finally beginning to move against me.

Waves of pleasure shimmered through my body as his other hand raked up the back of my arm. His fingers linked through mine on the ladder, curling around mine in a grip so tight his knuckles were bone white against the dark wood.

"I'm going to make love to you," he whispered, his lips skimming along my shoulder to my collarbone. "But I'm going to do it when we're both in our right minds. I want to remember every moment of it."

"Me, too," I whispered. "Thank you."

He laughed softly, his breath tickling my neck and sending shivers across my skin, even as an inferno blazed inside me. I tensed, biting my lip to hold back a gasp when a pinch of pain darted through me. It was erased as quickly as it came by the sure stroke of his strong fingers. I relaxed forward, dropping my forehead on the next rung of the ladder while his lips tugged at the fine hairs at the nape of my neck, his tongue tasting my skin.

The glow of our god engulfed us, wrapping around us like tendrils of golden smoke. The rightness of our bodies together shuddered through me. I'd been so worried about what I hadn't done, about not being able to keep up. But it took no thought. We were gods, we were the world itself, moving with a rhythm as natural as time, as the tides' ebb and flow, the wind through the trees. The heat of a volcano gathered in my molten core, building to a trembling crescendo until I could no longer hold the tension inside. I threw my head back against Xander's shoulder and let myself erupt.

Chapter Twenty-Two

Gwen

I woke when Aud clomped into the room and began tucking the others into bed beside me. The bed was made for giants, and we all fit easily. Peyton slid in next to me, for which I was grateful. There was a familiarity to our friendship, as if we'd always been friends. Being with her felt natural and easy.

"What time is it?" I asked, sitting up and squinting at the dark window. My head wasn't spinning anymore, and Xander was no longer beside me, as he'd been when I fell asleep.

"Late," Peyton whispered, pulling me back down beside her. "Way past midnight."

"Now that I've sobered up, you're all drunk?"

"Something like that," she said with a giggle. "You're a lightweight."

"Where's Xander?" I could feel him in the room, like a tether had joined us.

"Calm your titties, girl," Peyton said. "He's on the other side of the bed. What did you do to him earlier, anyway? He was practically giddy when he came back downstairs, and trust me when I say that word has never been used to describe Xander before in his life."

"Nothing." I sat up again, and my eyes were drawn to him instantly. He was sitting up on the far edge of the bed. He watched me, his lips twisted into a half smile, like he was trying to hold it in but couldn't. I couldn't hold my grin in check, either, though my face warmed at the memory of our earlier encounter. Gods, I couldn't wait to be alone with him again.

Aud leaned down between us and dropped Joaquin onto the mattress. She tucked him under and stood back, still clutching Valdan, his mane now as wild as ever, his red dress stripped down to the waist showing off the rippling muscles of his upper body. "I want a human for my dolly tonight," she said. "Who wants to sleep on Aud's pillow?"

"Oh gods," I muttered. "Please don't let her pick me."

"You want to be Aud's dolly?" she asked Valdan.

"Bro, he already volunteered to wear a dress," Zeke said. "I'll go."

"How about Joaquin?" Peyton said. "I'm afraid to go to sleep with him in the same bed."

"What is it with girls thinking I want to rape them?" Joaquin said. "Gwen was all freaked out about that, too."

"That probably says more about you than the girls you're around," Eliot said. "I'd take a good long look at myself if every girl I knew thought I wanted to rape her."

"Dude, I'm not interested in your lesbian sister," Joaquin said, throwing up his hands. "She probably has a tattoo above her twat that says, 'No Boys Allowed.' And Gwen knows I'm joking."

"It's not funny," I said through clenched teeth, glaring at him. He opened his mouth to protest, but I turned to Aud. "Please take him with you. He followed us here. He's not one of us."

"Mammy says she wants to keep an eye on this one," Aud said, exchanging him for Valdan. "I'll bring him to her room. But I want one for my pillow, too."

"She's going to take Finn again," Peyton whispered, her fingers clutching my arm under the blanket. "I just know it."

"Why isn't he shiny?" Aud asked with a frown, pointing at Finn.

"He just needs more time with us," I said quickly. More time, more closeness. I'd promised them I'd bring him closer and I'd fallen asleep instead.

"I want a dolly," Aud whined, scanning us. Her thick hand hovered over us. "You're the shiniest."

My heart skipped, but she didn't reach for me. Instead, she plucked Xander from the bed and held him in the crook of her elbow, his legs dangling. Joaquin hung from her other arm. At the thought of being separated from Xander, anguish tugged at my heart. I tensed, but Peyton pulled me back on the bed. "Xander will be fine," she said.

I swallowed hard, my eyes meeting Xander's. He gave me a sloppy grin that was very un-Xanderlike and waved at us.

"He's drunk," I said as Aud tromped out of the room.

"Shocker," Peyton said. Aud snuffed the enormous candle lighting the room, and we were plunged into darkness except for the moonlight streaming in the window.

"I stuck a rock in the door to keep it from closing completely," Eliot said. "In case we need to make an escape in the night."

"Good thinking, bro," Zeke said. "Let's hope we don't need it."

"You think our last piece will really just find us?" I asked, rolling onto my back.

"When we're all together in the morning, we should make the circle," Eliot said. "If we can call Heimdall to Midgard, maybe we can call one-ninth of him to Jotunheim."

"What do you think they'll be like?" Peyton asked.

"Probably not human," Eliot said. "Since they weren't in Midgard."

"And not an elf," Alvan said.

"Do you think it'll be a guy or a girl?" Peyton asked.

"I hate to ask," I said. "But isn't it most likely it will somehow be a giant? Since it's in Jotunheim?"

"As long as it's not Joaquin," Peyton said.

For a few minutes, everyone shifted around on the mattress without speaking. Soon I heard the steady breathing of the elves, and a soft snore behind them that I recognized as Zeke's. I was wide awake. I waited for sleep to claim me, but it didn't.

Peyton sighed, and I knew she was still awake, too.

"What if he passes out, and Joaquin hurts him?" I whispered, worrying the blanket with my fingers.

"Xander will be fine with Aud." She cupped my face between her hands and turned me toward her. "Joaquin will be with Mammy. And I know my brother. He'll sleep it off and be fine in the morning. I promise."

I closed my hands around her slender wrists, my thumbs touching the tender skin where her pulse thrummed in rhythm with my own. The breath caught in my throat, and my heart thudded slow and hard inside my chest.

"Will we?" I whispered. Her lips were so close to mine I could feel their warmth, could almost taste her bubblegum lip gloss. A painful yearning settled deep in my chest. My need for Xander had been raw and primal, something immediate and demanding. This was a quieter ache that touched some tender part of me I couldn't explain, like the feeling of being lonely even in a crowd, or the inexplicable sadness of watching the ocean by myself.

"Gwen?" she whispered.

"Yes." It was an answer to a question she hadn't yet asked, one I didn't want spoken aloud. And maybe she didn't either, because instead of speaking, she slid her small hand behind my head, drawing me closer until we touched. A wave of intense longing shimmered inside me at the touch of her lips, so incredibly soft that I melted like cotton candy on her tongue.

As when I'd kissed the others, nothing else existed. Her lips were gentle, her tongue sweet. I could almost taste the god on her breath, the warm glow of him that I no longer needed to see. It was there all around us, clinging to us, building in us, and shining from us. I sank into the yielding softness of her embrace, holding her slender body against mine with the care I'd show a precious thing.

I was lost to everything until I felt someone shift on the mattress, heard the rustle of the blankets followed by the thump of feet hitting the floor on the far end of the enormous bed. I pulled away, coming back to where I was.

"Can you keep going?" Alvan asked, grinning at us from where he lay propped up on one elbow behind Peyton. "I was enjoying that immensely."

Crap. I'd thought everyone was sleeping. I felt my face flare with heat and was glad he couldn't see it in the moonlight.

"That was Finn," I said to Peyton, searching her gaze for permission.

"Go get him," she said, squeezing my hand. "Bring him back."

I'd been so determined before, so sure I could do it. But now doubt plagued me. "What if I can't?"

"You can," she said, laying her hand over my sternum. "You're the heart. Our heart. You know how."

I nodded, though my stomach fluttered at the thought of facing him right now, after he'd heard me kissing Peyton. If I'd hurt him, how could I ask for his heart? What if bringing him into the essence of our god required more than I could give?

Peyton's hands pushed gently against my chest until I turned and slid from the bed, stifling a cry at how far the drop was. I landed on my feet, stumbled forward, and hit the floor on my hands and knees. Someone asked if I was okay, and after a second, I pushed myself up and wiped my hands on the satin dress I'd fallen asleep in. It would take more than a fall from a bed to stop me.

I had to get Finn back. Everything depended on him, on this. Once I had him, the last piece would feel us and come like a moth drawn to a flame. We could fix Bifrost. We could go home. I was willing to give Finn everything I had if it healed him somehow, healed the rift in us. We needed him, and he needed us. As the heart of Heimdall, I was the one who could reach him and mend whatever was broken between us.

I slipped out the door in time to see him disappear down the stairs. I padded down the hall on bare feet, hurrying to catch up. Since each step was as high as my shoulders, I had to lay face down on each one, hang my legs over, and drop a few feet to the next one. At the bottom, I was scraped and breathless. Finn had to have heard me following him, but he hadn't waited for me. I looked around, searching for him in the dark. The creak of the door alerted me, and I turned to find a slant of moonlight falling across the floor. I ran to the door on tiptoes, arriving just as Finn slipped out. I followed him, leaving the door ajar so we could get back in.

"Finn," I called when I made out his shape hurrying across the yard, his shoulders hunched and hands thrust deep into his pockets. He didn't turn.

My feet ached with cold as I ran across the damp grass until I caught up with him and slid my hand around his arm, pulling him to a stop. We stood there, facing each other for a second. The pain in his eyes was so raw, so visceral, that I shrank back.

"Finn," I breathed.

"What?" he asked, his voice cracking.

"Why didn't you answer?"

"You have other people to give you answers."

"I need you, Finn. You."

The muscle in his jaw twitched, and he looked off towards the woods. "Doesn't seem like you do."

"Where are you going?"

"I don't know," he said. "Away."

"Why?" This time my voice broke.

"I don't belong here," he said. "I'm not good at this stuff. This place, it's not right. It's from before God was even known to man."

I took a deep breath and reached for his hands, but he kept them deep in his pockets. I stepped close and wrapped my hands around his forearms instead. "Maybe it's okay that your god is not here," I said slowly. "We're in a different world. The people are different, the rules are different. Maybe it's okay that the gods are different. Your god is still in our world. Those rules work there. He'll be there for you when you get back."

"What if I need him now? Can I go back? Don't I have a choice in this?"

I released him and stepped back. "In what?"

"All of it. The things I see and feel…"

"It's hard for me, too," I said, wrapping my arms around myself, covering part of my grotesque scar with my hand. I'd been able to forget about it most of the night. Now, I felt exposed and ugly, aware of my inappropriate dress and the inappropriate things I'd done. Maybe Xander was my forbidden fruit, and now that I'd crossed some line with him, now that I knew what it was like to feel that good, I wanted to cover myself so Finn wouldn't know what I'd done.

The familiar urge to run rose up in me, but I pushed it away. I had faced giants. I could face my stepbrother.

I decided being honest was the best way to bring us closer. If I wanted him to be open with me, I had to open up to him first. "I'm not used to any of this, either," I said. "Especially this thing with all of you. I don't know how to do this, Finn. I'm just making it up as I go along, trying not to hurt anyone."

Finn didn't speak. We'd entered the forest where droplets of moonlight filtered down, moving as the trees swayed overhead. Cold stones cut into my bare feet, but I didn't slow. I couldn't lose Finn. The forest was cold and damp, so unlike the hot, dry air on the moss field. We stepped out into a clearing made by a massive tree that had fallen. Finn climbed up onto the trunk and sat, so I scrambled up beside him, awkward in my dress that now seemed so obscene. I held it closed as I sat next to him.

"I'm sorry," I said after a minute. "I'm sorry if I hurt you."

"I just wanted to get away," Finn said quietly.

"And I followed you."

"It's okay."

"Is it? You put so much distance between us, between yourself and the others. We know you're hurting. We want to make it better, Finn. You don't have to feel this way, to do this alone. Just talk to us. Talk to me."

"You don't need this," he said. "You're all so sure of it, so sure of yourselves."

I snorted. "I'm so far from that."

"You seem like it."

"Well, I'm not. The only thing I'm sure of is that I have to get back to my mom. I'll do all the things, everything Heimdall wants, to make it happen. I just want to go home."

"Me, too," Finn said, linking his hands around his knees.

"So what if we have to do things we wouldn't do in our world? We're not in our world. If I have to adapt to survive here and get home, that's what I'll do. We can follow human rules in the human world, and god rules in the gods' world."

"I don't know if I can do what I have to do here," he said. "I don't know if I'll survive it."

Heimdall had said we'd lose someone, but my heart balked at the thought. I couldn't lose Finn. When Mom and I had arrived at their house, he'd been the one to make me feel like maybe I'd be okay at last. Like maybe I could breathe again after holding my breath all those years, waiting for Mom to snap. He'd walked on the beach and talked to me, listened to me. Even when I'd told him we'd lived in storage lockers and begged for money, he hadn't looked at me like a freak. He'd accepted me just as I was, as simply as that.

"You will survive," I said fiercely, pulling his hand away from the tight hold he had on himself. I needed him to let go, to reach out.

I linked my fingers with his. "You're stronger than you think. We all are. We'll fix the bridge and go home because that's what we have to do. Okay?"

He looked at me a long moment, then nodded. "Okay."

"Good," I said, my heart suddenly slamming at what I was about to do. I loved Finn, and all the others, too. And I'd never thought my first time would be like this, in the woods with a tormented boy who could save the world if he'd just let himself go. But what did virginity matter when the fate of humanity was at stake? I had to do this, had to bring Finn close. And this was the only way I could think of. I just hoped it would work.

"You owe me a kiss," I whispered.

His shoulders stiffened. "What?"

"You kissed me when I was asleep. I missed our first kiss."

This wasn't like me. Or maybe it was, and I just didn't know it because I hadn't known what I was like. But with Finn, I wasn't shy. Terrified by the thought of it, yes. By how much it might hurt and what it might mean for us afterwards. Would I love him too much, more than I could bear? Would he love me that much?

But despite my fears, despite my heart beating so hard it made me dizzy, I wasn't afraid of *him*. I'd found my courage. He made me brave. With him, I wasn't inexperienced and inadequate. With the others, I was afraid to show myself and have them judge me. Finn had no one to compare me to, no measuring stick to hold me up against and find me lacking. I could be truly myself, could discover who that was.

Here, with no judgments and nothing stopping us, I could let go. I longed to be free, to be wild, to take him like a storm and make him rage back with the same abandon. But I had to free him from his own constraints first. I raised his hand to my lips and brushed them against the back of his knuckles.

"I'm sorry." He dropped his head, but I tugged at his hand, not wanting to let him slip away again and back into his head. I wanted him to be part of us, part of me. Maybe I'd misunderstood Heimdall, and he hadn't meant death. In a way, we'd already lost Finn. Was this what he had warned us about?

"Don't be sorry," I said, scooting over so our shoulders pressed together. "But let's have a do-over. This one will count as our first real kiss."

"I...I don't know how," he said, his face reddening. "I've never had a girlfriend. I've never even kissed a girl who remembers it."

"I'd never kissed anyone until I moved in with you. And I've never been with anyone, either." I slid my arms around his neck, my pulse throbbing in my throat when I leaned closer, smelling the clean, safe scent of his skin. "Kiss me," I whispered, closing my eyes.

After a slight hesitation, his hands landed on my waist, warm through the thin layer of satin. His lips brushed mine, soft and slow, and my heart ached with a need so deep it made the earth shiver. I met his kiss with my own, following his lead, letting him set the pace. Only when he began to pull back did I tighten my hold, pressing deeper and opening my lips for him.

His breath came faster as his tongue slipped between my teeth, tentative at first. I met it with my own, exploring his mouth as he did mine. I tugged the elastic from his hair, running my fingers through its silky length as he sighed with pleasure. Heat built between us, that golden light glowing inside me. When I buried my hand in his hair and drew him in, deepening our kiss, it shimmered and brightened as if I was feeding a flame with oxygen it had so badly needed.

I rose up and threw my knee over him, straddling his hips. My leg slipped from the fabric wrapped around me, exposing my bare thigh all the way up. Cold air swept over my skin, and I gasped in shock at the contrast between the outside world and the heat generating between us.

"Gwen," Finn gasped, pulling away, his hands landing on my sides.

"Don't push me away," I said, my heartbeat fluttering with fear. "Stop pushing me away. Let me in. I care about you, Finn. I want you to be part of this, to be part of us. Part of me."

"Are you saying…" He looked away, swallowing hard.

"Yes."

I slid off the log, pulling him down to the mossy ground. We sat with our backs to the log, and I slid my arms around him, laying my head on his chest and throwing my bare leg over one of his.

"I'm sorry it's hard for me," he said, his fingertips tracing a light circle over my knee, sending shivers racing through me. "I just…I watched my parents, and I always wanted what they had. That kind of love. I knew I'd find it one day, but I thought I'd be older than sixteen."

"So you're going to throw it away because you're not old enough?"

"What if I'm not ready for this?" he asked.

"I'm not, either," I said. "But it's happening. I'm not running from it."

He turned and stroked my hair back, running his fingers along my throat and my bare shoulder. A shudder rocked through me, and I closed my eyes.

"I love you, Gwen," Finn whispered.

My fingers found his, both of our hands trembling. "I love you, too."

He closed his eyes, releasing a slow breath. "I want you so much it scares me," he whispered. "I'm not trying to push you away, but it's the only thing I could think of. If I'm close to you, I want you. I want you so much I'm afraid I won't be able to control myself."

"Me, too," I said, stroking his cheek. The gold flecks in his green eyes seemed to glow in the moonlight, sending sparkles across every inch of skin they touched.

"What if we mess it all up because we're so young?"

I held his gaze, full of so much fear and confusion and desire. My fingers clenched around his. "Then we'll fix it."

"I want to be with you, Gwen," he said. "Forever."

I pressed my hand to his chest, feeling the hammering heartbeat there matching my own. "We will be. I promise."

"Gwen…are you sure? I mean, I don't know…Are you sure you want me? I don't know what I'm doing. Don't you think Eliot or Zeke or even Xander…"

"No," I said, pulling him down so we faced each other. "I want you."

"I've never…" He broke off and swallowed. "I guess you know that."

"I haven't, either," I said. "That's why I want you, Finn. This…it will mean the same thing to me as it means to you."

"I've never felt like this about anyone," he said, his eyes lingering on my lips, moving down along the line of my neck and shoulder, and to my breasts.

My skin ached for more than his eyes on me. I lifted his hand, running the tips of his fingers along the edge of the silky fabric of my dress. "Touch me."

He rolled over onto me, his hands moving over me with care as his mouth returned to mine. All the while he was slow and gentle, almost tentative. It was just what I wanted…until it wasn't. I wanted his tenderness and love. But I wanted more than that, too. I wanted him to lose control, to crash against me like the ocean battering the shore.

At last, I couldn't bear it any longer. I pushed him back and climbed onto him, stripping off the layers separating us until there was nothing between us. His gaze lingered on me a moment, and when he raised his eyes to mine, the same fire had ignited there. A thrill of triumph went through me—I had done that, had brought him back to life.

But more than that, a swell of love rose in me like a tide I couldn't hold back, threatening to wash me away. I wrapped my arms around him, clinging to him like he was my savior, this lost soul I'd called home. He'd come back to me, come back to claim me.

His arm clamped around my back, hot and strong, and he rolled us over. The touch of his skin against mine was almost unbearable. An inferno burned between us as our bare hips collided. With the frantic fumbling of two virgins, we found our way together, reckless and wild with desire. The relief of it burst like a flame over us, engulfing us.

At last, we were joined as we were meant to be. We were one. My heart tethered itself to his, my soul entwining with his. The two pieces of our god fit into each other the way our bodies fit together, my body devouring him as he took me in a way no one else ever would. The bond between us was like nothing I'd ever felt, forged as hard as diamond and just as beautiful.

Chapter Twenty-Three

Finn

Gwen fell asleep curled in my arms, her ivory skin now glowing like she'd rolled in gold dust. My breath brushed over her shoulder, and I watched chill bumps rise on her skin. I drew the sheet of satin up over her, tightening my arms around her. I hadn't meant for this to happen, but it didn't stop the joy spreading through my entire being at the thought of what we'd done. In all my life, I never would have imagined doing it like this, but I could feel how right it was all the way down to my soul. A peace like I'd never known saturated me. I had made love to the girl I loved, the girl I would love forever.

I pressed a kiss into the crook of her shoulder, linking my fingers with hers as she slept. We would make it work, like she said. Nothing could come between us. We'd be together longer than our parents, who were separated by death. Even death wouldn't separate us. I could feel it down into the hollow places in my heart that she had filled, in the marrow of my bones that had turned to molten gold when we joined.

A twig snapped in the dark forest and I tensed. Our love might protect us from the hurts other people experienced while dating and breaking up. But even our love couldn't protect us from whatever creatures might lurk in the forest.

I heard another footstep and pulled away from Gwen, cursing the golden light that lit up both of us, making us easy targets. Whatever was out here, I'd die fighting it to protect Gwen. I left Gwen under the sheet of her satin dress and hurried to pull on my pants. Just as I'd shoved my feet into my shoes, I heard a soft chuckle in the woods.

My old life crashed into me at full force. This wasn't a sweet dream. I was still me—Finn the artist, the loner, the religious freak. And she was still Gwen, the broken bird, the delicate daughter of a crazy mother. Gwen, who didn't know about people, and guys, and…I'd changed all of that. I'd thought she needed to watch out for my brothers. But in the end, it was I who had ruined her.

"Xander?" I asked, my mouth suddenly dry.

"No, dude, it's me," Joaquin said, stepping out of the shadows beside the log. His eyes fell on Gwen, and his grin got wider. "Well, well, well, what do we have here?"

"Nothing," I said, grabbing his arm and marching him back into the woods where we wouldn't wake her.

"Dude, you totally banged Gwen," he said, choking back laughter. "And on the ground in the dirt. You savage." He held up a hand like he expected me to high-five him.

I'd always tolerated Joaquin because it was the right thing to do and because I tried to be kind to everyone. I admired his skill on the waves, and I treated him with charity because he didn't have much in the way of friends, family, or money. And more than that, I accepted him. He was obnoxious, sure, but he was human like the rest of us.

In that moment, though, I'd never wanted to hit someone so much in my life.

"Don't be ashamed, she's hot," he said, dropping his hand. "I'd do her, too, if I were you, even if she is getting a little loose, if you know what I mean. You don't want to be left out."

"What are you talking about?" I asked, finally stopping a good ways off, where Gwen wouldn't hear us and wake up.

"You can't let your brothers have all the fun," he said. "But seriously, the chick is losing value, spreading it around to two guys on the same night."

Bile rose in my throat. "What?"

"You nailed her the same night as Xander. Don't get me wrong, you don't want to be last in line, but that's brave. I don't know if I'd want to follow in his footsteps."

"She wasn't with Xander," I said. "She'd never been with anyone."

Joaquin shook his head. "Is that what she told you? She's even more scandalous than I thought. I'm impressed."

My hands balled into fists. "She wasn't."

"Whatever you say," he said, holding up both hands. "I know what I saw, but believe what you want."

I didn't want to take the bait. I wanted to tell him to go to hell, but I couldn't. Every fear I'd ever had about girls came rising up. What had made me think I could be special to her? She'd gone off with Xander, like he said. He'd come back glowing and happy. And she'd been in bed when we came up, also glowing. Now that we'd done it, we were both glowing just like they had been. Had she tricked me? My stomach turned, and my hands began to shake. I couldn't even vomit, though I wanted to do that, too. My throat had closed off.

"Not that you can't hang," Joaquin said. "But dude, but from what I saw, Xander would be a hard act to follow."

"When?" I croaked, though I already knew. My chest was a hollowed-out cavity.

"Earlier, when he took her up to bed. I went to use the bathroom, and he had her bent over the ladder, getting it from the back." Joaquin thrust his hips, waving his hand in the air over his head like he was riding a bronco. "She was begging for it like a pro. 'Ooh, Xander, give it to me, I looove you, you're such a god. You're so big.' That kind of shit."

I grabbed him by the throat, all rational thought gone from my mind. "Liar."

"Ask him if you don't believe me," Joaquin said, half laughing as he tried to pry my hands loose. "Don't take it too hard, though. How were you supposed to know what a virgin feels like? You just lost your own V-card. She knows that. I'm sure she doesn't expect you to measure up to Xander."

Rage and pain pulsed through me in flashes coming too fast to push away, too intense to ignore. All I wanted was to shut him up, and I didn't care what I had to do to make it happen. My hands tightened, and I forced him to the ground.

"I'm sure she likes you better," Joaquin squeaked. "She probably just let him get her warmed up, so you could finish her off."

But I hadn't finished her off, as he put it. I would have known that, surely. And since I didn't know, that meant I hadn't.

My hands tightened as Joaquin flailed. He didn't deserve to live. He wasn't my friend. He was a giant. He'd tried to kill Gwen, and then he'd watched her hooking up with Xander.

But he'd told me. He'd been honest when she hadn't. I hadn't wanted to hear it, but friends told you that stuff.

Joaquin was still in there as much as I was still Finn, even with a god inside me. Saying he was Loki was like saying I was Heimdall. Joaquin was my friend, as awful as he could sometimes be. He'd lived a hard life, and he had a reason to be the way he was. Even with a giant inside, he was still as human as I was. I wasn't acting much like a human being right now.

I shoved Joaquin's head back against the ground and jumped up, staring at my hands. Joaquin rolled over, choking and holding his throat. I could have killed him. I would have. Wrath had taken me over, made me someone else, just like lust had taken me over with Gwen.

"I—I'm sorry," I said, my head spinning.

After a few minutes, he sat up and stared at me. "Dude, I was actually afraid of you there for a second," he said, standing and brushing himself off. "I didn't think you had it in you."

I sat back on my heels. Adrenaline was still rushing through me. My limbs started to shake again, and my stomach sloshed. Joaquin held out a hand, and after a second, I smacked it out of the air just so he'd stop waiting for a high five. "Don't mess with me, Joaquin."

"Me? Mess with you?"

"Can't you be serious for one minute in your fucking life?"

"Whoa," he said. "Fighting *and* swearing? I think I like this new Finn."

"That would make one of us." I slumped down to the ground, not caring if he wanted to go for my throat the way I'd gone for his. I didn't care if he choked me out and didn't stop until I had no breath left. I didn't care about anything. I'd thought what I had with Gwen meant something, but he was right. I'd seen her kissing all my brothers. She'd even kissed my sister. And yet, somehow, I'd let her convince me that I was special.

"Dude, don't cry," Joaquin said, sitting down beside me. "Everyone's first time sucks."

"I'm not crying." I pressed my knees into my eyes, afraid I really might cry if I didn't keep enough pressure on my eyeballs to make me see stars.

"Barb was mine," he said after a long silence.

"Eliot's girlfriend?"

"Yeah," he said. "Don't sound so shocked. I know she's hot and popular, but there was a time…"

"When?"

"Okay, fine, we were both drunk, and the only reason she hooked up with me was because Xander turned her down. The next day, sucker that I was, I got super psyched when I saw her number on my phone. Turned out she was just calling to say that if I ever told anyone, she'd spread it around school that I had herpes. And before you ask, I don't. But once that kind of thing gets attached to your name, it doesn't matter if it's true or not. You're never getting laid again."

"I wouldn't know," I said, hugging my knees tighter to my chest.

Except I could no longer say those words with complete truth. I'd given up my beliefs, my morals, for Gwen. For nothing. She would never love me the way my parents loved each other, having eyes only for each other. Instead, I could get in line and take whatever scraps of her heart were left after all my brothers finished with her.

I didn't realize I'd spoken my thoughts aloud until Joaquin slapped my back. "Give yourself a break," he said. "It's not your fault. And it's not really hers, either. You're both possessed by the god. Believe me, I know how much it sucks to get blamed for what they do while in our bodies."

"You're right," I said, lifting my head. "We've treated you like you did those things of your own free will."

"It's cool," he said. "I did attack Gwen. I don't blame you."

"You apologized. And we left you more than once, and you could have been killed. That would have been on us."

He shrugged. "Well, you're the nice one. I don't think the others care if I die."

It was true. They'd ditched him on purpose, and he could have been killed. And I'd gone along with it because that's apparently what we did in this world. But I was done with it. I wasn't going to follow along with my siblings anymore, not if it went against the truth I knew and believed. Murder was not something to be excused by our location. Neither was what I'd done with Gwen.

"It sucks being Loki," Joaquin said. "Even if you're possessed, you get to be part of something. You share your struggles. And dude, you're part of a *god.*"

"I don't want to be. Not if it makes me like this." Not if it meant leaving a friend to die, even if he was infested by a giant. He was no worse than the rest of us. We were all being controlled. None of us were blameless.

"You think I want to be like *this?* I'm the bad guy. No one even gives me a chance."

"I will," I said quietly.

"I obviously wouldn't have chosen Loki if I got to pick," he said, starting through the woods. After a second, I followed. "But it comes in handy right now, when I know exactly how to get us out of here."

My feet balked, my chest squeezing in protest, as if I were leaving my heart behind in that mossy clearing where a girl who looked like an angel slept, secure in the knowledge that I would be there for her in the morning. But how could I be? I couldn't face her right now. Not if she'd lied to me. And if she hadn't? That meant I'd taken something from her that she could never get back, that I had no right to take. I'd committed an unforgiveable sin while under the god's influence, and no one in my family would understand that. Joaquin was the only one who understood what that was like.

"Can we go back to our world?" I asked. Before Gwen had come to live with us, I hadn't known Heimdall was part of me. I could make that happen again. I just had to get away from it, clear my head so it wasn't so full of Gwen. I could still go back, but not now. Not yet.

"I thought you'd never ask," Joaquin said. "I'm done with being the monster. It's not my fault that's the hand I got dealt."

My blood cried out in anguish at being separated from Gwen, but I crushed it down, smothering it with thoughts of what we had to do now. After a while, it would get easier until I didn't even think of it, how it had been when I'd first started noticing girls. The temptations had seemed endless, but when I concentrated on art, Bible group, and surfing, I was so busy I hardly remembered anything outside those things existed.

I could do that again. Even if every step I took away from her hurt down to the roots of my teeth, I had a journey ahead, and I needed to focus if I was going to make it out alive. I knew it was the god that had made us both do it, but I couldn't help but be bitter. I'd wanted to save myself for my wife, and now I never would. Gwen would never share that precious gift with her husband, either. Maybe she didn't know better, but I did.

Joaquin was right. It wasn't her fault, and it wasn't mine. It was Heimdall's. I was done being his puppet, acting against my own free will. I couldn't erase what I'd done, but I could atone for it. When I got home, far away from the others, I would never acknowledge Heimdall again.

Chapter Twenty-Four

Gwen

I woke with a start. Scratchy moss, leaves, and twigs poked into my back. A shadow had fallen over me.

Stifling a scream, I scrambled backwards on my hands and feet. The satin that Aud had given me slid off, and I grabbed for it, frantic to cover myself. My intense vulnerability hit me as clear as a snapshot. I was naked, alone, defenseless, and in a giant's world.

"Oh, my," said a slightly high-pitched masculine voice. "I didn't mean to get that intimately acquainted so early in our journey, but okay."

After wrapping the cloth around myself, I stumbled to my feet. "Where's Finn?" I asked, my heart slamming in my chest.

"Whoever is Finn?" the guy asked. He was medium height and whip-thin, with dark skin and striking features. He wore what looked like something out of a Jane Austen novel—clothes I'd read about but never full pictured, like a frock coat, breeches, and a cravat.

"Finn," I said, growing more desperate. "My—my stepbrother." I swallowed hard, a funny feeling twisting in my stomach when I called him that. After what we'd done—the intimacy of it barreled into me, and I fought to stay on my feet. Finn, on top of me. Finn, inside me.

"I've only seen you," the guy said. "Actually, I've been looking for you for a long time." He stopped and scratched his head and squinted up at the trees. "I thought there would be more of you. The pull kept growing stronger, so I thought you'd added a new person each time. Tonight, it was all I could do not to run here and soil my shoes in the process. That's how strong the pull was."

"He was here when I went to sleep," I said, tightening the sheet of satin around my body and looking around, as if Finn might be playing a trick, hiding behind the log, and he'd jump out at any moment. As if Finn were the type of person who would do such a thing. But maybe I didn't really know what type of person Finn was at all. I hadn't thought he was the kind of person who would let me wake up alone.

"What did you do to increase your strength so much tonight?"

I blinked up at the guy, comprehension dawning. I'd brought in the last piece.

No, not the last piece. If Finn was gone, we were still missing one.

"You're the ninth member of Heimdall."

"Is that what's happening?" he asked, nodding slowly. "I knew I'd been called for something. So you're saying…I'm a god? Oh, my. I think I need to sit down." He started fanning himself with a white-gloved hand and sat heavily on the log. The log where I'd sat with Finn, where we'd talked, connected. Where he'd said he'd love me forever. Where I'd promised myself to him.

Suddenly, the sight of it made me want to cry…or hurl. I couldn't tell which. So many emotions were battling inside me that I couldn't process them while also explaining Heimdall to a newcomer. But I would not fall apart. I pushed down the raging storm inside and focused on what I had to do.

"You're piece of a god," I said. "And so is Finn. We need him. And you. And all of us."

"But I'm just a dwarf," he said. "I'm not a god."

"We're just humans," I said. Now that the shock of waking up with him standing over me had worn off, I wasn't afraid of him, but my heart continued racing. Instead of fear, anguish gripped me. I could feel Finn somewhere, could feel him stretching the connection between us so far it threatened to snap.

When I spoke, my voice was so normal it startled me. I should be screaming and tearing through the woods after Finn, blundering into giants' houses. Instead, I tightened my wrap dress and said, "There's a couple elves, too. Let's go inside and you can meet the rest of them."

"Oh, boy," the dwarf said. "I don't know if I'm ready for this."

"Maybe Finn's inside."

I knew it was a lie even as I said it. Finn was far away. The pain in my chest was small but sharp, as if someone had put a stitch in my heart and was pulling at the thread. My feet weighed me down, as heavy as stone as I trudged back to the giantess's house. What had I done?

The door was still ajar, just as I'd left it. When we walked in, a soft light glowed from the kitchen. There, we found the others sitting along the bench at the table, facing the door. A candle burned on the table, and even though their positions were casual as they sat with their legs dangling off the edge of the bench, their faces were as serious as a panel of judges.

Guilt jolted through me. I didn't need them to sentence me. I knew I had failed, and worse, had hurt us all. I'd done something unforgiveable.

What had I been thinking? I should have known this would make it so much worse. I'd made Finn do something he didn't want to do—something he'd never do. He didn't even believe in dating. How could I have seduced him like that, convinced him to sleep with me?

"There are so many of you," the dwarf said. He looked up at the others for a second then bowed. "I'm Smith. It's a pleasure to make your acquaintance. I was called by your magic."

"We've been looking for you all over the Nine Worlds," Zeke said, jumping down from the bench and shaking Smith's hand. "Well, not quite all nine, but for a long time."

"I got a signal tonight, strong as a beacon," Smith said. "I couldn't resist the pull, so it looks like you found me."

"Gwen found you," Eliot said, watching me. I was sure his eyes could see through me, could see what I'd done. They all knew. I'd gone off with Finn. They knew why.

And now he was gone.

It didn't matter that this dwarf was as much a part of us as Finn. He could have been the king of dwarves, and it wouldn't have made it better. He wasn't Finn. Yes, we needed Smith for Heimdall, but we needed Finn for us.

The rest of Heimdall's hosts were dropping from the bench, introducing themselves to Smith.

Xander slipped over to me, and a torrent of pain ripped through my heart. "Was it us?" he asked. "Is that why Smith found us?"

I didn't know what to say. Maybe it was partly us. I still felt a tie with him that was tighter than what I felt with the others. Except Finn. And that connection was tugging on my heart, tearing it with each pull as he drew farther and farther away.

I shook my head, grateful when Peyton joined us. "Where's Finn?"

I shook my head again, but I couldn't speak. My throat was broken, a tight fist of pain that wouldn't unclench.

"What's wrong?" Zeke asked, joining us with a frown. They must have all sensed it. That's why they were up and waiting, even though it wasn't even light out yet.

"Go away," Peyton said, pushing at Zeke's chest with a flat hand. "And you, too, Xander. Gwen needs some girl time. All this testosterone is enough to suffocate us girls."

A flicker of hurt crossed Xander's face. It multiplied ten-fold by the time it reached me, hitting me like a slap. I stumbled back, struggling to swallow past the ache.

"We're going upstairs to talk," Peyton said.

"But where's Finn?" Zeke asked. "And what happened to you?" His eyes scanned my disheveled appearance. "I mean, you were with Finn, so I know it's not what it looks like."

"Finn's off being Finn," Peyton said. "And Gwen needs to talk to me. Now chill and get to know our new addition. We'll be right back."

She grabbed my arm and pulled me towards the stairs. I followed, my legs numb. We were both still in our makeshift dresses, and it took a while. By the time we reached the top, I was tired down to my bones. "I just want to lay down," I said. "I barely got any sleep. We'll talk in the morning."

"No," Peyton said, herding me towards the bathroom. "You're not going to push us away like Finn did. You're going to take a bath because your hair is full of leaves and you're all dirty. And I'm going to sit there because that's what friends do. You spill. I listen. Got it?"

I nodded, letting Peyton take me into the bathroom and follow me up the ladder and down into the bathtub, which was still filled with the cold water I'd used before. I was too tired to care.

I hesitated, though, not sure how to take a bath in front of Peyton. It wasn't like in movies, where I could hide under the bubbles and she could discreetly look away while I talked. If she sat outside the tub, we'd have to yell. I might as well be shouting my shame from the rooftops.

"Gwen, I bathed you for three months while you were sleeping off the dragon venom," she said, planting a hand on her hip and glaring. "Give me a little credit here. I'm not going to ogle you or gawk at your scars."

"Sorry," I muttered, pulling off the dress, which I'd had tucked around me like a towel. I felt more exposed now, more naked, than I ever had before. Before, I had scars. Now, I had shame. I was sure she could see it on me, hanging heavy on my shoulders like a shroud. I quickly sank down into the cold water, tensing as it hit my tender places.

"Finn's gone, isn't he?" she said. "I can feel it. Like, there's this emptiness. So I guess you didn't—oh." Her eyes widened, and I followed her gaze.

There was blood in the water.

"Oh," she said, softly this time. "Shit. Gwen."

She sank down to her knees beside me, soaking her dress.

"You'll get blood on your dress," I said, turning my face away.

The water sloshed as she sat down next to me, scooting close and sliding her arm around me. "Sweetie, I so do not care about that right now. You're hurting. What happened? I mean, I can guess what happened, but…with Finn? *How?*"

I closed my eyes, but tears squeezed from under my lids. "I did it wrong," I whispered. "I was trying to fix it, but I messed it up."

"I know it doesn't feel like it, but it'll be okay," Peyton said, leaning her head against mine. "It will."

"How?" I asked, swiping at the tears on my face. "He left, Peyton."

I'd given him everything, given it all to make us complete. And I'd gotten what I wanted. I'd drawn the last piece to us.

But I'd lost Finn in the process.

Chapter Twenty-Five

Peyton

We sat in the bathtub for a long time, until our skin was pruney and we were both shivering. Gwen mostly just cried, and I held her. I couldn't believe my brother. I mean, I could. He was probably mired in self-loathing right now. But still. He could have thought about someone else for a change—about us. And Gwen, especially. If I'd have picked one of my brothers to take a girl's virginity and skip out on her, Finn would have been the last on the list. My other brothers weren't above that sort of thing, but Finn? No way. I was surprised he wasn't on one knee with a ring right now.

"Maybe I am a slut, like those girls said," Gwen said, resting her head back against the wall of the tub. "I mean,

I've kissed all of you. And you have a girlfriend. And Finn doesn't do girlfriends. What kind of person does that?"

"A person with a god inside," I said. "Now, stop feeling guilty about that. The only one who should feel guilty about our kiss is me. I'm the one with the girlfriend."

"I'm sorry."

"Me, too," I said. But after a minute, I shook my head. "Actually, I'm not sorry we kissed. I'm sorry I have a girlfriend, and I'm definitely sorry I cheated on her. I should have broken up with her like Eliot said. But if our kiss brought us closer, and therefore helped draw our last piece to us, how can I be sorry?"

"I don't know," she said glumly.

"Plus, I wanted to kiss you," I said. "And it was a pretty fab kiss. No regrets."

She closed her eyes, and a tear worked its way from under her lashes. "So many regrets."

I squeezed her shoulder. "No regrets between us," I said. "Not ever. Deal?"

The corner of her mouth tugged into a sad smile. "Deal."

"Remember when you said free will could be selfish sometimes? I think that's what's happening. Finn is not the guy who's going to hit-and-run, okay? He's not. He didn't leave because he didn't want you or because he doesn't like you."

"You can't know that."

"Too bad, because I do. Whatever he said to you, I'm sure he meant it. He's just… Fine, you're right, he's a dick. There's no excuse. He's a selfish, scared little boy."

She closed her eyes again. "I didn't say that."

"You didn't have to," I said. "He left after you hooked up, and you're sitting here crying. No further evidence needed."

She was quiet for a minute. "What do we do now?"

"We go find him and kick his ass. We're so close to getting all of us together and getting back to our world, and then he runs off? No. Screw that."

"We're going to hold him hostage? Peyton, I'll never be able to look at him again."

"Then don't. But I bet in a few days, you'll get over this stage and move on to the pissed off stage. Then we'll drag him back kicking and screaming and tie him to a goat if we have to. He's not ditching us to fix Bifrost by ourselves. We can't, anyway. And I, for one, would like to get back to the land of hot showers and Starbucks."

Gwen shivered against me. "A hot shower would have been nice."

"Do you even realize how much we've missed? Three months, Gwen. Three months of school. Christmas. All our birthdays—yours, mine, and the not-twins. We're all sixteen now. We'll all probably have to repeat a grade. Who knows? Alej might have found a new girlfriend by now. And what are our parents telling the school? That we suddenly moved in with a mysterious uncle on a faraway island? Don't you think people got suspicious when we disappeared with no warning?"

"That seems like the dream now," Gwen said. "This is reality."

"Okay," I said. "Then the reality is I'm really freaking cold. Let's get out. You need a good long sleep, and when you're ready, we'll go after Finn." I stood and pulled her to her feet.

"I'm ready to get back into some real clothes," she said, staring down at the satin sheet like it had betrayed her. It floated in the water, sad and frayed at the edges, the previous night's shiny glamour gone. It seemed like a good metaphor for our group.

Chapter Twenty-Six

Gwen

We'd barely pulled on our clothes when a heavy thud shook the house. It was just getting light out, the sky still a deep morning blue, and I'd been looking forward to a couple hours of sleep. Instead, it sounded like I was going to get trapped in the rubble when the house fell down.

"Come on," I said, grabbing Peyton's hand as another thud rocked the house.

"Who's in my house?" bellowed a voice that was so big and booming I thought it had to be one of the gods.

"The others," I said, running for the door. "Quick. We need to get back to them."

We ran down the hall and jumped down the first step. The staircase unfolded before us like a mountain. It would take way too long to jump down every step. But we kept going, pushing ourselves to go faster. Run a few steps, jump. Run a few steps, jump. I was so focused I forgot to get woozy from the height.

My heart sank as a crashing sound came from downstairs. One of the guys yelled, though I couldn't tell which one, and an arrow of fear pierced my side.

Come on, come on, run out the door…

"I guess Papa Giant's home early," Peyton said, leaping down the stairs in front of me.

I forced myself to keep going, concentrating as hard as I could on the others. Maybe if I could call a goat by the sheer force of my will, I could call the other pieces of my god. It would've been nice for Heimdall to give us telepathy. I could feel them down there, terrified and angry. Most of all, I could feel Xander. I grabbed that thread and yanked on our connection as hard as I could. Maybe I could tell him to meet us at the bottom of the stairs. They couldn't run outside anymore because a giant was in the hallway at the bottom of the stairs, blocking off the front door.

"Who invited a god into my house?" he thundered. Upstairs, a pair of feet hit the floor. If we didn't reach the bottom before Aud or Mammy came down, they'd knock us over and send us tumbling to our deaths. They wouldn't look where they were going. They'd be busy worrying about Papa Giant, as Peyton called him.

"We're just leaving," Xander said.

The giant bellowed, shaking the whole house as he stepped into the kitchen.

"Uh-oh," Peyton said as footsteps approached the top of the stairs.

Five more to go. Peyton only had three.

Mammy's form filled the stairway, blocking out the pale light filtering in the windows from above. I heard the unmistakable sound of someone falling to the hardwood stair below me.

"Peyton," I cried, running forward and leaping down, cursing the stupid stairs. Four to go. Now three. Mammy thundered down the stairs towards us, taking them two at a time, shouting at her husband.

I stumbled over Peyton on the second-to-last step.

"I think I twisted my ankle," she moaned. "I couldn't see where I was going when I jumped. It's too dark."

"Get up," I said. "You'll just have to use the other foot."

"Help me over to the edge and go get the others."

"Shut up and put your arm around me," I said. My insides were tugging so hard I thought I'd be turned inside out if I didn't see the others soon. I grabbed Peyton and stood, dragging her to her feet.

The stairs shook under Mammy's footsteps. Someone screamed in the kitchen. My heart beat so wildly I couldn't think straight. Two steps to go.

"Jump," I said to Peyton.

We jumped together, and both of us hit the step with a clatter of elbows and knees. Peyton screamed.

"We can't stop," I said, dragging her to her feet again. She was sobbing loudly when suddenly, at the bottom of the next step, the twins appeared. I'd never been so happy to see their crazy Viking faces in my life.

"Catch," I yelled, and I heaved Peyton over the last step just as Mammy's foot loomed above me. I screamed and covered my head. Strong hands grabbed my shoulders, wrenching me off the step. A giant foot landed where I had huddled. Valdan's strong arms wrapped around me, and he kissed me hard on the mouth.

"Thank me later," he said with a wink, setting me on my feet.

"The door is closed," Zeke yelled behind us. "We can't get out."

"Is there a window we can reach?" Eliot asked.

Xander was supporting Smith's weight as they limped towards us. "They're higher than the doorknob," he said.

"Should we all join together and see if it works?" I asked. "Maybe all of us together can defeat a giant."

"We're still missing Finn," Peyton said, eyeing the latch above.

Mammy had stepped into the hall and was trying to dissuade Papa Giant from murdering us, but he didn't seem convinced. Any second, he was going to push her out of the way and stomp us like bugs.

"Lift me up," Peyton said. "I'll hang on the doorknob and turn it with my weight."

"You're hurt," I reminded her.

"Yeah, but I'm not dead," she said.

"I'll go."

She planted a hand on her hip and gave me a look. Even with one foot lifted off the ground, wearing leathers from head to toe, and her roots growing out, she could make anyone cringe with her evil eye. "I will not be the weakest link," she barked. "I'm not afraid of heights. I'm a cheerleader, and I've been on top of enough pyramids to know what I'm doing. Now, everyone get in here. Zeke, Valdan, and Alvan, on the bottom. Eliot and Xander, you're on level two. Gwen and Smith, stabilize me while I get up there. Snap, snap!"

We all huddled together, and the glow started immediately. I felt better, too, as if I'd been holding my breath and could finally let it out. In seconds, Xander and Eliot were standing on the hands and shoulders of the elves and Zeke. A second after that, Peyton shot straight up to the top like she was about to execute one of her cheer routines. But instead of standing on one leg to show her balance, she was doing it because her ankle was messed up. And instead of thrusting her pompoms into the air, she reached up to grab the door's latch that would lead us to freedom.

Seconds later, she scrambled onto the latch. Bracing her feet, she lifted the latch, and the door swung open a few inches. Smith grabbed it, but I stopped him. "Wait for Peyton."

As if she'd heard me, she turned, a look of panic crossing her face just before she toppled off the latch. With a shriek, she landed on top of the pyramid, and everyone tumbled to the floor. I could hardly see which one of Heimdall's host was which over the golden glow covering us.

"I'll never be cheer captain now," Peyton growled, hauling herself from the tangle. "Rookie mistake."

The others all scrambled to their feet just as Papa Giant roared in fury and pushed past Mammy. The elves yanked open the door, and we all dove out, then stopped.

At least a dozen giants stood outside.

Chapter Twenty-Seven

Gwen

"Fuck," Xander muttered behind me.

"Looks like we're just in time for breakfast," said one of the giants in the same thick, slow accent Mammy had. They varied in size from about seven feet to what looked like seventy, and they were all blinking at us with stupefied, hungry expressions. Giants may have been slow, but their size alone made them terrifying. That, and the fact that they wanted to kill and eat us.

"What do we do?" I asked, grabbing Zeke's arm.

"Maybe we can outwit them," Eliot said, his face pale but determined.

"I'll take an elf," a giant said, cracking her knuckles. "They're bigger. More meat."

"We're so dead," Smith whimpered, clinging to Alvan.

Alvan let out an ear-splitting whistle. "Our chariot is on its way," he said. "We just have to stay alive until then."

"Thor's hammer would come in handy right about now," Eliot said, shooting a hopeful look at Valdan.

"I'm ready to battle a giant," Valdan said, turning to Alvan. "Let's do it."

Peyton had split her lip in the tumble, and blood was leaking from the cut. Her hands trembled as she wiped her pink hair back with her wrist. "I guess this is it," she said in a small voice.

"You're all crazy," I said. "They're big and slow. We can run between their feet. We just have to be careful not to get stepped on."

The door was yanked open behind us. "What are you doing in my front yard?" Papa Giant thundered at the others.

"Come quick," a loud whisper came from the corner of the house. I turned to see Joaquin gesturing for us to join him. "While they're distracted with each other."

"Why are you hiding humans?" a giant thundered at Papa giant.

"Not giants," Valdan said, his chest swelling as he and Alvan held up a giant hammer between them. "Gods."

I had no idea where the hammer had come from, and I didn't really care. They could fight the giants. I was going for the getaway car.

"What's Joaquin doing here?" Xander asked. "I thought he was upstairs in the mother's room."

"Does it matter?" Zeke said, scooping up Peyton and slipping along the house towards Joaquin. "He's helping us."

"How do we know that?" Peyton asked. "There's probably ten more giants on that side of the house."

Alvan and Valdan dove into the yard, and a battle cry went up from the giants. Their roars of fury knocked my head sideways with the sound waves. I was pretty sure my eardrums were rupturing. The ground trembled as a giant crashed to the ground behind us.

"Let's go," Joaquin said. "I borrowed a ride for us."

I stumbled when I reached the corner of the house. A sleek black horse-like creature stood waiting. It was at least twice as long as a normal horse, though, and with twice as many legs. Its powerful muscles rippled under its skin as it turned a massive, bridled head our way.

"What the hell is that?" Peyton squeaked from her perch in Zeke's arms. "Is this like that movie *Splice,* but it's a centipede-horse hybrid?"

"Is that…Sleipnir?" Eliot said, his eyes popping behind his glasses, a grin spreading across his face. "You borrowed Odin's horse?"

"They're getting away," a giant yelled, pointing to us.

"So are we," Xander said, picking me up and throwing me over his shoulder. He ran for the eight-legged horse at breakneck speed.

A giant came charging our way. Alvan and Valdan raced after him, swinging the hammer at his legs. It smacked into the back of the giant's thigh, and he bellowed and spun around to face them. But they darted past and sprinted towards us. I had no idea how the horse, huge as it was, could carry more than three or four of us, but I'd risk it over being slaughtered by angry giants.

Joaquin was already on by the time we arrived. Xander heaved me on and I pulled him up behind me. Zeke shoved Peyton up into my lap and scrambled onto the horse, which seemed to grow longer each time someone mounted. Eliot shoved Smith up, and the twins took a flying leap onto its back. With a lurch, the horse began to rise, kicking its legs to churn up the air around it. Its powerful body reminded me of the dragons we'd ridden, but I didn't have time to admire it. Eliot was still on the ground, a giant just inches away.

"Wait," I screamed, reaching for him. I began to slide, and to my horror, my body slipped from the horse. Valdan's hands clamped around my ankles and I screamed, swinging upside down. My hands connected with Eliot's outstretched ones, our fingers clamping together like two wires in a circuit. A charge shot up my arms just before a jolt of pain as my shoulders wrenched under Eliot's weight.

I screamed again, feeling the pressure building as my arms strained not to rip from their sockets.

The horse wasn't rising fast enough. The giant was almost on us. She grabbed for us, but we swung wildly in the air, and her fingers only snagged in Eliot's shirt. With a ripping sound, his shirt was suddenly gone. His glasses slipped down his nose, and terror welled in his eyes.

"I'm letting go," he said.

"Don't you dare," I growled. "Or I'm breaking up with you on the spot."

"I'm not letting you go down with me."

"Then you'd better not plan on going down."

"Hold on," Zeke yelled from above. "We're pulling you up."

The giant swiped for us again. We were yanked upwards, and her fingers missed us by inches. Eliot's hair blew back and his glasses tumbled away.

I felt my arms separating from their sockets as Eliot's weight tugged on me when Valdan hauled me farther up. I screamed, a fireball exploding in each shoulder. And then I was across Valdan's lap, and he and Alvan were dragging Eliot onto the horse's back.

"Good grip, human," Valdan gave my backside a playful whack.

"Can you please stop hitting me and fix my shoulders?" I choked through a sob.

"I hurt you?" Eliot asked.

"I'm alive," I said. "Please tell me someone here knows how to push my arms back where they belong."

"I do," Joaquin said. "Let's just find somewhere with a few less giants who want to kick my ass for betraying them and defending a god."

"Thank you," I whispered, closing my eyes. Flying was not my thing. I was almost grateful I had pain to distract me.

It seemed like hours before we set down at the spot where we'd come into the giant world. Everyone climbed off Sleipnir, and Zeke gently lifted me down.

"Are you really going to let Joaquin touch you right now?" Peyton asked. "He's probably going to break your arms."

"What's your problem, Barbie Girl?" Joaquin asked. "I've apologized like a hundred times for hurting Gwen, but you keep treating me like shit. I've done everything I can to show you I'm not out to get you. I just want to be part of this. I know I'm not hosting the same god as you, but I can be part of your little posse until we get home. I'll pull my weight."

"He did just rescue us," Eliot said, eyeing Joaquin warily.

"That's right. I didn't have to do that. I could have left you there, but I just saved all your asses. So maybe you can shut up for five minutes and let me help your friend. Or hey, I can take you back where I found you and dump you off, and you can make it out on your own. Good luck."

311

"No," I gasped. "Please. If you fix my shoulder, you can come with us."

He looked at me a long moment, and my heart thudded with fear. I forced myself to keep my chin up and hold his gaze. The last time he'd touched me he'd had a knife in his hand, and I'd been tied to a chair. Now, I was the one with the power—the power of a god. I had nothing to be afraid of.

I kept telling myself that as he knelt beside me and placed a hand on my shoulder, gripping my arm at the same time.

"How did you get Sleipnir?" I asked through clenched teeth, trying to distract myself.

"I borrowed him," Joaquin said, and with a quick thrust, he shoved my arm back into place. I screamed as pain jolted through me.

Xander was on Joaquin in a second, but I held up a hand, breathing hard. "I'm okay."

Xander seemed reluctant to let go, but Zeke pulled him off Joaquin.

"You borrowed Sleipnir from Odin?" Eliot asked. "Does Odin know that?"

Joaquin grinned and stuck out his freakishly long, pointy tongue, swiveling his head from side to side. "That depends on if he's looked for him today."

"Great, now we're on Odin's bad side?" Peyton asked. "Pissing off Papa God has got to be even worse than pissing off Papa Giant."

"It is," Joaquin said. "But he won't be pissed at you. Ready for the next one, Gwennie?"

"Please don't call me that."

"What do you want me to call you? Eve the temptress?"

My heart skipped in my chest. "What?"

Joaquin knelt on my other side. "I ran into your missing piece this morning," he murmured. "He told me about your little seduction dance."

My stomach lurched, and I clutched my middle, trying not to puke. "What did you do to Finn?"

Xander stepped toward us again, his hands in fists, his eyes flashing.

"I didn't do anything, dude," Joaquin said, holding up both hands. He couldn't keep the smile off his face, though. "But I heard you did."

"What's he talking about?" Xander asked, confusion flickering over his face.

"You didn't tell them?" Joaquin asked. "I thought you shared everything."

"Just fix her arm," Peyton said. "And stop trying to stir up trouble."

"Tell me exactly what happened with Finn," I said. "Where is he?"

"He went home," Joaquin said, gripping my shoulder and arm. "He felt too guilty, and he wanted to go back to Midgard and hide from this. Meanwhile, I came to your rescue when he ditched you. That's worth something, right?"

He drove my arm back in, and I gasped in pain, gripping my shoulder and doubling over, fighting nausea. I had to admit, the other one felt better already, though it was still sore as hell.

"It's a start," Eliot said. "And thanks for fixing Gwen's arm. How'd you know how to do that, anyway?"

"Sometimes Loki has me do things that require such knowledge."

"You mean torture," Peyton said, her hand on her hip.

"Hey, I did what I said I would. You said I could be part of your group. So you'll stop ditching me, and let me in on the plans, right?"

"You can't replace Finn," I said.

"I wasn't trying to," Joaquin said.

"Then tell me what you did to him."

Joaquin held up both hands. "Why's it always my fault? You thought I did something to Rosa, too. I'm not going to mess up my chances. I didn't do anything to Finn. He made his own decisions, and he's where he wants to be. Going home."

I glared at him, wanting to blame him for Finn leaving. But it was my fault, not his. I dropped my gaze and turned away.

"If you so much as laid a finger on Finn, no amount of good deeds will save you," Xander said. "Just give me a reason to get rid of you."

"I don't see why you're still defending him," Joaquin said. "He ditched you. I wanted to be part of this and he didn't. He left, and I came back."

None of us could deny the truth in his words.

"Too bad you can't pick who gets to be part of your god," Joaquin said. "You could just trade me out for Finn."

Eliot cleared his throat, squinting at Joaquin. "How did you know we'd need to be rescued?"

My heart stumbled in my chest. He was right. Joaquin should have been in the house with us, as unaware as we were of the approaching giants. He shouldn't have been running around in the woods meeting Finn or stealing Odin's horse.

"What?" Joaquin asked, his face a complete blank.

Eliot watched him, squinting without his glasses. "You came back prepared to carry us all out of there, and we appreciate that. But how did you know we'd need to fly out in a hurry?"

"It's obvious," Joaquin said. "You were in the land of the giants. Of course you'd be in danger. The faster you could get out of Jotunheim, the better."

"I don't suppose you know any giants you could have alerted to our presence," Xander said.

"How would I know any giants? I'm new here, just like you. How many gods do you have at your beck and call?"

"It doesn't matter," I cut in. We had to focus. If we let every little thing come between us, we'd never make it home. "We're out of danger now, and we need to find Finn."

"Yeah," Joaquin said. "You might need my help in getting him back."

An uneasy feeling settled in my belly as we climbed onto Sleipnir. We needed to get out of Jotunheim before we became snacks for a hungry giant, but Eliot was right. Joaquin had gone to a lot of trouble just to get us out. There was no reason for him to do that unless he knew we would need to be rescued. But he was the last person who had seen Finn, which meant that we needed him around. If I had to play nice to get what I wanted from him, I'd do it. It wasn't the worst thing I'd done on this journey.

I felt a little better when the elves shoved Joaquin back on the horse and took the reins. At least we were in good hands.

As the horse rose, Xander's arms tightened around me. "Tell me you're okay."

"I'm okay," I said. "By the time we get home, I might not even be scared of heights at all."

"I meant your arms."

"Really sore," I said. "But Joaquin did what he promised."

"So I could join your little club," Joaquin said. "Now that I'm a member, I get all the benefits. Right, Gwennie?"

"You're really testing our bargain," Zeke said. "You better shut your mouth before we change our mind in midflight."

As much as I wanted to snap at Joaquin like everyone else, I held my tongue. If we didn't have Joaquin, we might not find Finn. Why didn't anyone else get it? It wasn't like I wanted to be his bestie, but I could play whatever part I had to if it brought back our last piece. And I wasn't that keen on pissing off a volatile giant.

"I said you could come with us," I said. "And here you are. I can't make you part of Heimdall."

"Maybe Finn can," he said. "He doesn't want his part. If I got to host a god, I'd be a little more gracious. We could trade."

"The only way out is to die," I said.

"So if he died, his share of Heimdall would be up for grabs," Joaquin said. "Interesting."

"We can toss you off the flying horse, you know," Zeke said. "You'd probably get sent back to your acid cave if your body died."

"But the elves have two gods," Joaquin said. "Maybe I could have Loki and a ninth of some lame god."

"Where did you leave Finn?" I interrupted.

"What?"

"Where did you leave him?"

"I left him in Yggdrasil," Joaquin said. "Why?"

"I don't think that squirrel is good for him," Peyton said. "He got all weird after it talked to him the first day."

"If Finn's in the tree somewhere, he might be as hard to find as in one of the worlds," I said. "We never found Rosa. The tree stretches through all Nine Worlds. It could take years to find him."

"I found you," Smith said.

"Because we had a stronger bond then," I said.

"So, do what you did before to make the bond strong again."

Chapter Twenty-Eight

Gwen

I pulled my hands into my sleeves and shrank inside Xander's arms. After what happened with Finn, there was no way I was risking it again with someone else. We'd just have to be close in other ways. The elves were good at squishing us into our little huddle.

"If Heimdall said we can't go home until we've succeeded, can we get back into Midgard?" Peyton asked.

"If we can't, then he can't," Eliot pointed out.

My heart thudded at the thought. Home. Life hadn't always been good there, but it had made sense. I just wanted to be home now, to curl up in my mother's arms and tell her I was sorry for all the things I'd blamed her for since we arrived at the Keens'. To see her and know she was okay, that we could get through anything together, as we always had. Now, I had all these people around me, and she only had Neil, practically a stranger.

"Where do we even start?" Zeke said. "Finn could be anywhere."

I turned to Joaquin. "Where in the tree did you leave him?"

"I don't know, on a branch?"

"Give me an excuse to throw you off this horse," Xander said.

"We share everything," I said. "That's why you wanted to be one of us. If you want to be part of the group, you have to be willing to share, too."

"Are you really sharing everything?" he asked. "Or are you still treating me like shit?"

"We'll share," I said, forcing myself to hold his gaze and sound genuine. Guilt flared through me, though. I wasn't used to lying and manipulating people. I wasn't the trickster here. Or maybe I was. I smiled, but not too big. It had to look sincere. "You'll be our honorary ninth member."

"Until you find Finn," he said, turning away. "Then you'll ditch me again."

"We won't," I said. "You'll be one of us. But it goes both ways. You have to treat us the way we treat each other."

His gaze slid over my body. "I can treat you the way your brothers do. Is it my turn tonight, since I'm the new guy? Or do I have to wait for my turn in the rotation?"

"I'm going to kill him," Xander said, reaching forward and grabbing Joaquin's throat. Joaquin flailed his arms, trying to hold on to the horse and pry Xander's fingers loose at the same time.

Dammit, why couldn't we have telepathy? He was messing up my whole plan.

"If you kill me, I can't tell you where Finn is," Joaquin gasped.

"Let him go," I said, grabbing Xander's arms. "We need Finn more than you need to shut him up. Don't let him get to you."

"See, Gwen wants me," Joaquin said the moment Xander released him. "She may not admit it, but she's the one protecting me now, isn't she? She's seen me naked. She knows I'm a giant in more ways than one."

Peyton snorted behind us, but I just smiled, wishing I could tell them what I was thinking. Wishing I could open my mind to them and we could all communicate like we had one brain—Heimdall's brain. He'd told us not to let anyone come between us, and I'd listened. Not even Joaquin's nasty words could get to me. I'd given up everything to bring all nine of us together, and I wasn't going to let it be in vain. We would get Finn back whatever it took.

"Just saying," Joaquin said. "It'll bring us closer, right? I'll be like a real member. That can be my initiation. If you have someone else on the rotation, you can still fit me in for a special occasion, can't you, Gwennie? After all, I saw you getting busy with Xander last night, and then Finn told me all about your little roll in the leaves. Every. Last. Detail."

"Where is he?" I asked through clenched teeth, struggling to control my own anger. He was pushing it pretty far considering I'd just saved his ass. It was almost like he wanted me to throw him off. Which just made me suspicious as to why he was being such a dick. Had he sensed that we were playing him? Was he testing us?

"Throw out the dead weight," Peyton said. "He can't be one of us, and he'll never tell because he doesn't know. He's tricking us."

"You're using me," he shot back. "Maybe I know and maybe I don't. If I'm really one of your team, you should want me here no matter what I can or can't do for you."

Xander grabbed me around the waist and heaved me up, pushing me behind him into Zeke's arms. I fell in a tangle with Peyton, a cry of protest leaving my lips as Xander grabbed Joaquin and swung him off the side of the horse. Sleipnir swerved sideways, banking in the direction of the unbalanced weight. Zeke's arms wrapped protectively around Peyton and me, and Smith swore in another language.

"What the hell, dude?" Joaquin yelled.

"Tell us where Finn is, or I drop you," Xander said. "Your choice."

"I fixed Gwen," Joaquin whined. "You said you'd take me with you."

"We changed our mind," Xander said. "What's it going to be? Are you feeling lucky?"

He released his hold on one of Joaquin's arms. I lurched forward, but Zeke held me back. "If he knows, he'll tell," he said.

"What if he doesn't?" I asked. My heart twisted at the thought of Finn stuck somewhere, stranded or trapped. If Joaquin knew where to find him, we couldn't lose him.

Joaquin flailed, kicking the side of the horse in the process. It veered sharply, and my stomach dropped. Was it possible for a horse to buck off a rider while flying?

"My arms are getting tired," Xander said. "Last chance. Where is he?"

"At Bifrost," Joaquin said. "I left him at your campsite trying to figure out how to get back into the tree."

"Can I drop him anyway?" Xander asked.

"No," I said. "He's helped us. Give him a chance."

And we needed him. Why didn't anyone else see that?

Peyton snorted. "How many chances are you going to give him?"

"We all make mistakes."

"This seems like one of them," Peyton muttered.

After a while, Sleipnir began to descend into the chasm where the lava river flowed. It was black on top, as if the lava were cooling. Above, Bifrost looked about the same as the last time I'd seen it, but it was somehow subdued. The air didn't shimmer as energetically, the water barely flowed, and the flames flickered lazily instead of blazing. If we didn't find Finn—and fast—there would be no bridge to fix. The giants would storm across and swarm our world.

"He's here," I cried, straightening. "Don't you feel it? The pull?"

"I do," Xander said.

"This is our last piece?" Smith asked.

"Hurry," Peyton said. "We can catch him before he gets back into the tree."

The horse rose, his legs churning the air until he touched down on the mossy hillside. At the top of the bluff overlooking the river stood Finn.

The moment my feet touched down, an intense current of electricity caught me up, conveying me towards him. The god part had taken over for the moment, my human shame and hurt forgotten. "Finn," I cried, running up the mossy hill.

He turned slowly, his face set and grim. When he saw me, he held out a hand to stop me. His expression was guarded, closed off, as if he no longer knew me. "Don't come closer," he said.

I stopped, feeling like he'd punched me in the throat. He knew me better than anyone on earth. I knew him better. How could he look at me like a stranger?

"I'm sorry," I said, my voice choked. "I'm sorry I made you do it."

"It's not your fault," he said, shoving his hands into his pockets. "It's my fault. I should have been able to control myself. If not for my sake, then for yours."

"I never asked you to control yourself. You don't have to feel bad for my sake."

"Good people avoid temptation."

"Is that all I am to you? A temptation?" I squeezed my hands into fists, letting my nails cut into my palms to keep myself from running to him, fitting myself to him where I belonged. We all fit together to complete this puzzle.

His face fell. "You know you're more than that. But I should have kept you pure. It's my job to protect you."

"Finn…I don't need protecting from you." I stepped towards him, but he stiffened and stepped back, closer to the edge.

"You obviously do. If I was a better man, I would have stopped myself."

"You're a good man," I said. "Stop telling me what you should do, or feel, or be. I don't think any less of you. I love you even more than I did yesterday. I love you for what you are, not what you do or should do. Don't you see that?"

Peyton joined me, and the temperature in the air spiked. The flames in the bridge flickered higher. As the others came up the slope, I could feel the pull of each of them—the longing to be with them, to draw Finn in with us.

So could Bifrost. It brightened as we gathered closer together.

"You better not be thinking about jumping," Zeke said to Finn.

"I can't get back into the tree," Finn said, turning his face toward the chasm below. "I can't go home. There's only one way to get free of Heimdall."

"It's true," Joaquin said. "Dude, I wouldn't blame you. We understand."

"No, we don't," Xander growled, stepping forward.

I gasped as Finn stepped back again, his gaze flickering over the group.

"They replaced you already," Joaquin said. "I can't take your place, but I can help them. I'm the honorary ninth member. Gwen even says I get full benefits."

"That's not true," I said sharply, willing Finn to look at me. I tightened my fists, my nails biting deeper into my palms. I could not let Joaquin distract me from Finn right now, no matter what he said.

I could feel the wave of rage rolling off Xander, boiling up like the lava below. He was barely keeping himself in check.

"We can't replace you," Zeke said to Finn. "You're not just part of Heimdall. You're part of us. You're Finn, our baby bro."

"He knows his name," Joaquin said. "And he's not a baby. He's a big boy. He can make his own decisions. He doesn't want this. You should respect that."

"I can make my own decisions," Finn said with a nod, like he was reciting a line he'd told himself so many times it had become meaningless.

"Are you sure this is your decision?" Peyton asked. "The Finn I know wouldn't commit a mortal sin."

Finn flinched, and I wondered if he was thinking he'd already committed one. "I'm sorry," he said, his face full of misery. "Maybe Heimdall can find a better host."

"If you release your part of Heimdall, you'll be free of his control," Joaquin said. "He'll go into another host, someone who can help them. Someone stronger."

"Shut up," Xander growled, stalking towards Joaquin.

Joaquin backed up, moving toward Finn at the edge.

"No," I cried, running between them.

"Do the right thing," Joaquin said.

Finn turned towards the ravine.

"Finn, no," I cried. I rushed forward and threw my arms around him.

"Get off me," he growled, his voice nothing like his usual soft-spoken tone.

"No," I growled back.

As if my charge had released the others from the grip of fear for Finn's safety, they started forward as well.

"He can make his own choices," Joaquin said. "You really want to make him miserable for the rest of his life? Finn's in pain. If you really loved him, you'd want to put an end to that."

Xander grabbed Joaquin, slamming him to the ground.

Finn wrestled to free himself from my clinging, aching arms. Every second I held on to him felt like the last I'd be able to hold on. Pain seared into the sockets that had been disconnected earlier. Finn stumbled, and my head swam when I saw the drop below. This time, Thor wouldn't be there to save me.

"Don't do this," I said to Finn.

"*You* don't do this," he said.

"We can help you. No, we can get you help."

This time, I would know not to just go along like I had with Mom. I'd wanted to protect her from outsiders. I'd known that I had to keep them from seeing how sick she was. But that had been a mistake. I wouldn't make the same one with Finn. We would get him help.

While I fought to hold on, Xander and Joaquin were grappling with each other, too.

"Let me go," Finn said, going still. "You're going to get hurt."

"You don't think losing you will hurt?" I wrenched Finn away from the edge, my heels digging into the stone at the edge of the cliff. We stumbled, and for a second, the lava below seemed to reach up for me, rising sickeningly towards us. Ignoring my stomach's lurch, I closed my eyes and threw my weight backwards.

Finn took several stumbling steps sideways before losing his balance. Together, we tumbled to the ground. The pain when my shoulder hit the unforgiving stone was so intense I didn't even register that we'd crashed into Xander and Joaquin. Not until I heard two screams. One from behind us and one plummeting into the chasm below.

Chapter Twenty-Nine

Gwen

Zeke sailed over my head, diving for the cliff edge. Peyton screamed again, rushing to join him. The cliff beside us where the two boys had been fighting stood empty. I dove for the edge as my heart burst inside my chest. Zeke was already there, kneeling at the precipice. My brain refused to compute. Two seconds ago, there had been two grunting, cursing boys wrestling with solid, muscled bodies. Their presence had filled the world. Now, the cliff was too stark, too barren, to comprehend.

"Gwen, be careful," Finn said quietly, his hands on my waist, holding me from going too far forward.

My fingers frantically clawed at stone as I tried to reach the edge, my nails tearing from my fingers. I didn't know I was screaming until it abruptly stopped in my throat. "Xander," I gasped, pulling myself to the edge.

Zeke held tight to his wrists. Xander stared up at him. There was something passing between them, some understanding.

Zeke pulled hard, and Xander leapt up onto the cliff edge. Zeke fell back on the ground, an expression of pure wonder dawning on his face. He jumped to his feet. "Did you see that?" he asked. "I jumped like ten feet through the air and caught Xander with my bare hands! That's impossible. I should have been pulled off the edge."

"But you weren't," Xander said. "We weren't."

Suddenly, they were both laughing, doubled over with it. Zeke clapped Finn on the back and threw his arm around him, pulling him over. Finn fell to the ground, and a second later, the adrenaline inside me took over and I joined in, as hysterical as they were. And then the others were crashing into us, falling to their knees, all our arms around each other, our tears falling on each other's faces.

Five minutes later, we'd begun to calm down. Something shone through us, a vibration of the highest energy. We were all together. We were glowing faintly, the golden light throbbing from our skin like a sunset. The swell of elation soaring through us nearly bore us up into the air, like Heimdall had done when he came to see us.

"We're all together," Peyton said, sitting on her heels. Her eyes widened. "We did it."

"I didn't mean to knock him off," Xander said, his laughter fading. He stared down at his hands.

Silence fell over the group.

"You didn't," I said after a long moment. "I did." My stomach turned, and I thought I'd be sick. I'd killed someone. Not just a giant, but the person he'd inhabited.

"We did," Zeke said, his hand closing around mine. "All of us are responsible."

"It was an accident," Peyton said quietly.

"I guess we did as Heimdall wanted after all," Eliot said.

Finn stared down at his hands, pinching his lips together.

We'd killed someone. A kid from our school.

The old instinct rose up in me as it did every time things got hard. It was the instinct to get in the car and drive, to get away from these people staring at me. These people whose concern felt heavy suddenly, something I couldn't bear. It was too much to deal with.

But I wouldn't run this time. I had a job to do. I had to be brave and face this. Instead of shrinking, I forced myself to stand, to face them with my trembling knees, my scarred arm, and my useless, dangling hands.

"It's my job to pull us all together," I said. "I'm supposed to be the heart of the group, and I haven't been doing a very good job. I've been too confused by my feelings for you. All of you. And I didn't deal with them very well."

"You did fine," Eliot said.

I gave him a quick smile, focusing on his steady gaze to give myself courage. I could feel the whole of the group as if it were an extension of myself, could feel each of them move as if they were limbs of my body. I nodded. "Heimdall warned not to let anyone come between us, and I think I'm the one who did. I didn't mean to, but I should have been more open. I wasn't trying to hide. I've just never talked to anyone about my feelings. It wasn't the kind of thing I talk about with my mom, so I'm not good at it, but I promise to do better. I'm the heart of Heimdall, the essence. We all need to come into his essence to be complete."

"That sounded dirtier than you probably meant," Zeke said with a crooked grin.

My face flamed, but I was grateful for the lighthearted comment that allowed me to breathe through the intensity of my feeling of exposure. "What I mean is, we need to stick together. We're finally all here. We need to make sure we stay together. And if I ever start to mess up, I need you to call me out. Be honest with me. And I want to be completely honest with all of you." I turned to Finn. "Can I tell them?"

He looked like he might hurl, but he nodded, his lips tight. This journey had changed us all. I didn't even feel like the same girl who had worried what the popular girls thought of her jeans, the same girl who had spent most of her life with no one to turn to but her unstable mother and the characters in novels. Now, I was scarred inside and out. I was a murderer and a seductress. I was the heart of a god.

"I guess I felt like I was being pulled in a different direction every time I was with one of you. I…I like you. All of you. I can't choose anyone over anyone else. You're all amazing, beautiful people. So if you want to be with me while I figure this out, I'm honored. And if you don't, I completely understand."

"You want to be with all of us?" Zeke asked, looking around at his siblings.

My heart pounded so loud I could hear it rushing in my ears. "Yes," I said. "And…I slept with Finn. That's what brought him close enough for a moment that Smith could find us. I'm sorry that it hurt you, Finn. I wish I'd realized that wasn't the right way to bring you close. But I can't wish I hadn't brought you to us. Because now we're together, and we can finally fix this bridge and go home."

Home. Hot showers, cheeseburgers, ice cream. Mom.

God, I had to get home to her.

But at the same time, I knew that once we left this place, once we were back in Midgard, we couldn't be together the way we were here. No one there would understand. We would not be allowed to be together there.

The group pulled together in silence, as if they were experiencing the same doubts and longings. We were bound together now. There was no use labeling things here.

We weren't a homeless girl or rich kids, lesbian or stepsibling, or even elf and human and dwarf. We'd pieced together all the parts to complete Heimdall. Together, standing on that bluff, we weren't nine individuals. We were a god.

***

To find out what happens next, order book 3 HERE.

If you'd like to be the first to know about future releases, cover reveals, and opportunities to beta read and get ARC copies, click here to join my RH Readers Club.

From the Author

If you or someone you know is contemplating suicide, please get help!
The National Suicide Prevention Lifeline, open 24 hours a day. 1-800-273-TALK (8255) or (866) 859-4440

You matter.

***

I would never have written this book without the support and encouragement from wonderful readers like you! After writing book 1, I was unsure if I should carry on with Gwen's story, but I had so many amazing reviewers ask for more that I had to give y'all what you asked for. If you enjoyed this book, please consider leaving an honest review!

Reviewers are magical unicorns to writers—our most precious source of feedback on whether to continue a series and what to put in it! Click here to leave a review and may unicorn dust rain down around you!